"You don't h
Mitchell," sh
come first."

He nodded. "As it has a few times this week. Things are slow for me right now," he added, finishing off his roll and licking his fingers. "Might even be fate, huh?" he asked, smiling over at her.

She knew he was teasing her. Making light of the incredible amount of time he was investing in a new client who hadn't even yet signed a contract.

Her heart opened wide, and with an intensity she couldn't stop, she said, "I will always be here for you, Mitchell. No matter what or when."

He glanced her way, nodded. And pulled into the medical center parking lot.

That last look, it had been brief, but Dove felt it to her core.

It was like he'd just returned the vow. Silently.

But she'd heard it loud and clear.

It was as she'd known.

They were soulmates.

Dear Reader,

Welcome to Alaska! The Colton family here pulled me right in with their outdoor adventures. With parent brothers who, with their wives, dealt with tragedy together and forged new lives in the wilderness, raising daring, outgoing siblings/cousins who work together to bring adventure to others. And who step up to face danger at every turn just because it's the right thing to do.

And welcome to Mitchell and Dove's story, too. I love these two characters. They're so completely different. And wonderful, compelling people in their own ways. I had no idea how they'd interact, or manage to stay on the page together, but they took care of it all for me. And taught me some things along the way that enriched my life. I hope they do the same for you.

Tara Taylor Quinn

COLTON'S
SECRET WEAPON

TARA TAYLOR QUINN

ROMANTIC SUSPENSE

Special thanks and acknowledgment are given to Tara Taylor Quinn for her contribution to The Coltons of Alaska miniseries.

Harlequin®
ROMANTIC SUSPENSE™

Recycling programs for this product may not exist in your area.

ISBN-13: 978-1-335-47155-0

Colton's Secret Weapon

Copyright © 2025 by Harlequin Enterprises ULC

Harlequin Enterprises ULC
22 Adelaide St. West, 41st Floor
Toronto, Ontario M5H 4E3, Canada
www.Harlequin.com

Printed in Lithuania

MIX
Paper | Supporting responsible forestry
FSC® C021394

A *USA TODAY* bestselling author of over one hundred novels in twenty languages, **Tara Taylor Quinn** has sold more than seven million copies. Known for her intense emotional fiction, Ms. Quinn's novels have received critical acclaim in the UK and most recently from Harvard. She is the recipient of the Readers' Choice Award and has appeared often on local and national TV, including *CBS Sunday Morning*. For TTQ offers, news and contests, visit tarataylorquinn.com!

Books by Tara Taylor Quinn

Harlequin Romantic Suspense

The Coltons of Alaska

Colton's Secret Weapon

Sierra's Web

A Firefighter's Hidden Truth
Last Chance Investigation
Danger on the River
Deadly Mountain Rescue
A High-Stakes Reunion
Baby in Jeopardy
Her Sister's Murder
Mistaken Identities
Horse Ranch Hideout

The Coltons of Owl Creek

Colton Threat Unleashed

Visit the Author Profile page at Harlequin.com for more titles.

For one of my longest-standing friends, one who knew me then, Cinci Davis. It's no mistake that as I was writing this Alaska book, you were cruising her waters! Our paths are forever crossed.

Chapter 1

Summertime. Eighteen hours of daylight. Hiking, fishing, flying to do. And Mitchell Colton sat in his cushy law office on Main Street, waiting for noon to arrive so he could take the rest of the day off and get to it all. June and July had already passed him by, and there were so many more adventures he wanted to get to before winter hit.

The lull in business at his Shelby Law Office, while not a problem financially, did not bode well for him. He needed to be busy. Or be outside.

He'd prefer to be busy. In his experience, lulls generally meant an avalanche was coming. As the only corporate law firm in town, he'd have to handle the ramifications for every business, all needing him ASAP, were something to happen that affected the Main Street merchants. An online scam, say, that somehow hacked into Shelby's internet service and stole customer information.

Finishing the revisions on a series of privacy policies for several of his clients with online offerings that mirrored their brick-and-mortar stores, Mitchell shook his head at the dark route his thoughts had taken. While it was his job to foresee possible pitfalls and do all he could to protect his clients from falling prey to them, he most definitely did not need to borrow trouble.

And…there it was.

Trouble.

Glancing up from the email he'd just sent, with the up-dated privacy policy attached, he saw the woman parking her little 1968 Meadowlark yellow Mustang right out in front of his place.

And hoped to God she wasn't headed his way.

Dove St. James. Local yoga queen.

In black leggings covered only by a thin, very thin, see-through-thin veil of what she might think was a purple skirt, a black crop top that ended right below her breasts, and lavender flip-flops that had more glittery junk on their straps than any one pair of shoes should bear, she was head-ing straight for his door.

Every inch of her slim, toned body was on display. Like some kind of billboard advertisement. Take a class with me and you, too, can be exactly who and what you want to be.

He did not relish taking on the completely untraditional woman as a client. Even for the minute it would take to refer her to someone cheaper in Anchorage.

As though staring at a train about to wreck, Mitchell swallowed, unable to not watch her very purposeful prog-ress toward his establishment. The long auburn hair, as wild and free as the woman was, seemed to wave at the world with every step she took.

He hadn't heard of any trouble at Namaste, the Main Street yoga studio the twenty-seven-year-old owned and operated. In a rented second-floor studio above the Repo— a secondhand shop he *did* have as a client. Surely, if there was a problem requiring his legal expertise, he'd have heard about it by now.

Most particularly with the lull and all. Mitchell tended

to overconcern himself with problems that weren't his business when he didn't have enough to keep his brain occupied.

His outer door opened. Stuart, his paralegal who also handled reception, had the day off. A long weekend.

"Hello?" Dove called in that singsong voice of hers that reminded Mitchell of her free-spirited mother. He'd never understood what Whaler—officially known as Bob St. James—had found so enchanting in his now-deceased wife. Free spirits were great for children. But young ones had to grow up. To be equipped to face life realistically.

Thinking of Dove's father, a retired whaleship captain and the current owner of the only boat rental company down on the pier, St. James Boats, and a man Mitchell respected, he called out, "In here."

For Whaler's sake. If the ship lord's daughter was in trouble, Mitchell would do what he could to help.

The woman burst in through the opened door like a swirl of leaves in a storm. Smelling like…he didn't know. A cross between lavender and rose with a bit of peppermint thrown in. Certainly not any perfume with which he was familiar.

Not horrible, though. So thinking, he nodded toward the seat in front of his desk, figuring she'd earned herself a minute of his time. Mostly because of her paternity. And a tad due to the scent she'd brought in.

"You know my father," she said, looking at him square in the face with her wide green eyes.

"I do."

"He speaks highly of you. Respects you."

Sitting back, Mitchell straightened his tie, dropped his arms to his chair, and watched her. He'd seen her around town. With her shop just down the street from his, knowing her identity was pretty much inevitable. But with the five years between them, he'd never had an occasion to actually socialize with the woman. He'd graduated high school before she'd entered.

"He's in a bad way, Mitchell," she said and then followed the statement with, "Mitch. I like Mitch. Sounds much more accessible. Can I call you that?"

Accessible? What the hell? "No," he said, moving nothing but his mouth. "I go by Mitchell."

Her tongue darted out along her lips as she nodded. "He's been drinking more and more since my mom died a couple of years ago. He's pretty much drunk all the time now."

Mitchell was aware. He'd heard, but he'd seen, too. And while he felt real sympathy for the guy, he said, "I'm a lawyer, not a doctor. Or mental health counselor."

She nodded. "I know. I'm here because he's losing his business, Mitchell. I've tried everything I know to do, but nothing is working. One of his longest-standing employees, Oscar Earnhardt—you know him?"

"I thought Whaler fired him."

"He did. He had to. Oscar's got as bad a drinking problem as Dad has. I think he thought that since Dad was drinking, he got a bye on his own situation. His wife left him, which made things worse. He quit showing up to work, or would show up drunk, and tourists would be left with a precious vacation day wasted because there was no one to facilitate the boat rental they'd reserved. Dad cut him slack again and again. Warned him. The last straw, though, was when he wrecked one of Dad's most expensive and sought-after boats. There could easily have been customers in it with him, and as much as Dad hated to, he had to let him go…"

Mitchell figured, with as fast as words were bursting out of her, that she'd rehearsed the whole thing. Figured it was only polite to let her get it out. It wasn't like he was in a huge hurry to find out how she thought he might be of assistance to Whaler. He'd help if he could.

"The other couple of guys working for him don't know nearly as much as Oscar did about the area. You're a Colton, grew up in the field of tourist adventures with RTA, you know how important that kind of knowledge is to someone on vacation up here."

At the mention of Rough Terrain Adventures, the company founded by his father and uncle and currently run by one of his older brothers and his cousin, and the segue from there back to Whaler's business, Mitchell frowned.

Again, lawyer. Not professional adventurer. Though, he knew the area as well as anyone else in his family. And was out in it, on his own solo adventures, every chance he got.

"I've been hoping the loss of his job would help Oscar sober up, which would let Dad hire him back, but so far, not at all. And if Dad loses his business, I'm going to lose him."

She had problems. He'd give her that. "What is it you think I can do?"

"You helped him form his corporation years ago. He said then that you'd talked to him about things you, as a corporate lawyer, could do to help him with parts of running it, too. But Mom was already sick then, and he'd been worried about the money."

Mitchell raised his eyebrows at that one. He was to believe that years later, and with the business failing, Whaler suddenly had more money?

"Dad did well in his career," Dove said. "He'd invested enough to provide for him and Mom into retirement, but we're still paying off her medical bills, so I can't pay you much, but I'll sign over a portion of the company to you. Or you can write up some contract that gives you a portion of the proceeds until your fee is paid. I'll pay you myself, if you can take monthly installments—small ones… I just need your help. Please."

For a second there, unable to miss the woman's sincere distress, Mitchell considered any possibility that he could give her the positive response she was so desperately seeking.

A split second.

While he knew a whole lot about running an adventure company for tourists, his expertise came in preventing disaster before it happened, or cleaning up messes after they'd been made. As a corporate attorney, he could help with investments and suggest various ways to make them, but clearly there wasn't enough cash flow to get started.

Sometimes dealing with employee relations was the key, and again, getting someone sober wasn't in his wheelhouse.

Mitchell gave her the respect of appearing to seriously consider her request before he said, "I sympathize with your situation, but I'm just not seeing where the Shelby Law Office can be of any help here. If your father had come to me sooner…" He let the sentence fall short. Shrugged.

Not sure that, with Whaler's drinking, he'd have been able to help even then.

And, as her shoulders slumped, Mitchell wished that, like Stuart, he'd taken the whole day off, too.

He was telling her no. Dove's heart put up roadblocks, which caused a major pileup of emotion. She couldn't just give up. And Mitchell Colton was her last resort.

She'd dreaded coming to him. Had known what a long shot he was.

Holding her lips together by sheer force of will, she lifted her head slowly. Breathing in deeply through her nose as she did so. Tapping into learned resources to calm herself.

And made it right until Mitchell's face came into view. *No* was written all over it. But something in his eyes wasn't...cold.

Maybe not warmth. Or compassion. But her heart, which never lied to her, recognized an understanding that unleashed her desperation.

Tears sprang to her eyes. And spilled over, too. Before she had any conscious sense they'd broken free. "My father needs your help, Mitchell," she said. "You're his last hope. And until you've taken a look at things, how do you even know there's nothing you can do?" She blinked against the tears, talking through them. "How would you ever get new clients if you didn't at least vet them? Maybe there's something you'd know how to capitalize on. Could even be a lawsuit or something that he could bring for something." That last pie-in-the-sky scenario was accompanied by a large, inelegant sniffle. After which she helped herself to a tissue from a box on the corner of his desk.

Blew her nose. Took another and wiped her eyes. And wondered if he kept the box there because he was used to making his clients cry.

Words continued to spew rapidly through her mind, and once they'd started to break free, she couldn't hold them all. She'd bite some back and, while she was busy doing that, others slipped through. "Isn't this some kind of discrimination?"

Cringing inside at the absurdity, she knew she couldn't take it back and so went forward with it. "Refusing to even take a look at a possible case? And isn't your oldest brother a cop? I wonder what he would think of his little brother breaking the law?"

As soon as the words were out, she knew she'd gone too far. And still she couldn't back down. Or completely stop the tears that were filling her eyes. More of a trickle than a flood but still there.

"All I'm asking is that you take a look," she said then. Finding a small piece of zen in the midst of her storm. "Please." She looked him straight in the eye. "I know you and my dad are on good terms. He's on the verge of losing everything," she said. "And that would kill him."

"What is it you expect me to find?"

She'd thought she'd made that obvious. "I don't know. If I did, I'd already be implementing a plan and be on my way to saving the business." Her heart flooded with hope, as her stomach clenched with tension.

He hadn't said no a second time.

Nor had he given any indication that he was changing his mind.

"Does Whaler know you're here? That you're asking me for help?"

There was that. The man had a way of getting right to the challenge. Which was what she needed from him, right? "Do you think I'd be here if he did?" she countered. "Or be here without him right behind me, apologizing to you and telling me to mind my own damned business?" He knew Whaler. He'd get the point.

Still sitting back in his chair, arms lying casually on the rests, he continued to study her. Not all that much of a phenomenon, actually. Dove—who'd been raised almost exclusively by her free-spirited mother while her father had been out at sea—had been getting stares since before kindergarten. Had been taught from birth that her choices were not to be dictated by what society or popularity prescribed. Life wasn't measured in terms of an endeavor's success but rather by how fulfilled something had made her feel. Or how happy.

And pursuant to that standard, she was in the midst of what could end up being her biggest failure of all time.

"How do you propose that I get a look at things without him being aware of my doing so?"

Finally, an answer she had. "My father's going to be taking a charter of tourists out tomorrow. A half-day cruise of photography students from Anchorage who've been assigned to get various types of images of the glaciers. They're leaving at seven in the morning. You could show up after they leave. I can let you into his office." Her chin came up as she said that last bit. Perhaps issuing a challenge.

While she didn't know Mitchell Colton well, he was surprisingly different than she'd expected. Analytical and serious, yes, but there was that hint in his expression of more.

Still waters running deep. The cliché came to her. Along with her mother's reminder that clichés became such due to the fact that they spoke to a universal truth.

There was no hint of anything beneath his surface as he sat up straight and said, "Is seven thirty too early for you?"

Dove's mouth dropped open. Afraid to speak, she slowly closed it. Had she just heard correctly?

The way he was watching her, brow raised, gave her the sense that she should go with a *yes* just to get out of the tension flooding the room before it drowned her.

"No," she said. Just as she'd been taught to follow her heart, she'd also learned how important it was to put on her big-girl panties when life got tough.

"Then, I'll meet you there, tomorrow morning, at seven thirty."

Nodding, silent—for fear of somehow cracking the very thin layer of ice upon which she stood—she rose and turned toward the door.

"Dove?"

His voice, the way he'd said her name, slid through her. Not so much with the fear she'd have anticipated but with something just as forceful. So much so that she stopped in her tracks. Stood frozen, her back still to him.

"No funny stuff," he said then. At which she did fly around.

"What?" Her frown spoke of her genuine perplexity.

"No oil incensing, candles burning or any other means to manipulate an outcome that you might not like."

Had he not sounded so genuinely serious, she would probably have been offended.

"I guess that includes voodoo dolls?" she asked, tongue in cheek. And couldn't quite stop her droll tone. She managed to keep a straight face, though. For which she was immensely proud.

She was kind of taken aback at the slight sideways tip of his head and the possible hint of a smile turning up the corners of his lips, as he said, "Yes."

With a nod, she turned back to the door, eager to make her exit before something happened to change his mind.

"Dove?" he called a second time. Sounding more as if he was calling out to someone he knew. Curious, in spite of herself, she turned back again.

His expression had changed. There was no mistaking the seriousness there as he said, "This is only a cursory glance, out of respect for your father. Don't get your hopes up."

"I understand," she told him and then bugged out before he could call on her a third time. She fully grasped that from his perspective, there was no reason for hope in the matter between them.

But he didn't view life in quite the same way she did. He likely saw the world analytically. With an eye to preventing danger or damage. And that was fine. For him. To her way of thinking, if one gave up hope, one might as well stop breathing, too.

Chapter 2

Suit or cargo pants? Mitchell faced the question Saturday morning as he finished a workout in his home weight room and headed for the shower. Not looking forward to the seven thirty appointment at St. James Boats.

Wearing his lawyer hat, suit every time. But if he wanted to make the most use of his time, he'd take a quick look around St. James Boats, fulfilling his obligation to Dove, and then help Whaler's business by renting a fishing boat and heading out toward the sound. Which meant cargo pants.

Wouldn't be the overnight hiking adventure he'd planned for his weekend, but a way to salvage the day just the same.

Definitely cargo pants… Cargo pants if he was okay with being a self-centered ass. Whether he was wasting his time, professionally speaking, or not, he'd agreed to give the woman a few moments of his expertise. He wasn't going to disrespect her by showing up ready to fish.

Which was why, half an hour later, Mitchell was the only person at St. James Boats in dress clothes, tie, and leather dress shoes—expensive ones—that had already been splashed on twice. They most definitely didn't have the sole necessary to efficiently traverse the dock he was touring.

The area was overrun with the end-of-summer tourist rush. Not the best time for him to be there, but Dove had requested he visit then due to the six-passenger glacier charter Whaler was captaining that morning. Meaning Whaler wouldn't be privy to Dove's request for Mitchell's help.

Dove was thorough. He'd give her that. She might be as flighty as her name implied—as evidenced by the elastic-waisted purple and pink balloon pants she had on with a crop top and tennis shoes—but when it came to her father's livelihood, she'd educated herself impressively.

To the point that, after the tour of the docks—including a listing of every boat's use, power, sleeping capacity, and value—and brief introductions to the two full-time staff members who were busy with customers, he had a sincere interest in following her into the office and getting a look at the inner workings of Whaler's business.

"Unfortunately, it all goes downhill from here," Dove said as she led him into her father's office. "I've tried to make sense of what I could, but when I saw that even if I sorted out the various receipts, reservations, charges— basically I need an accountant for that—the problem is bigger than paperwork and bank accounts." She threw up a hand, and his glance caught on the plethora of rings spanning every one of her fingers.

Most, he was guessing, remnants of her mother's home-made jewelry business. Having spent so much of her child-hood exclusively with her Mom, Dove couldn't help being like the woman.

She'd stopped talking and was watching him stand there.

Clearly, she was waiting for him to figure out what to do, to start looking at ways a lawyer might be able to help, rather than thinking about rings and…her slender, soft-looking hands.

Straightening the knot on his tie, reminding himself why he was there, he said, "I've actually got a couple of ideas."

That was the truth and not one he'd planned to share. With twofold reasoning. He'd need Whaler's cooperation, which meant anything he might think to suggest was a moot point until Dove talked to her father. And he didn't want to give the false impression that he could help when he wasn't yet sure that he could.

His gut clenched with tension when Dove's eyes widened and a very definite new light came into them. "You do?" she asked. Her hands clasped together in front of her breasts as she said, "I had such a strong impression that I had to see you, and yet I was still so worried. I should have had more faith."

"I didn't say I could help, Dove," Mitchell was compelled to point out. "Just that I have some thoughts to pursue that will determine if I can. Or can't."

She smiled. Nodded. "I understand," she said but didn't look as though she did at all. "You take your look. Do what you need to do. And then let me know our plan."

What the hell?

"We don't have…" he started then stopped when she shook her head, waving both of her hands in front of her face.

"I know," she said, her tone still light and breezy. "But I've been given all the signs I need. You'll find what you need to know how to help. And I'll be right here, ready to take on any task you have for me. As soon as you have it."

With that, she moved to a small wall space that wasn't cluttered with boxes and papers, boat parts, file cabinets or the desk and chair that took up most of the room. Sliding down the wall, she sat on the floor, legs crossed, hands on her knees, palms up, and closed her eyes.

He could be gone before she knew it. Just quietly head out. Get in a day hike. Far away from any and all doves in the world.

It was the sensible thing to do. Full of logic and good business sense, too.

He took a quiet step toward the door. Stopping, he pictured her opening her eyes to find him gone.

And dropped his dress pants–clad butt in her father's greasy old chair.

Breathe. In through the nose. Out through the mouth. Deep breaths. Relax. One muscle at a time. Toes first. No, better make that neck. Breathe. Cleansing breaths.

Until she could get to her crystals and have a private session of hot yoga.

Losing focus once again, Dove refused to open her eyes. To give up. In spite of the bad karma emanating from the man seated behind her father's desk.

Seriously. The man was filling her aura with his negative energy. She could only imagine what it was doing to his. She should offer him a session.

Imagining the tight layers they'd have to get through to even find his spirit, she figured the long process would be a fair trade for his help at St. James Boats.

Deep breath. Eyes closed. You don't need to look at him. He's there. His tension is suffocating you. No reason to open your eyes. Even if you saw what drawer he was reaching into, you wouldn't know the significance. Breathe. Do. Not. Open. Your. Eyes.

When Dove realized that she was expending far too much precious energy on keeping her eyes closed, she opened them.

Energy was the one thing she absolutely did not have to

waste. Without it, she had nothing to offer her clients. And without them, she couldn't afford to live.

Negativity! Negativity! Negativity!

Deep breaths!

Slower ones.

You hyperventilate and he's really going to think you're a flake. Not worth his time.

Stop.

Blinking, Dove put an end to the destructive self-talk. Reaching into the big pocket on the right leg of her pants, she pulled out her cell phone and the vial of lavender oil she'd also stashed in there with it that morning.

Uncapping the bottle like she'd seen her father do to a bottle of whiskey—with shaky hands and obvious urgency—she didn't even try to hide the small glass bottle held up to her nostril as she inhaled. All the way to her core. And then again.

Recognizing the familiar scent, her body instantly settled. Started to relax. Delivering a shot of zen. Her stomach relaxed.

And her gaze wandered over to Mitchell Colton. A wave of euphoria hit then. A sense that all would be well.

The man really was too gorgeous for the small town of Shelby to handle. At least, unattached as he was. His physical form, features that depicted ruggedness and a sense of dependable astuteness at the same time, was overpowering.

Add to it the deep timbre of a voice that seemed to assure you that it spoke the truth and eyes that held a surprising depth, and a woman could hardly be blamed for having a swoon or two.

He gathered a slew of papers together. Straightened them into one pile.

Was he done?

She didn't want to ask. Didn't want to interrupt.

And desperately needed to know their plan before her father returned. She might only get the one shot to convince Whaler that engaging Mitchell Colton's services was not only a good idea but paramount if his business was to survive.

Someone was bound to tell Bob St. James that the town's only corporate attorney had been taking a tour of his docks. Maybe even ask him if he was thinking about selling the place.

Which meant Dove had to get to him first.

With a positive plan.

It only worked with that plan pre-established and first steps ready to implement…

"I'm missing a couple of boat invoices." The deep timbre broke into her thoughts.

Panic hit her. She knew nothing about her father's bookkeeping other than the drastically bad state she'd found it in.

"*Ladybird* and *Wicked Winnings*. You have any idea where they might be?"

Euphoria hit again. Just a small wave. Reminded her that it was there. That she just had to access it. Trust. Refuse to let fear have any portion of her brain. "*Wicked Winnings* was actually a win," she said, half smiling at the memory. "Dad bought a couple hundred raffle tickets because proceeds went to support the leukemia foundation." Leukemia. The earthborn darkness that had taken her mother back home far too soon for Dove's liking. "A boat maker in Anchorage had put the small trawler up as a prize. A buck for a chance to win a boat? It seemed like everyone in the state bought into that one. The guy ended up buying enough tickets himself to pay for twice what the boat had cost to begin with. He got the write-off for his business. And he gave my dad the boat. He knew about my mom."

She was surprised Mitchell didn't know the story.

He'd turned to face her, his gaze alight with what felt like real interest. "When was this?"

She shrugged, not always that great with earthly time passage. "Ten years, maybe?"

He nodded. "I was in law school."

Right. He'd won a full scholarship to Harvard. She'd still been in high school, and every teacher, the principal, pretty much anyone who was vested in getting students to study and get good grades, had held up the possibility of a Harvard scholarship as potential reward.

She'd forgotten about that. Studied him anew at the memory.

The man, for all his surface living, had more layers than she'd expected.

Interesting. But not pertinent to the moment. Or his purpose in her life.

He was still looking at her. It felt like he was touching her, too. In what seemed to be a kind way. Unless she was self-imposing her own needs onto him.

Seeing herself starting down a path upon which she would only get lost, Dove gave herself a mental shake and forced herself to focus on the more mundane—but vitally important. "*Ladybird* was Mom's boat. She used an inheritance from her grandmother to buy it after she got sick. She used to take me out on the water and…"

No. Stick to the mundane.

"She left it to my father in his will—"

Emotion welled, but anything else Dove might have said was interrupted by the sound of her cell phone alerting her to a call.

A particular call.

From a problem she was tackling by begging Mitchell Colton into helping her father.

Brad Fletcher.

He's looking for a soul to steal. The line from the famous song filled the room. She'd set the ringtone to remind her not to let the man trick her into captivity.

Fear struck her. She let the phone ring twice. She had to answer it. Wouldn't let him think he'd intimidated her. *He's looking for a soul to steal.* The line of the famous song played a third time. Giving her a boost of strength. She needed at least one more.

"Are you going to get that?" Mitchell's voice pulled her out of her haze. Drew her gaze in his direction.

And she didn't need the fourth ring.

Filled with confidence, she said, "Hello?"

Mitchell didn't mean to eavesdrop. The office space Whaler had chosen for himself among the buildings on his little property was about the size of a cubbyhole.

He still couldn't make out all of the words booming from Dove's phone. A *take it or leave it* and *best you're going to get.*

It wasn't so much the words that had him tuning in. It was the tone of voice he heard over the smartphone in Dove's hand.

That, and the way her hand was shaking.

A sign of fear or weakness at odds with her tone as she said, "I've told you, Mr. Fletcher, I'm not interested. Please do not call again."

She was pushing to end the call as she issued the last word.

Timed perfectly. Like a movie scene that had had many takes and film editing to make it so.

Her phone calls were none of his business. Except that she'd asked for his help. Beyond that, he'd heard a threatening tone that had raised the lawyer in him. "What was that about?" he asked, without a hint of apology.

"Brad Fletcher. My dad won't take his calls or open his emails, so he's taken to calling me. He wants to buy St. James Boats. I've told him multiple times that we aren't interested in selling. And the offer he just made was so low, no way I'd accept. He keeps warning me about the business losing equity and that when I'm forced to sell, he'll get it for half of what he just offered."

Mitchell's radar had been up just from the man's tone. He liked the situation even less with Dove's added information.

"There was menace in his tone, Dove. You need to be careful. Block his number. If he shows up here, call the police." His lawyer's brain was going at Mach speed. They could file for a restraining order...

On what grounds? A phone call? A tone of voice? Because the man hadn't actually issued a threat. Except by way of stating the obvious. Whaler's business was failing. The longer he waited to sell it, the less it would be worth.

Unless Mitchell found a way to help St. James Boats succeed.

"I just need to take care of things here," Dove said, glancing around the office. "If Dad can start turning a profit again, we don't need to worry about the business losing value."

Her words so oddly aligned with his own thoughts that the response popping into Mitchell's head seemed perfectly logical.

"I might be able to help with that."

He regretted the words the second he said them. Most

particularly when Dove flew toward him. Threw her arms around his neck and hugged him.

Before stepping back. "Thank you," she said. "What's next?"

"You go do what you normally do in a day and give me time to get that far."

She was already heading toward the door. And Mitchell's gut tightened. "Dove?" he called her back a second time.

She turned. "Yeah?"

"I'm serious. You be careful with that Fletcher guy. Block his number. And if he shows up anywhere near you, err on the side of caution and call the police. Tell them I told you to, if it comes to that."

Sometimes it helped to have a big-brother cop.

With a nod, accompanied by a smile so huge it felt like another hug, the woman finally left Mitchell in peace.

And five seconds later he was on the internet via his phone, looking up every Brad Fletcher within the area code he'd been able to make out on Dove's screen.

He might never come up with a feasible plan to get Whaler's business back to health, but he could damned sure see to it that the old captain's daughter didn't fall prey to its demise, too.

Chapter 3

Freed from chaperoning Mitchell Colton in her father's office, Dove got to work helping out on the docks. While she didn't know anything about general maintenance or fixing the boats—her father had always insisted that was men's work—she'd been helping with tourist check-in on and off since her father had used his savings to buy his own boats and start the business.

She had also adjusted her class schedule at the studio to free up Saturday mornings when her father had been forced to let Oscar go.

The adjusted schedule was temporary. As was, Whaler hoped, the termination. He was ready to rehire Oscar as soon as the man got sober.

Holding the position open was part of what was hurting the business. While most of the revenue came from boat rentals, Whaler used to make good money with the chartered excursions he and Oscar had run on a regular basis. He'd had to take those outings off the St. James Boats offerings at the start of the current tourist season. With Oscar gone, and as much as Whaler was drinking, he'd made the responsible choice, in terms of client safety.

The best choice, of course, would have been to curtail his own drinking. Something he was managing to do on a case by case basis as special requests came in for excursions. He'd blow completely sober before he went out and when he got back, too. An hour later, no way.

As she headed to her studio before lunch, needing an hour of self-provided therapy before her afternoon classes began, Dove still hadn't heard from Mitchell Colton with any kind of plan. She found herself thinking not about what that silence meant in terms of her hopes but about the fact that the lawyer hadn't pointed out the most obvious solution.

Bob St. James had to sober up.

With a failing business that wasn't going to happen.

If he was sober, the business would bounce back.

Catch-22. Which comes first, the chicken or the egg. She'd been diving headfirst into emotional pools of bad energy with her lack of solutions every time she thought about convincing her father to try and go even a day without getting drunk.

But if Mitchell could find a way to help her save the business in the interim, her father would sober up. She just had to believe that.

On a wave of hope, she climbed the stairs to her studio, key in hand to unlock the door. And stopped just short of reaching to slide it in the slot it matched. The doorknob was tilted at a downward angle. And the quarter-inch gap between the jamb and the front of the door told her that it wasn't latched. Pulled closed, but not tightly.

Curious more than anything else, she pushed a shoulder against the door. Hanging back enough that if someone was inside, she could call out and be heard by Repo customers at the bottom of the stairs.

When no sound came, she cautiously took one step and then another. Could be there'd been a leak from her bathroom and maintenance had had to get in to fix it before it damaged goods in the store below. The plumbing was old. She'd put in requests to have it fixed but hadn't pushed because she couldn't afford to have her rent raised.

She also hadn't delivered a key to the place after she'd had the locks changed shortly after moving in. She trusted her landlords implicitly. Not so much the taxidermist who'd had the space before her.

She'd spent a month ridding her studio of bad energy before she'd moved a single thing in. With salt in a bowl at the door, scrubbing every corner and then applying pinches of salt in each one of them, burning incense and essential oils, leaving windows open when the air outside was fresh, leaving music playing twenty-four seven at frequencies that were proven to relieve tension, she'd finished by changing the locks.

Four steps was what it took to get around the wall that faced the studio's front door and blocked the peace of the classes from those entering. There was also a wall filled with cubbies in which clients stored their personal belongings—suffused with energy from their everyday lives—before entering the studio itself.

Four steps and Dove froze. Gasping for air. Eyes flooding with tears, she found the strength to move her head, allowing her a glimpse from one end of the studio to the other.

The entire space had been trashed. Literally. The expensive sprung wood floors she'd put in were covered in what looked to be an entire garbage truck's worth of everyday items human beings threw away. Piles of it. A crushed empty toilet paper roll. Empty cans. Broken and stained food containers. A ripped egg carton.

And the smell...spoiled food? Used hygiene items?

Covering her nose and mouth, she stood there, tears

streaming down her cheeks. Unable to comprehend what she was seeing.

Feelings always came first. They spoke the loudest within her.

And in that moment, all Dove knew was despair.

Mitchell's plan was half-formed and weak at best. He'd found problems with the leasing agreement Whaler had signed years before, giving him lifetime access to the dock space he used. The fishing captain had been charged illegal fees over a period of years. Enough so that the money would be a boon.

St. James Boats needed employee contracts that better delineated a benefit package that would serve the two men who worked for him but also save the company money.

Mitchell could oversee contract negotiations under which Whaler could use the equity in *Wicked Winnings* to borrow enough money to buy two new smaller boats to be rented out for private fishing charters—currently St. James Boats largest income stream. But without Whaler sober and at the helm of his operation, Mitchell didn't see much hope of any of it making a big enough difference to save the business.

That particular message wasn't first on his list as he climbed the stairs inside Repo to speak with Dove before her afternoon classes started. Assuming she was adhering to the schedule he'd just accessed on the Namaste website.

He'd also spent time that morning doing some research on Brad Fletcher. And did not like what he'd found.

Mitchell was equally displeased as he saw the studio door standing open—allowing anyone to enter as they pleased. He'd just warned Dove to be extra careful. Keeping her studio door closed and locked while she was in there alone was part of that. She could unlock it when it was time for class.

Muscles tensed beneath his shirt, he pushed on the door with one shoulder. And was hit simultaneously with an eerie silence... and dreadful smell.

In two strides he was around the wall blocking the entry from the studio and ran straight into Dove's back. Catching her shoulders between his hands, he held her upright long enough for her to give a backward jab of her elbow straight into his rib cage.

And barely had the wherewithal to protect his area as she spun with a knee already poised to hit. Hard.

"Oh!" Her exclamation was part of a hiccup as she looked up, her gaze—wide-eyed and blank—connecting with his.

Aware of the destruction in his peripheral vision, Mitchell tuned out any specifics as he saw the tears dripping down Dove's face.

Had he been too late? Fletcher had done something to her?

Filled with an anger that was foreign to him, he softened his hold on her arms, though not letting go as he feared she might need his support. "Are you okay?" he asked.

His gaze intent, he brushed by his own mental *Of course she isn't* to get the information he needed first. Had she been physically compromised in any way?

When she just stared up at him, he rephrased the question. "Are you hurt?"

Her eyes cleared some as she frowned. Opened her mouth slowly. And said, "Not physically."

Relief flooded through Mitchell. More than any he'd ever experienced in court when a questionable verdict came back in his favor.

With the confirmation that he wasn't rushing her to emergency care, he took his first good glance over her shoulder and tensed all over again.

"Who did this?"

Dove shrugged. But it was the desolate look in those big green eyes that caught him. "I just got here and found it like this," she said. "I think the lock on the door was broken." Her voice was threadbare. Sounding nothing like the woman who'd spent the past twenty-four hours challenging him to step up.

Strands of that long auburn hair, wet with tears, were sticking to the sides of her face. He pushed them back over her shoulders. Like somehow that was the first task toward making something better.

What, in her life, he could improve, he had no idea.

Only one thing was clear to him.

Pulling out his phone, Mitchell tapped the contact for his older brother. A lieutenant in the state major crimes division, Eli didn't handle break-ins, but he'd get someone over to the studio who did. More than that, he had the means to quickly find out where Brad Fletcher had been all morning.

To look for any evidence there might be of him or someone he hired having been on Main Street.

And to have someone keep an eye on the man in the meantime.

Mitchell was there. His phone to his ear, though he hadn't yet spoken. She had no idea who he was calling. Or why. She just stood by him, shaking, until he said, "Come on, we've got to get you out of here."

Still in shock, she wasn't even sure he was talking to her, until his grip on her elbow brought her to an awareness that he wanted her to move toward the door.

She went. At that moment, she knew of no reason not to do so.

Until she was standing out in the hallway, listening as he said, "Eli." In a tone urgent enough to shake her up and out of the stupor she'd fallen into.

Eli. He'd called his brother, the cop.

He broke into a concise accounting of the past few minutes, detailing the state of her studio, while trying to lead Dove away. With awareness slowly coming back, Dove dug her heals in. She needed to hear Mitchell's conversation, and she wasn't leaving until she could find a way to block off the door of the studio.

No way she could have any of her clients seeing the space in its current condition. The traumatic sight could leave a permanent scar that would block the good energy they came to her seeking.

She had to call them all. Immediately. Prevent them from experiencing the horror still assailing her in waves.

Thoughts tumbled one after another, until she heard, "Bob St. James is a new client..."

He'd officially taken them on? She'd told him his bill would have to come in monthly installments. She'd gladly sign on to paying them for the rest of her life if that's what it took.

Relief and horror mingled inside her.

With a hand still wrapped around her elbow, Mitchell took another step toward the stairs. She held her ground. And he said, "Have them get eyes on Brad Fletcher."

The name tore through her. And she moved with him to the staircase. She could stand guard and prevent any of her students from seeing the degradation in their peaceful place from the bottom of the stairs just as easily as she could the top. Should have already thought of that.

Brad Fletcher?

"I looked into him this morning," Mitchell spoke softly, but with authority into his phone. "He owns boat rental places up and down the sound, with Shelby being a noticeable hole in his monopoly, and, due to our location in relation to the glaciers, a definite drain on his tourist population. He issued a very clear threat to Bob's daughter, Dove, this morning. Cushioned, but clearly there. I heard it myself."

They were halfway down the stairs. And in the next second, Mitchell had hung up. "Eli's on it," he told her. "The police will be here in a minute or two, and then we need to get you out of here until they know more."

She needed to back up a step. "My dad's business is cutting into this Brad Fletcher guy's profits?" she asked, refusing to go down another stair until she had her answer.

Mitchell's gaze met hers. "Most definitely."

She'd searched the man on the internet. Knew he had similar businesses to her father, but every town had similar businesses to those in other towns. How Mitchell had secured actual financial information, she had no idea, but he was good. Far better than she'd expected if the past minutes were anything to go by.

But that wasn't all. Looking him in the eye, she asked, "You're taking us on?"

He held her gaze. Didn't speak. And her tension escalated. "You just told your brother that my father was a new client."

He nodded. "He is at the moment. Because I've taken your authority to seek my assistance at face value. But what's going to happen when Whaler gets back from today's cruise and hears about what you've done?"

Right. His question was valid. But there was no way

she was going to lose his help. "You leave my father to me," she said.

She'd call in every single card she had, if that's what it took, to get Bob St. James to concede on this one. She might not wield enough power over his heart to compel him to stay away from the bottle. But even if she had to remind her father that her mother's last wish had been that the two of them carry on their family unit so that she could smile down on them together from her place in heaven, she'd do so to get him to see that his drinking had left them no other choice but to seek help.

Because she couldn't continue to hold the two of them together without it.

Mitchell heard the very real determination but also the load of bravado in Dove's assertion that she'd handle her father. As right as she was about Whaler's dire straits, she had to know that part of the reason for the current situation was the man's refusal to admit he needed help.

With anything.

Including his drinking.

Which meant that the only one who could help the old fishing captain at the moment was Bob St. James himself. And Whaler just didn't seem to have what it took to face the truth.

Or to have enough internal strength left to do the work required to fix things.

Two officers were entering the building as Mitchell and Dove hit the bottom of the stairs. They took down Dove's brief statement. Asked a couple of questions. And reminded her that with Shelby's low crime rate and no need for CCTV or alarms, they didn't have a lot to go on. They'd secure the scene. Dust for fingerprints. But without a witness, there was no telling who'd vandalized the property.

When the officers went upstairs, Mitchell stayed close to Dove as she called clients to cancel the day's sessions, determined to give her the assistance he could before getting on with his weekend plans.

It appeared that the biggest challenge facing St. James Boats—and currently the most critical one—was Brad Fletcher. Who was not in Mitchell's lawyerly wheelhouse. Investigative efforts had to run their course first and foremost. Something which Mitchell had just set in motion.

So…he'd helped. Fulfilled whatever prophecy Dove thought she'd envisioned pertaining to him. He just had to make sure that she was safe until the police had eyes on Brad Fletcher, and then he'd be off on a boat. Or hiking some remote neck of the woods that would be treacherous enough to discourage anyone else from seeking him out.

Just until Monday. Then he'd be back in the office and willingly at the beck and call of anyone and everyone who could benefit from the talents and skills he had to offer.

They'd reached their cars—he'd deliberately parked next to hers—in silence. Her proclamation to leave her father to her, still lingered between them.

"I'm going to follow you home," he told her unequivocally. Until she heard back from those processing her studio, she had no way of knowing what kind of danger, if any, she might be in.

Still, he hadn't needed to tell her his plans. The streets were public property. Anyone could use them. He just hadn't wanted her to freak out if she saw him right behind her as she turned into the drive of the small house she rented by the marina. Or saw him parked out front until she got inside.

Stopping as she reached for the handle on the door, she turned to him. "I'm not going home. I'm going to the marina to see my father, and I'd rather you didn't follow me. It'll go better if I have a chance to talk to him without him seeing you hanging around."

"He'll have heard by now that I was there this morning." They were in Shelby, not Anchorage. There were few secrets in their small town. And word traveled fast.

"Yes, but no one knew why," Dove said, seemingly unfazed by his point. Her confidence impressed him. As did her, "No need to make him feel as though we're ganging up on him before the conversation even begins."

She really believed she had a chance to get Whaler's approval of her plan.

The realization gave Mitchell pause for the second it took him to remember that Dove also thought that sitting on the floor with her eyes closed and taking deep breaths made the bad things that happened in life go away.

Or that cleansing auras could change someone's life. When, clearly, it was actions taken every day from choices made—either deliberately or not—that determined one's course.

He was facing just such a choice. And knew that his course would take a downward spiral if he watched her drive off and then heard that something happened to her on the way to the marina. "I'll follow you long enough to see you make it back safely and then keep driving," he told her. "But only if you allow me to call and make arrangements for someone to check your house and then see that you get home safely tonight." The words came without forethought.

Not a usual occurrence for him. Or one of which he was fond.

Dove's eyes narrowed on him. The way she studied him,

as though she could see things others couldn't, made him feel like he did when a fly was buzzing around him. He needed to swat the intrusion away. Keep his space to himself.

And was about to tell her so when her gaze cleared, and she nodded. "I would appreciate you making that call," she told him. Surprising him yet again. "And if you could have someone let me know when I can get back into the studio to start cleanup, I'd be thankful for that, too."

Cocking his head, he watched her, looking for something more ethereal attached to the words, but discerned nothing more than a practical request. And so he nodded and said, "I'm happy to do so." He wasn't just being polite. He felt good about helping the woman.

Brushing the thought aside, Mitchell took a few quick steps to his own vehicle and had the engine started before he pulled the door closed. Not trusting Dove to actually give him a chance to position himself behind her.

She did, though. Waiting to pull out into traffic until she'd had a nod from him, and then stopped at a yellow light when she saw that he wouldn't be able to make it through the intersection without stopping.

The woman might be flighty, what he'd call woo-woo, even, but she appeared to put value in keeping her word. As did he.

A nice note with which to seal the ending of their short acquaintance.

Chapter 4

There was nothing nice, or particularly noteworthy, about the situation in which Dove found herself. Within minutes of watching Mitchell Colton drive away, she was once again in her father's office. Pacing. Which she hated. On the floor in the lotus position would be the better choice.

But anything that reminded Bob St. James of his wife—which Dove did just by existing, so no need to exacerbate that by practicing her teachings in front of him—made the downward spiral worse.

"You like Mitchell," she said, for the third time in as many minutes.

With another tip of his whiskey bottle at his lips, Whaler swallowed. Smacked his lips and nodded. "'S right, I do," he said, the slur already obvious in his diction. "But no reason for him to be in here."

The petulant tone, along with another swig, did not bode well. But Dove had no other option but to take him on. And words came to her.

"Fletcher called again, Dad…" she started, only to have him cut her off with a wave of the hand holding his bottle, on the way to his mouth.

"Call all he wansh. He can't toush ish place," the man said, full of whiskey-induced bravado.

"Mitchell heard the conversation," she said then, raising her voice only a notch and instilling the sternness she'd heard her mother use on Whaler a time or two when he'd been working himself too hard. "Found it to be threatening enough that he called Eli to check into the guy. Apparently, Fletcher is a shady character."

She stopped short of telling her father about the break-in at the studio. Only because, due to his drunken state, she feared what foolish thing the man might do to avenge her.

Whaler's grunt gave her hope. She rode it for the few seconds she needed to breathe and ready herself for battle.

"Mitchell's smart, Dad. And noticed some other things while he was here. Things he can help with. I think we need to take him up on his offer." She chose the words carefully. "Before Fletcher tries anything more than just threats."

Whaler put the bottle on his desk. Hard. "No."

Standing still, she faced him. "Dad—"

Slamming his hand down on the desk, Whaler stood, too. Slurring some very strong words the gist of which she understood.

He had the right to make his own choices. Even if they were the wrong ones.

In any other circumstance, Dove would have looked him in the eye, nodded, told him she loved him and walked out.

She couldn't do that. They'd reached the end of the road.

A brand-new thing between them. With no set protocol to direct her.

So Dove did what she had to do to maintain her own inner harmony. Which would give her the equilibrium to deal with Whaler's lack of any kind of peace. Sliding down to the floor against the wall, she closed her eyes. Took slow, steady breaths. Envisioned the sun shining, bringing warmth to her skin. Chasing away the shivers of anxiety that were fighting to take control of her.

Other than the occasional sloshing of liquid as her father lifted his bottle to his mouth, she sat in silence. To his credit Whaler just let her be.

Respecting her need for a personal time-out?

Or just glad that she'd quit harping at him?

More likely, her decision not to walk out had gotten through to him. At least enough to clue him in that something was more wrong between them than it ever had been before.

And he was leery of waking a beast inside her?

The thought brought another singe of tension. And the threat of tears. The last thing she wanted to do was bring any kind of negative emotion to her father. He was already being eaten alive by the grief life had brought him.

Which was precisely why she had to stay her course. To help him find some joy again. Next to her and her mother, he loved St. James Boats more than anything else. If she could just give him a glimpse of what it would be again with Mitchell's help, then maybe he'd lay off the bottle enough to help them make it happen.

She just had to show him that there was joy left to be had in his life.

If the stars fully aligned for him, maybe he could even get to a point where he'd be open to counseling. And be restored to the healthy man he'd been before her mother had gotten sick.

Peace settled over her, and she inhaled the silence. Taking comfort from knowing that her father was right there, breathing in with her. Breathing out.

In between swigs from his bottle.

And that was okay, too, just for those moments. Because

there was always a point in Whaler's drinking when he hit the mellow stage, as she'd learned to think of it.

It came after aggressive, and before he passed out.

A plan became obvious as she cleared her mind and the cloud of negativity. She had to sit quietly with her dad and wait for the mellow stage.

Sometimes it took longer than others. Depending on how much or how quickly he was drinking. Straight out of the bottle, as rapidly as she was hearing it rise to his mouth, she figured another ten minutes or so ought to do it.

He was checking out for the day. She recognized the signs.

Something on the cruise must have triggered his grief. Anything could do it. The sound of a bird at just the right time could remind him of a picnic he'd had with her mother when they were in high school. A wave might be a replica of one they'd first dunked Dove in when they'd taught her to swim.

"They'uz ha-ha-ving a grand time."

Dove's eyes flew open as her father spoke. Centering on him immediately. "Who was?" she asked, truly wanting to know.

To somehow get inside his pain so she could help lead him out of it. Even as her logical mind made note of the fact that they'd arrived at mellow. Which meant she had about fifteen minutes before his chin dropped to his chest.

"People. I made 'em laffff. Your ma…ma…" His attempt to speak was interrupted by a big belch. And without even seeming to realize it had happened, he continued, "Ma… motherrr…she said I was…good…at thhaaat."

With a sad smile and a nod, Dove said, "Yes, she did. She used to tell everyone what a great time you'd show them if they booked a trip out with you."

Whaler's gaze found her then, his eyes bloodshot and weary-looking. "I missh her sooo mush."

"I know, Dad. I do, too. And that's why we have to get through this together, just like Mom said. You and me, we stick together, so she can look down and see both of us at once." She spoke softly but didn't let herself pause long enough for him to flop to another train of thought. "And that's why I need you to do something for me. I can't just sit here and watch this place fall apart. I want to be here more. Help out more. But I don't know nearly as much as you do. And Mitchell, he's an adventurer just like the rest of his family. Yeah, he's got a law degree and sits in an office during the week, but on weekends, from what I hear, he goes it alone even more than his family does. He does it out of love for the land, the sea, the adventure, just like you do. That's why I need him here for a bit. Helping out. Just until we get through this rough patch, and get Fletcher off our tails." Whaler was still conscious, still watching her, so she pressed on. "I need you to sign a contract that will let me be an equal signer on St. James Boats, Dad. That way, if you're having a bad day or are out at sea, I can make decisions here and help you fight off the Fletchers in the world. Just like Mom would do."

Crawling on her knees, she stopped right in front of her dad, putting her hands on his knees, and looked up at him. "Please?" She wasn't just fighting for his life, but for her own, too. She was half him. He was all the family she had left.

"Not highing law, juss 'venture." His eyes were cloudy, but he was still with her.

She didn't move. Didn't speak. She wouldn't lie to him. When he lifted a hand and put it in her hair, softly cupping her head, she couldn't stop the tears that sprang to her eyes. No matter what, he was her father, and she loved him.

"'Kay."

Eyes widening, she sat encased in stillness. As though a veil of safety had enclosed her. "You'll sign?"

Looking her in the eye, he nodded.

And Dove jumped up, rushing to his computer she searched for a contract, filled in some blanks and within a few minutes had it printed and ready for him to sign. But before she gave him the pen, she made the call for the police escort Mitchell had arranged for her, telling her father that she had to talk to the police about her call with Fletcher—true—just not the reason for her call. And when the officer arrived, she gave Whaler the pen. Dove called in the college boy her father had helping out that summer and, with the cop and the deckhand as witnesses, had her father sign his name.

It was possible that, once sober, Whaler wouldn't recall a whit of what had transpired over the last half hour. And equally possible that he'd wake up in the morning and remember it all.

Either way, with document in hand, she had her chance to save his business. And him.

Against all odds, the stars had led her right again.

It was like her mother had always taught her.

She just had to hold on to hope.

It would show her the way.

Mitchell's phone beeped a text at just after eight Saturday night, the moment he stepped up and onto a cliff face overlooking the sea, eight thousand feet up in the Chugach mountain range. The only place he knew of where he could get service.

Why he'd headed in that direction, he didn't want to contemplate. His family was used to him disappearing without leaving word during his time off. Most particularly during the summer when temperatures were mild and days were long.

But with only another hour plus before sunset, if he was going home that night, he had to start his downward trek so he'd be hiking on more level ground by the time it was fully dark.

The sleeping bag hooked to the bottom of his pack told a different story. The plan was to sleep alone up in the mountains where no one would find him. To rest without everyone's cares on his shoulders.

So why was he checking his phone?

He asked the question silently, not seeking an answer, as his thumb pressed the screen to open his messaging app.

Dove St. James.

A contact he'd added that afternoon. Just in case she needed him to put in another call to Eli. To use his influence with the ABI major crimes office in Shelby regarding the ongoing investigations into Fletcher and the studio break-in. Not that there'd been a major crime.

Yet.

Prevention was Mitchell's job. One he took to heart with utmost dedication.

She'd sent two messages. One a single sentence: Dad's on board. Followed by the second, which was a photo of a rudimentary contract, giving Dove St. James power of attorney rights for St. James Boats. It wasn't notarized but had two witness signatures.

Without the notary, Whaler could argue the validity of

the contract in court. But unless the older man could argue convincingly that he'd signed under duress, he'd have a hard time winning.

And with a local cop as one of the signatories, a duress claim was unlikely to fly.

Another text buzzed against his palm. Dove's name flashed on his screen. As though the woman really did have some kind psychic connection and knew he'd been thinking about her.

Stopping that thought before it could settle, he shook his head against illogical intrusions and read.

I've been cleared to get back into my studio. I plan to be there at 7 tomorrow morning. Can you meet me afterward? Say, 9? At your office?

On a Sunday?

Seriously?

He read the missive a second time.

Hesitated to answer.

Then it hit him. Her timeline was good. Best that he get her taken care of and out of his hair before regular office hours on Monday.

In the event that urgent business hit his desk at the start of the week, he'd have his little sidebar done.

Sunrise was scheduled for just after five Sunday morning. He could bed down, get several good hours of rest and make it back to town and shower by nine, easy.

Unless he just met her at her studio at seven. No one should have to face the devastation he'd witnessed there alone. He could talk to her about St. James Boats while they straightened her place up. And then he'd have the rest of the day to head to the glaciers. Strap on his new cram-pons and head out on the ice.

He should test out the cleats before embarking on a lon-ger solo ice adventure with them.

Decision made through logical choice, Mitchell was in his bed at home by one in the morning and up at six. Was showered, dressed in jeans and a long-sleeved flannel shirt and leaning against the back wall outside of Repo, waiting for Dove when she arrived at five to seven.

He couldn't help but watch as she approached him. In purple leggings with a lighter see-through purple skirt made out of some kind of thin netting and a purple long-sleeved tightly fitting top that ended just above her belly button.

Did she dress purposely to make people stare at her? Her aim every morning when she looked in the closet was to appear as bizarrely as she could?

Had she any idea how sexy she looked?

Her purposeful stride spoke of determination, not a come-on.

She was about three feet away from where he stood in the doorway when she asked, "What's up?"

He shrugged. "I figured we could talk while you clean."

With a raised brow she glanced at his clothes. "You don't look dressed for business."

Looking her straight in the eye, he cocked his head at her and asked, "You want my help or not?"

She nodded, put her key in the door, swung it open, and glanced back at him. "Always. Just trying to figure out if I'm paying by the hour yet, or not."

Couldn't the woman accept some help without making a major event out of it? Let him ease his conscience some before he broke it to her that there was no point in her paying for his legal services until she had her bigger problems resolved. "The clock hasn't started yet" was all he said, as he held the door and followed her inside. ·

Chapter 5

Dove was fully prepared for cleanup duty. She'd spent an hour meditating that morning, separating self from other as one's aura did not have to take on another's. Blocking herself from the negative energy into which she'd be walking. She had a small lavender sachet tucked into the middle of her bra, between her breasts. And knew what music she was going to cue the second she walked into space that was her own.

In spite of the fact that another had inflicted harm there.

One sight of Mitchell Colton and she was grasping to hold on to her calm. Bending her head, she inhaled like she was taking in the last air left on earth. Focusing on the lavender scent wafting up to her, she walked through the back hallway of Repo and up the stairs to the second floor and her damaged sanctuary. The Repo maintenance guy had installed a brand-new lock for her the day before.

Her thoughts more on the lawyer than awaiting messes or new locks, she went with what was hitting her strongest. The man looked too good in a suit. Put those muscled arms and broad chest in a shirt that delineated them, rather than a jacket that hid them, and you had a whole new set of problems.

Or at least, in that moment, Dove did.

Wow.

All of the adventuring Colton men were fine specimens of the male ideal, but Mitchell... She'd had no idea he was so well endowed.

Turning to say something pithy, to rile him and get herself into a different mode, she stumbled on the step instead. He'd been closer to her than she'd realized. Her gaze had been shooting downward, to meet his gaze steps below. And instead landed on the fly of his jeans.

Which much more clearly hugged what it held than suit pants had done.

Wow.

Endowed indeed.

Infused as she was with the sight and the thoughts it engendered, she nevertheless made it into her studio without gagging over the sights and smells awaiting her. Dipping her head for sniffs of lavender again and again, she proceeded across the room to the counter and cupboards that served as desk, storage and sound system station. And zeroed in on feeling her own strength over the destructive emotions of whoever had violated her space.

"The police wanted me to check to see if anything's missing," she said. "Detective Welding was going to accompany me here last night, but I told him I'd rather look in the morning. I'm supposed to call him with a report. He said they took a look and saw my sound system untouched and laptop still hooked up under here..." She pulled out the keyboard drawer that slid from under the countertop, opened the computer and saw the home screen flash on normally, and continued with, "So they aren't expecting me to find anything gone. And without that, there's really no evidence for them to act upon at this time."

She was talking too fast. Glad to see her electronics

where and how they belonged. She hadn't even noticed them the day before.

But the rapid speech was more a result of the tsunami of sexual desire that had hit her on the stairs.

Mitchell Colton? Really?

Good to know her spirits had a sense of humor. And were using it to help her get through the process that lay immediately ahead.

"You have cleaning supplies around here?"

Even Mitchell's voice was sending pleasant shivers through her. With a grin, and a quick thanks to the loved ones she couldn't see, Dove bent to the cupboard below her laptop and pulled out a bucket filled with environmentally friendly cleansers, sponges and towels.

Pulling out a filled spray bottle and a couple of cloths, she passed the rest to the man who'd come up to the counter beside her. "You okay?" he asked.

"Yeah! Fine!" Her tone was a little on the squeaky side. He didn't know her well enough to know that, though. "Just eager to get this done, for obvious reasons, of course," she said as she sprayed and dropped to her knees to get the smears of what appeared to be ketchup off her cupboard. "Let's get to work. I want to hear your ideas and will do whatever it takes to implement them as soon as possible."

She might not be able prevent some of the things that happened around her or even, in part, to her. But she did have control over her own response to them. And of the thoughts and topics that she allowed to hold her focus. She could refuse to linger on that which brought negative energy into her heart. To replace such things with positive thoughts that were also relevant.

Like the fact that Mitchell Colton had ideas to help her save her father's business. And that nothing within her own minimally lucrative business had been damaged. Cleanup only cost a few dollars in supplies. And some elbow grease.

Her sound system and laptop, which could have imposed prohibitive costs, were fine.

So thinking, she stood, cued up the playlist that had come to her during her pre-cleanup meditation that morning. And focused on the golden glow that shone from the wood of her cupboards as they became cleaner than they'd been since she'd first rented the place.

She should have thought to polish them sooner.

And had just found a reason to be thankful that some unknown entity had spurred her on to getting it done.

Spending time alone with Dove in the quiet of her studio was not an easy thing. Mitchell found himself almost thankful for the smells of rotten food that permeated the areas he was working on—anything to keep his feet, and thoughts, firmly planted rather than flying around among the clouds painted on a back wall. Or falling into the trance the music Dove had playing was trying to suck him into.

Shame on her for that one. Trying to manipulate him into...what?

Helping her? She already believed he was on board to do that.

To...*desiring* her? No music needed for that one. The clothes had it covered.

And she hadn't given any hint of coming on to him. Or even noticing that he was male. He was a lawyer. He was help that she needed to save a business. Not a sexual being.

On his hands and knees, he was halfway across the floor when he heard what sounded like a cow mooing. He glanced over to see Dove standing near the end of the wall of cupboards she'd been cleaning, staring at her phone.

She had a moo as a ringtone? A new thing. He certainly hadn't heard the sound in her father's office the day before.

But then, she'd had a call. It appeared that whoever was currently communicating with her had texted.

Getting back to his work on the floor, Mitchell cut off all thoughts of Dove St. James. Whoever she talked to was no business of his.

Her feet walking on his clean floor, heading toward him, was. He looked up as she reached him, saw her handing her cell out to him.

He took it. Glanced at the screen, and then, recognizing the number, gave it his full attention. Switching immediately into work mode, he stood. "Fletcher dropped his offer by ten thousand overnight," he said aloud what she already knew, while his mind drew the obvious conclusion from the maneuver. The shady businessman was upping the pressure he was putting on Dove. Severely.

A person generally only did that when they believed they had someone over a barrel. When their target was running scared and ready to respond to being squeezed.

Pulling his own phone out of his pocket, Mitchell called Eli. Just like his older brother called him anytime he needed lawyerly advice for a case.

The call was short. Succinct. One sentence from him. And one back. Mitchell had eyes on Dove the entire time. The white lines around her lips, the stark glint replacing the usual warmth in her eyes held him there. As though, by a phone call, he could assure her that she'd have no reason to fear.

And that it was his job to do so.

Neither impression was valid.

"What did he say?" she asked as soon as he lowered his phone from his ear.

Mitchell paused, choosing his words carefully, as was his way, and Dove said, "He said something you didn't like."

She was right about that last part. Which anyone watching him closely could have discerned. That did *not* mean she had any special powers enabling her to read people.

Him in particular.

"Your face got stern," she said, helping him along.

"Brad Fletcher has no alibi during the hours this place was vandalized." He gave her a longer version than Eli had delivered. "He says he was out fishing. Alone. A team has been assigned to keep eyes on him."

Her cheeks paled as her eyes continued to seek something from his that he knew he didn't have to give. For a split second there, he almost wished his did.

Until she said, "We have to get to my dad."

We. Not *I.*

Blockades shot up inside him. Even as warmth oozed between them at the familiarity. At being considered a part of something that meant so much to someone.

He shook the thought away.

Because she was right. Whaler needed to know what was going on, to protect himself if nothing else, and the lawyer he'd thought he'd just hired was the proper man for that job.

Not the daughter with whom he had emotional investment and who might try to soften the blow.

"I'll drive," he told her, dropping his cleaning supplies on the counter and heading toward the door. He waited until she'd collected her purse and joined him and then, with a hand at her back, and eyes taking in everything around them, he escorted her out to his car.

Working. Only working.

Pro bono work, possibly.

But still, one hundred percent work.

His earlier conundrum with an unwelcomed awareness of the auburn-haired woman in her out-there clothes had nothing to do with the very real concern currently flooding through him on her behalf.

"He's not here." Dove's voice sounded…off…as she swept through the small space of her father's office. As though the man could be hiding under the threadbare carpet beneath his desk.

Standing in the doorway, Mitchell put a lid on the tension spreading through him. Logic and planning were his guides in life. Emotions did not dictate his reality. "Where does he go when he's not at home, at the bar or out on one of his boats?"

With it being Sunday morning, they'd already checked all three, as Dove had determined them to be the most likely spots to find him. Home first, passed out. Sleeping off Saturday night at the bar. Then the bar, passed out, either slumped on a table or in his truck, not having made it home. The office was usually only when he was close to being sober. But when he wasn't loaded, his favorite place to be was the water.

"He comes here," she said, turning to face him. Her long hair framed her in what appeared to be fire in that first second. Like she was alight with fear. Maybe because her eyes were alight with it. But the rest of her…all the purple, the netting…he had the most bizarre impression of an angelic part of her, there to pull herself out of the earthly flames.

Or one calling out to him to do so.

That sense of need pushing through him kicked him into gear. Whaler had grown up in Shelby. Knew every inch of the town and most of the people in it. As far as Mitchell had ever known, the man had no enemies. At least not local ones, he amended with a thought to Brad Fletcher. Anyone who'd been in the bar the night before could have taken him home. "So we wait," he told her. "Home, here or the bar?"

Wait for an hour or so, he planned silently. Then he'd call Clint Schumer, owner of the local bar where Whaler had his own stool, to put in a quiet feeler as to the man's behavior the night before. Hopefully find out who he'd left with.

Schumer was a client. And one he could trust to keep their conversation confidential, even in Shelby. The last thing he wanted to do was embarrass Whaler. The older man was already undermining himself with all the drinking.

"Here." Dove's answer was longer than usual in coming. "If he's already out, he'd come here rather than going home during daylight."

She moved a couple of piles of paper materials and lifted herself up to sit on the space she'd cleared on top of a credenza facing the door.

Instead of settling on the floor. The choice bothered him. Left him no choice but to try to fix the problem.

If he slid to the floor and closed his eyes, would she follow suit? He was nixing that one before the idea had even completed itself. Giving himself a strong mental shake, he said, "You're worried."

Great. Stating the obvious when he should be helping her get back to her usual way of taking things on the chin. The woman had a reputation in town, and if everything he'd witnessed in the past forty-eight hours was anything to go by, it was well earned.

She'd nodded and was sitting forward, fingers curled over the edge of the credenza on each side of her, swinging her feet.

"I don't think you need to be just yet," he said, cautiously. Not wanting to lie to her but… "Law enforcement has had eyes on Brad Fletcher since yesterday—before you and your dad signed that contract." She'd put not only the date but also the time on the signature line.

And a guy like Brad Fletcher likely didn't do all of his own work. He'd pay for the dirty stuff.

"You're concerned," she said. "Even when you just said that you didn't totally believe what you were saying."

What the hell? She thought she was some kind of mind reader?

"I need you to be honest with me, Mitchell."

He needed to go. To tell her he was the wrong guy to help with her problems. To apologize. And try to find a lawyer from a nearby city who might be willing to take on St. James Boats when the Fletcher dust settled. He'd even offer to pay the person himself.

Looking for an out, he went for the obvious. Taking offense. Lifting his chin, he gave her a piercing courtroom look and said, "You calling me a liar, Ms. St. James?"

No lawyer worth his salt—or at least Mitchell—would work for a client who didn't trust him. Or for a client he couldn't trust to act according to societal norms. Dive-bombing others' silent thoughts was not okay, as far as he was concerned. Most particularly not if one was going to believe one's magic knowledge over their victim's own words.

"No, Mitchell, I'm not calling you a liar." Dove's face softened as she issued the answer. A smile even teased at the corners of her mouth. "I'm just paying attention to your posture, your tone of voice. You're uncomfortable, which tells me that you know more than you're saying."

A body-language reader, not a mind one. Some of the tension she'd mentioned seeing in Mitchell eased away.

He'd taken a course in understanding the language himself. It helped him to read others during critical negotiations.

And it didn't hurt in conversations with his siblings and cousins, either. Or their poker games.

"I don't *know* anything," he told her, taking a seat in her father's chair, as she'd had him do the morning before, and turning it to face her. "I just don't like how much lower Fletcher's offer was overnight. In business negotiation terms, he'd only do that if he felt like he had an upper hand to the point of assured victory. It doesn't track that he'd hurt your father, though, if he's believing that he's on the verge of getting what he wants—which is your father's signature on a business deal."

Dove slid down to the floor, her back against the wall, but kept her eyes wide open and trained on Mitchell. "I was more worried that he's hurt himself," she said. "He's usually able to carry on, drive on the right side of the road even, when he's been drinking—not that I ever, *ever* condone him doing so—but he was pretty beaten up yesterday. Missing my mom. And then, with me getting him to sign that contract… Do you think he'd, you know, hurt himself on purpose?"

The meaning behind her question was completely clear to him. As was his answer. "I do not. Your mother's death has hit Whaler hard. He's in a bad spot, I grant you that, but a man like him, he just keeps going until he doesn't. He gets up every day. He comes to work when he's supposed to be here. And I'd bet you a hundred bucks that he's never forgotten to tell you *Happy Birthday*."

Her gaze widened, and a full smile broke out on her face. "You're good," she said softly.

Relief flooded him, and Mitchell sat back, prepared to

wait the hour out with her and then make his phone call. "You aren't taking my bet?"

"Hell, no. I don't have the hundred to spare."

He did.

And he'd give it willingly—more than once—to see that smile stay on her face.

Unfortunately the fates she was so fond of didn't always provide smiling moments. No matter how rich you were. There were just some things money couldn't fix.

And some things a practical lawyer would never be able to do.

Hooking up with a breezy woman like Dove St. James being top of the list.

Chapter 6

In his jeans and flannel shirt, Mitchell Colton looked a whole lot more like he belonged at St. James Boats. And in her world.

Dove didn't kid herself into thinking that he was there to stay. But she was thankful for the time he was giving her. He had no obligation to give up his Sunday to sit with her while she waited for her father to show himself.

And yet he seemed to sense that she couldn't talk boat business until she knew that Whaler was accounted for. Hoping her dad would join in their business meeting might be too much for her to ask, but Dove was planning to do so. Holding onto hope was how she lived, no matter how illogical she seemed sometimes, nor how unrealistic and foolish.

No matter what Mitchell Colton thought of her.

She'd never let others' opinions of her matter. A gift instilled in her by her mother who'd taught Dove from birth to live authentically. Raising her with an awareness that she'd be far happier listening to her heart—trusting herself—rather than worrying about society's whims, or letting those around her influence what she wore, ate or thought.

She refused to allow her sudden awareness of Mitchell Colton to change that. The feelings she'd had in the studio...and they were still lingering in the aftermath...had been nothing more than a way to ward off negative feelings while cleaning up the results of vandalism.

"Why mooing?" Mitchell's words fell easily between them, pulling her gaze from the doorway back to him. The lawyer seemed to have left the room. A man who was curious sat in his place.

"Mooing?" she asked, frowning.

"Your text notification."

Right. The text with the lowball offer. "Like the devil looking for a soul to steal, the line from the song that's his ringtone, the text notification is set just for Brad Fletcher's number," she clarified. And then told him, "The song reminds me instantly I'm talking to the devil, you know, since it's real time direct contact. Text lingers. Sits there with you. So, in ancient mythology, the divine mother is represented by the cow. She is the giver of life. And it's there to remind me that anytime that man tries to contact me the spirits are there with me, to provide what sustenance I need, while I deal with the devil. Takes away his ability to overpower me."

She didn't expect Mitchell to understand. But she had to assert herself fully into the air between them. She couldn't afford to lose any part of herself to him. Not even for business purposes. If she didn't stay true to herself, she had nothing to offer anyone.

And the attraction she felt for the lawyer...it had to be kept in its place. An anomaly. Nothing more. Unless she could find a man who respected and admired all of her, she was better off alone. Which was why she hadn't had a date in longer than she wanted to contemplate.

"I don't know much about ancient mythology, but setting a ringtone to trigger a mindset is kind of impressive." Mitchell's tone drew her gaze back to him another time.

Her initial thought, that he was mocking her, had already dissipated before her eyes pointed straight toward his. She warmed inside all over again. It wasn't sexual, though that awareness was there every time she looked at him now, but more spirit to spirit.

"Did it help?" he asked.

She nodded slowly, holding his gaze in an attempt to understand more about what was going on between them. Until he looked away and pulled out his phone.

Various ringtones sounded within seconds, and she continued to watch him. Not sure what to think. Experience told her he was playing with her.

Her heart told her he was being sincere.

Could she trust her emotions in the moment? With the vandalism, Fletcher's menacing pressure, her father missing and that odd attack of sexual awareness, she most definitely needed an aura cleanse. And she definitely should not make any potentially momentous decisions until she'd had time to detoxify.

While she sat with her impressions regarding Mitchell Colton, he was engrossed with causing his phone to emit a myriad of sounds. Some soothing, some decidedly not.

She sat in the moment, letting the present happen around her. Until he said, "Preventing disaster before it strikes is half my job. I'm thinking I need separate tones for each of my brothers. For my cousins. And some of my problematic clients, as well."

Soft chills spread through her. Followed by a mellow warmth. And she smiled a little as she asked, "You consider your siblings and cousins problematic?" Since she'd never had either, and he had a plethora with whom he was reputed to be close, she was truly curious.

Without looking up from his phone, or ceasing the sound

bombing, he shook his head. "They just expect me to see potential issues and prevent them if I can, though I don't know if any of them are consciously aware of doing so."

"Then, wouldn't just one tone do it for all of them?"

The next shake of his head snared her attention. She couldn't explain the sudden pull from him to her except that somehow the conversation had become personal. Almost intimate. "Why not?" she asked, sitting forward as she focused entirely on him, needing to hear his answer. He was giving her a private piece of himself. And that mattered.

"Because they're all different. I'm aware of their individual pitfalls, and I think it might be productive to have rings that remind me of them prior to our communications."

Leaning back against the wall again, Dove stared at him. Mitchell Colton was truly taking her seriously.

Learning from *her*?

She wasn't sure anyone had ever done that outside her studio. And at Namaste, all anyone came to her for was cleansing and calm. Things they could do on their own if they'd trust themselves enough to try. And had the discipline to make it happen.

An intrusive beep sounded, interrupting her happy mojo, and she looked over at the phone and then raised her gaze to the man's face in time to see his frown.

Fear speared through her. "What's wrong?" she asked. Deep breath.

He shook his head, then, tapping his phone screen a couple of times, held the cell up to his ear. "I set an alarm for nine. Clint Schumer is a client of mine. I trust him not to mention our conversation to anyone."

Clint Schumer. Owner of the bar that had become her father's second home. "You're calling him about my dad?"

Just like he'd phoned Eli, not once, but twice, without first cluing her in.

Dove needed to have a word with him about that. After she got over being grateful for his help. His initiative. And the contacts he had who took him far more seriously than they'd take her.

Mitchell was nodding, then, tapping his phone screen a couple of times, held the cell up to his ear and said, "Clint? Mitchell Colton here." Dove stood up and walked over to her dad's desk. Stood there. Saw him lower his phone to tap the Speaker icon and set the device on the desk and then say, "I'm calling to make a discreet inquiry," he said.

Dove heard the bar owner reply with, "Of course. Who do you need to know about?"

As though it wasn't the first time Mitchell had made such a call.

Some of those preventative measures he'd just been talking about? The wondering helped distract Dove from the sound of the lawyer's voice mentioning her father's name. Asking when he was last in the bar.

"I haven't seen him since Friday night," the man said. And Dove's good vibes dropped to her toes. Slithering away even as Clint continued with, "Someone said he was in yesterday afternoon but didn't stay long."

"Any word as to who he might have been with? Did he leave with anyone?"

"No, but I can ask around," Clint offered. Asking no questions at all. And Dove understood why Mitchell had called the bartender first.

"I'd appreciate that," Mitchell said. "Call me on my cell if you hear any more."

"Will do," the deeper voice said, and the call ended.

Leaving Dove staring at the man who'd just the day

before agreed to take her father on as a client. Would he change his mind?

The question lurked but wasn't the one screaming so loudly in Dove's mind, forcing her to ask, "Where in the hell is my father?"

Just before she burst into tears.

Mitchell wasn't good with the crying. Its unpredictability made him uncomfortable. And its lack of problem-solving capabilities interrupted his ability to process concisely.

Dove's tears seemed to multiply the effect on him tenfold.

Disliking the situation in which he found himself, Mitchell stood. "We need to focus," he said aloud. Realizing, even as he spoke, that the words weren't his best effort. "Where else would your father go? Who might he be with? Or have seen or heard from him?"

Blinking a couple of times, Dove sniffled. Wiped her face and said, "Any of his crew. They were still here when I left yesterday. The police had the vandalism report ready for me and had questions to ask as well, so as soon as the contract was signed, I left with Detective Welding..." She paused. Seemed to go inside herself, and he suspected he was losing her again until she said, "Oh! And Oscar Earnhardt. They meet for beers every Saturday afternoon. Always have for as long as I can remember."

Frowning, he stared down at her. "Oscar Earnhardt who he fired for driving a boat while drunk and then crashing it?" He'd gleaned the further information about the incident when going through Whaler's jotted notes in his friend's file. And he and Dove were getting further and further apart from each other with each contribution to the current conversation.

She nodded, and he used his own body-language-reading skills to try to assess her current reliability. Her shoulders were back. She was looking him in the eye. And her voice was stable as she said, "They've been drinking buddies for years. It's how Oscar came to work for Dad in the first place. They'd met at the bar. Back then, the whole time Mom was alive, actually, he only went to the bar on Saturday afternoons because Clint has always had a sailors' happy hour. Oscar enlisted in the navy right out of high school but blew out his knee during his first year at sea and was put on permanent desk duty. He got out as soon as his tour was up, came here, and my dad took him under his wing. Oscar understood that my dad had to fire him or risk losing the business to potential lawsuits…"

Mitchell was leading her out the door by the time she got to that part. He'd heard enough to know that they had to find Oscar Earnhardt. It sounded as though if anyone would know where Whaler might be, it would be his drinking buddy.

It wasn't the first time he'd heard the story of the bottle being a stronger bond than career or money.

"Where does Oscar live?" he asked when Dove shot a questioning glance up at him. It didn't make good business sense for Brad Fletcher to have harmed Whaler, but the way facts were suddenly lining up, Mitchell could see possibility in the theory.

Most particularly if Fletcher somehow got word about the contract Bob St. James had signed the day before, giving his daughter legal right to make decisions for the company. With Whaler out of the way, the uptick in pressure Fletcher had put on Dove that morning made more sense.

The sailors' happy hour—something Whaler had been participating in for years—would have been easy for

Fletcher to find out about. A few questions in town or at the docks could easily have provided the information. Everyone knew Whaler. And if someone working for Fletcher posed as an old friend...

"Last I heard, Oscar's got a room at the Shelby Inn," Dove's response to his question interrupted the thought. "But it's up for sale," she continued, "so I'm not sure if he's still there. He's in the process of going through a divorce. His wife and son are still living in their small home not far from the docks."

She'd wrapped her arms around herself as she spoke and slid out the door he held open. A sign that she was holding back? Or just giving herself a much-needed hug?

Activity down at the dock looked much as it had the day before. Customers waiting for boats to be readied for them to climb aboard for a day of fishing. Whaler's two current employees making the work look easy. For a second there, Mitchell envied them both. Spending their days at or on the water. The condition of the boats their main responsibility. But only for a second. He'd be missing his job, his clients, by end of day one. The idea of having a boat waiting for him at the end of the day was a good one, though.

Something to think about as he had Dove climb into the passenger seat of his expensive sedan to head out to the renovated hotel. Better that than give any brain time to the warm soft touch of her skin he'd felt when his hand had brushed her bare side above the waistband of her skirt thing and the bottom edge of the long-sleeved crop top as he'd led her out of the office.

What was he doing? Escorting the flighty woman around town searching for her drunk father when he should be on his way to the glaciers to test out his new footwear.

His current behavior was so out of character, he almost

told Dove she'd need to go alone as he climbed behind the wheel and smelled lavender coming from the seat beside him. But how could he just walk away?

Most particularly with her thinking that he was going to be taking on St. James Boats as a client.

The thought calmed him. Going the extra mile for a client was not new to him. On the contrary, it was completely ordinary. Almost predictable.

He'd just never had a client like Dove St. James. It wasn't him that was out of character. It was her lifestyle, requiring him to meet different needs, that had his normal routine in flux. As soon as they found Whaler—and had a business conversation that would go along the lines of letting the police get a handle on Fletcher before contemplating any business moves they could make—he'd be free to get to his own Sunday pursuits.

Down the road, if Whaler was willing to listen to any of Mitchell's suggestions to generate cash flow for his business, the sea captain could meet him at Shelby Law Office.

And Dove St. James would be wholly out of his life.

Oscar was still in his room at the inn. And wasn't at all welcoming when he answered the door with his growl of "What?"

But as soon as Mitchell told the man why they were there, his expression changed from sourpuss to open concern. And for the first time in a long time, Dove's heart went out to the navy man.

Oscar's drinking had caused seemingly unending pain for his wife—a client of Namaste—and had endangered Whaler's business as well. But Dove was beginning to understand that while raising a glass to your mouth was a choice, it wasn't always a logical mind that drove a person's choices. Sometimes overwrought emotions were in control. Impulses. Physical addictions.

Something she'd been blind to for too long. Because she wanted to believe that her father could be well by just not raising that glass. Cured from one minute to the next.

But with the thought of losing him taking over her mind, she knew that the only way to save him was to see him as he really was.

Which meant she had to see Oscar in that new light as well. Rather than through the many layers of pain she'd helped his wife clear from her spirit.

Not trusting herself to be as efficient as Mitchell would be in the current situation, she stood outside the doorway with the lawyer, and listened silently to the conversation taking place.

Oscar had seen Whaler the afternoon before, briefly. The former St. James Boats employee had had a job interview in the next town and had had to leave the bar shortly after Whaler had arrived. Whaler had walked out with him to wish him luck, and Oscar had assumed the older man had gone back into the bar. But he hadn't looked back to confirm that. Or couldn't remember having done so, at any rate.

He also hadn't been offered the job he'd applied for. But he had another really good possibility on the table. The news drew out a genuine smile from Dove as she told the man thank-you and followed the expression of gratitude with "And good luck with the next interview. Just be yourself, and you're sure to get it."

As long as he didn't show up drunk. Oscar, sober, was an excellent seaman. Was a walking encyclopedia of southern Alaska and most particularly glacier facts. And was a people person, too. As critical as it had been to get him away from St. James Boats after the accident, the business had also suffered for Oscar's leaving.

Tension filled her space, encased her, as she hurried with Mitchell back to his car. She couldn't move fast enough to escape it.

And had never felt so alone in her life.

She couldn't seem to access the spirits that she knew never left her side or the air around her.

"Can we check Dad's house again?" she asked even before Mitchell had his door shut. "Just in case?"

Nodding, Mitchell looked at her, and she didn't want to hear his words when he opened his mouth to speak. Had to restrain herself from covering her ears.

An action she'd allowed herself many times in her life when she knew something was going to come at her that she didn't deserve and chose not to take in.

"And then I'm going to call my cousin, Kansas," he told her, the hint behind those words ripping through her.

She'd known what was coming. Turning a blind eye to the truth was different from deflecting mean-spirited opinions that bore no merit. Life had to be lived with eyes open. With awareness. Or there'd be no true joy. Or real peace.

Kansas was a cop, too. Just like Mitchell's brother.

"She's search and rescue," she said quietly, stepping into the facts slowly.

Mitchell's long look was speculative. She withstood it. He nodded.

She could be heading straight into hell. He needed to know if she was going to be okay.

She wasn't. Not if they didn't find Whaler.

Was this the time when she lost the ability to believe and her spirits left her?

Would Mitchell stand in the fire with her? Or would

she be there all alone? She couldn't ask the question. Not even of herself.

So she nodded.

And he started the car.

Chapter 7

Whaler wasn't at home. With a quick look around, Dove determined that he hadn't been there since they'd looked for him there earlier that morning. On the way over, she'd called several people she knew that kept in touch with Whaler. The guy who rented space from him at the marina to sell bait to Whaler's customers. Both of the men who still worked for him. The woman Dove had hired to clean her father's house twice a month. And his doctor of forty years. She reached the man just as he was leaving church.

No one had seen or heard from the business owner since Saturday afternoon.

Mitchell was itching to call Kansas in, had been ready to do so for more than an hour, but Dove insisted on checking out one more place. "He might have stopped for a bite at Roasters," she said, standing in the middle of her father's living room as though she couldn't decide where to put herself. "One of my mom's friends works there, and when he's particularly lonely, he'll go order some pie and chat with her in between customers. Not that he'd be eating pie, as drunk as he was…"

Her voice dropped off, and Mitchell paused on his way to the front door. He looked at her face and felt a rush of the horror he read there, as an almost physical being.

"I never should have left him in that state," she whispered, eyes wide and almost blank as she stared at him. Her long amber waves fell around her as her shoulders closed in on her petite, shapely frame, and Mitchell was directly in front of her before he'd had the thought to go there.

Taking both of her shoulders in his hands on instinct, he straightened them, bending his head until he could see into her eyes and then raised himself, pulling her gaze up with him. "From what I hear, you'd never leave him at all if you didn't leave him in that state," he said clearly. Succinctly.

Staring at him as though through the eyes of a frightened child, she nodded. Nodded again. And he felt her muscles engage beneath his fingers, pulling her together. Upright. Ready to stand on her own.

"Let's go to Roasters," he said then, as though nothing had just happened between them. Needing to convince himself that it hadn't.

He was just out of his comfort zone. Reading far too much into normal, everyday occurrences that were happening in the midst of disruption, coating their time together with uneasiness.

Time that he hoped would be drawing to an end before afternoon hit but held out little hope when no one at Roasters remembered seeing Whaler since Friday.

He'd just pulled out of the parking place on Main Street, not far from the café, and had turned the corner to take them back down toward the marina when he heard Dove gasp and then shout out, "Stop!"

His foot was already pushing hard on the brake by the time she'd finished the command. Shooting forward against his seat restraint, he turned to look over at her.

"That's my dad's truck," she said, her voice breathless-sounding. And hopeful, too.

Mitchell shot forward, turning down the side street he'd been about to pass, and sped toward the truck. Dove was out of the car before he had the vehicle in Park and, leaving his car running in the middle of the road, he followed quickly behind her.

Praying that, if Dove found Whaler slumped over the steering wheel, the older man was still alive.

Her father wasn't in his truck. Nor was there any sign of when he'd exited the vehicle. Could have been an hour or two, or the day before.

"The engine's cold so it's been here more than a few minutes," Mitchell told her, but she knew he was stretching the time for her benefit.

Something she both appreciated and needed him to not do. Whatever was lying in front of her, it was her job to get through it with as much faith, hope, joy and peace as possible. Not to crumple beneath the weight of it.

"It's been at least an hour," she stipulated, more for her benefit than his and headed up to the house in front of which her father had parked.

"You know who lives here?" she asked, as Mitchell showed up beside her.

"Nope."

"Me, either." But she couldn't let the unknown stop her. With Mitchell standing right behind her, his car still running in the street, she knocked.

A few times. Until an older woman called out to her from behind. "He's a captain, out to sea. Won't be back for another couple of months."

She turned to see a seventyish woman, dressed almost stylishly in linen pants and a blouse and jacket—probably just coming home from church Dove realized—standing on the sidewalk between them and her father's truck. "I live across the street," The woman said, "and saw you through my front window."

Dove wanted to smile at the woman. To thank her. And ask questions. But felt the sting of tears too sharply to do anything more than nod.

"Do you know how long this truck's been parked out front?" Mitchell jumped in, covering her weakness.

"It was here yesterday afternoon when I got home from playing bridge. Hasn't moved since, that I've seen."

Saturday afternoon. Again. Dove's heart took a dive so deep she struggled to stay upright and moving forward.

Except that Whaler needed her. She was all he had left, and she was not going to fail him. Or the spirit of her mother who would be there, guiding her, if she'd let it.

If she could access it.

She had to access it. To find her center and be fully present. No matter what it cost.

Even if it meant finding enough good feeling to supersede the bad by turning to a man she hardly knew and had no business leaning on.

He'd been put in her path for a reason. It wasn't up to her to question why. Not then. Not yet.

And so when she felt Mitchell's hand at her back, his palm against the strip of bare skin between her crop top and skirt, she landed right there with it. Absorbing his touch. Going with the flow of warmth it gave her. And let him lead her back to his running car.

Mitchell was already on the phone by the time he slid behind his steering wheel. Heading down the street and around the corner, he stopped just a couple of blocks from the local office of the Alaska Bureau of Investigation. As far as he knew, his cousin Kansas, a search and rescue state trooper, didn't have a current case, so probably wasn't at the office.

But he'd bet Eli was. And he didn't want to pull his older brother's attention away from his major crimes duty another time if it wasn't warranted.

"Hey, cousin, what's up?" Kansas answered her cell on the second ring, sounding wide awake and ready to go as always.

"I'm not sure. Maybe nothing," Mitchell said, more in deference to Dove sitting next to him, hearing every word, than his own take on the situation. By his calculation, something was most definitely up. He just wasn't sure it was within Kansas's wheelhouse.

"You wouldn't be calling me on Sunday morning if it was nothing."

Watching Dove he said, "Whaler St. James hasn't been seen since yesterday afternoon. He's not home, at work or at the bar. No one who works for him has seen him. And his daughter's studio was vandalized as well. Welding's working on that. There've been some less than friendly offers to buy Whaler's business issued to his daughter as well as Whaler, from a businessman named Brad Fletcher. Eli has had a team watching him since yesterday. The most recent text from him came before eight this morning."

He paused, sent an apologetic look to Dove, who'd been staring out the front windshield during his entire missive, and said, "We just found Whaler's truck parked outside the house of a deployed sailor. Neighbor said it's been there since yesterday afternoon. Whaler wasn't in a great state the last time he was seen yesterday. I'd even say worse than usual." His opinion. But based on facts. He finished with something they both knew, more for Dove's sake than anything else. "Local police aren't going to do anything about this until more time has passed. He could have just wandered off."

"And, if you mean by he *wasn't in a great state* that he was drunk, then he could have fallen while he was wandering and might need help," Kansas said, stirring up an influx of affection within Mitchell. His family, their closeness, was a pain in the ass at times, but he loved them all. Would die for any one of them.

Sitting there with Dove, who had no one but a failing father who was missing, Mitchell realized how lucky he was. Feeling grateful for the first time in a long while, rather than just accepting life as it came and giving his best to it.

A good man didn't just sit with his wealth. He gave back. And as Kansas told him she'd head out and see what she could find on Whaler, Mitchell hung up the phone and turned to Dove. "This is going to sound like overkill, but my family and I...we don't ever take chances when it comes to someone's safety..." He paused as she turned and looked into his eyes. Tried to read what her gaze was telling him. And got nothing but openness.

"Every Colton home has top-notch security," he said, speaking without carefully choosing his words. And stopped himself as he was about to further expostulate. She didn't need to know why his family lived as they did. Eli and Kansas in law enforcement were reason enough.

He was going to help Dove. He wasn't there to bond with her. To tell her he knew about tragedy. About living with those who'd experienced inexplicable loss.

Eli might be the only one of the siblings and cousins who remembered their aunt Caroline, having been five when he and their father had found Will Colton's seventeen-year-old sister murdered, but every single one of the Coltons lived with the devastating grief that day had wrought.

Will's parents, Mitchell's grandparents, had been found that day as well. Slain in their bed. Years before Mitchell had been born. He'd never had the chance to know them, but the shadow of their deaths had shaped every day of his life.

None of which mattered to Dove or the current situation. It just served as information Mitchell could use to understand and predict his client's current needs.

Pseudo client. There'd been no official business arrangement made as of yet. And wouldn't be until the owner of the company was found.

But he'd said he'd help her. Which, by his own moral code, obligated him to do so.

"I don't think it sounds like overkill to call in your cousin," Dove's words pulled his head out of his ass and back to the car where he'd started to make an offer and had then just stopped.

"She's in search and rescue, right?" Dove continued, her pinched face in contrast with the calm tone. The fact that she was repeating something they'd already discussed was telling.

She had to be worried sick. And there he sat, thinking about himself.

"She is," he confirmed, to give her the moment she'd obviously been seeking. And then said, "I have a guest suite in my home. I want you to move into it until this is resolved."

She sat back, her body rigid, a clear indication of rejection. Reading the response, he didn't give her a chance to express it. Just kept right on talking. "Free of charge," he said, trying to hit every one of her upcoming arguments before they became such. "I'm on the outskirts of town, but just. It'll only be another few minutes' commute to work. A little farther to the marina, maybe. The place is big enough that you wouldn't be encroaching on my space. And most importantly, you'll be safe while we get this thing figured out."

The tension in her face, her shoulders, hadn't eased a bit. "The suite is there for just this purpose," he said then came up with his closing argument. "Several of my clients have used it over the years."

Truth… Barely. Clients who'd also been friends. Having moved away and come back to visit. Or needed a place to stay while damage to a business had been repaired. Once when a house didn't close as soon as expected and the rooms at the Shelby Inn had been sold out.

None of which mattered. He'd inferred that she was a client. Her shoulders should be relaxing. They were not.

How long could Whaler's truck sit on the street, awaiting his arrival? Weeks? Months? Should he see about having it towed back to the sea captain's home? The marina?

"Of course I'll stay in the suite," Dove said then, her gaze flecked with gratitude but filled with unrest. "Gratefully. And I'll do whatever housework or anything else you need done, I'll cook your meals, whatever to show my gratitude. I just… The fact that you called your cousin, and thinking I might be in danger…you really think something's happened to my dad, don't you?"

Right. He'd hoped they were going to let that lie for a bit. Until Kansas had a chance to do her thing. "I think it's possible," he told Dove.

She nodded then said, "It's more than that. He's in trouble. I can feel it."

And for a second there, until he came to his senses, Mitchell was certain he felt it, too.

* * *

Dove had no idea what kind of a bill she was racking up with her and Whaler's new attorney, but didn't care. Fate had driven her to his door on the longest shot she'd ever taken. Every good thing that had happened since was because she'd let hope guide her.

While she hadn't even dreamed that her circumstances had been about to turn so horrible so quickly, she'd been fully aware that she'd been in need of pursuing her last-ditch effort.

Just as she knew that, until she heard news of her father, she had to stay busy. If one of the boats had been missing, she'd have taken another and sped to all her father's favorite coves. She knew every one of them. Or if his truck hadn't been found, she might have driven every road out of town, for as many miles as it took to find the old vehicle.

As it was, she wanted to knock on the doors of all seventeen hundred homes in Shelby. Instead, she told Mitchell that she had to get back to her studio, finish removing all signs of vandalism, and then give the space a thorough spiritual cleanse. She accepted his offer to help make the studio appear normal for her classes in the morning.

When it became clear that he had no intention of leaving her alone, she opted to forgo the most important work until morning. And even agreed to him waiting outside her small house by the marina as she packed a bag for the next day or so. But when he went to load her things into his car, she finally spoke up, insisting that she take her own car to his place. She might be in need of assistance, but she would not become dependent. No way her spirits would be leading her to *that*.

Though she'd only had oatmeal and fruit for breakfast at six that morning, she wasn't hungry when Mitchell suggested that, before leaving town, they get something for lunch. But because the chance to sit and watch for her father, or anyone she knew who might have seen him, was too good to pass up, she agreed to lunching at The Cove— a place right on the water, not far from the marina or her house—and ordered the fresh salmon salad she always got.

When her mother had been alive, their small family had dined at the somewhat dimly lit, quaint restaurant at least once a week. The water called to all three of them— though in different ways. To her mother, it brought a sense of peace and wellness, of enough space to store all of life's answers. To her father, the sense of adventure that he'd always craved.

Before all he'd craved was the contents of a liquor bottle.

For Dove, it was a combination of the first two. And a reminder of a third. The danger that lurked and could take a life with little warning. As disease had taken her mother.

If she'd been fully present she might have thought it would be awkward, being at The Cove at all that day—with her mother gone, her father's business on the brink of collapse and him missing—let alone sitting at a table for two by the window with the lawyer.

Maybe because she was on and off numb, her comfort wasn't even an issue.

If he was embarrassed to be seen sharing a table alone with a woman in what most would consider unfashionable purple attire, he certainly didn't show it.

"You've been nothing but kind to me," she said, reaching with all the might she could muster to stay focused on that good feeling. "I'll find a way to repay you, Mitchell. It's important that you know that."

Unfolding his napkin and putting it in his lap, he shrugged then said, "I don't charge for kindness."

The statement made her smile. Inside and out. It didn't quell the fear slicing through her. But it helped ease the immediate sense of impending doom enough for her take a couple of bites of her salad when it arrived.

He seemed okay with letting her control the conversation while they sat together. So she asked about his family. He'd been born in town, but she knew his parents and aunt and uncle had moved from California when Eli and Parker had been little. The family was well known for their adventure tours. That had not only helped keep Shelby on the map but had contributed to the success of St. James Boats as well. Unfortunately, it also prompted the interest of outside businessmen like Brad Fletcher.

"I was born here," Mitchell confirmed when she mentioned what little she knew about Colton family history. "So were Spence and Kansas. My cousins. Our fathers are brothers."

She'd known that much. Wanted more. But couldn't clear her mind enough to get there.

"And Lakin, of course," he added. "She's the real gem among us."

Dove's heart caught at the warmth she heard enter Mitchell's voice when he mentioned his adopted sister—a woman who'd been two classes behind Dove in school—and a native Alaskan who exuded love.

"I heard she'd been abandoned at a grocery store," Dove said, and then, with a quick intake of breath, needing to take back the crude words, ended up choking.

Which caused her to miss Mitchell's initial reaction to her rudeness. "I'm so sorry," she said, taking a sip of water as her coughing subsided. "I am most definitely not myself." Which was scaring the crap out of her, and lending strength to the negativity invading her system.

Reaching over the table, Mitchell used his napkin to wipe the tears from her cheeks, caused by the coughing. "No need to apologize," he said. "Lakin would be the first one to tell you about how she came to us. I'm convinced that she considers her story to be her lucky talisman, though she's never admitted that. She was three when she was found alone at the grocery store. Friends of my parents fostered her while authorities searched for her parents, and my parents ended up adopting her. She's been the light in our family ever since."

The way he said that, as though his family had been lacking light, caught at Dove. She wanted to ask him about the darkness she sensed but didn't trust herself enough to know if she was sensing him, or just projecting her own current state onto him.

Before either of them could say more, Mitchell's phone rang. Because he'd placed it on the table when they sat down to eat, Dove saw the name flash on the screen: *Kansas*.

Her stomach clenched around the few bites of food she'd taken. Staring at the phone, she willed herself to take a deep breath. Could barely draw a shallow one.

Mitchell grabbed the phone and went out to the reception area to take his call.

And Dove sat alone, trying to think about her mother, about her family in that restaurant, and picking out the different tables where she had memories of them together. To draw on what she knew rather than accessing any of the emotion that led her through life, certain that doing so in that moment would release the fear waiting to drown her.

When Mitchell appeared in her line of vision, heading her way, she was still breathing, thinking about a birthday she'd celebrated at the table in the corner. She couldn't remember how old she'd been. But she remembered the purple glitter birthday hats she and her mother had worn. Her dad had been out to sea. But he'd radioed in before she went to bed that night.

Mitchell didn't have a radio. He had a cell phone. Still in hand.

Heart pounding, she glanced up as he reached their table. Got nothing from blue eyes staring straight in hers. No warmth. No fear. No strength. Or weak knees, either.

"Tell me," she said.

Wondering what it meant when he sat first, instead. Had they found Whaler? Was he...

"Kansas found drag marks in the back alley, behind the bar."

The last place her father had been seen.

"They end abruptly right next to a pair of tire tracks that left rubber and debris behind. As though a vehicle accelerated rapidly. A truck, most likely, based on the tire tread. But a newer one."

Relief hit for a brief second. She grabbed a breath while she could and said, "Not my father's truck."

He shook his head. Didn't seem to find the news as good as she did.

Because her father wouldn't have hauled himself away. Someone else would have done that. In their own or a stolen vehicle. Made more sense that way.

She didn't want sense. She wanted her father home. Passed out drunk if it had to be that way, but home.

Was that the lesson she was there to learn, then? To be more tolerant of Whaler's drinking? To accept the liquor as part of their lives, rather than constantly trying to get her father to leave it behind?

Fine then. She'd make peace with the bottle.

Did you get that? She wanted to scream the words aloud.

Settled for the silent communication that wouldn't get her thrown out of polite society. *I get the message* she added for good measure, just in case someone out there in the spirit world was having as bad a day as she was.

"Kansas is heading up a search and rescue team, and they'll be heading out shortly, starting from the bar. Welding and his partner are going to be canvasing the area, talking to everyone who was in the bar yesterday."

Feeling her face start to tingle from tension, Dove forced herself to relax back in her seat. One muscle at a time. Starting with her neck. Her cheeks. Her fingers. Not in any of the orderly ways she taught. Didn't matter. Toes. Elbows. Any relaxing at all.

Lavender. Remembering that she had it on her, she shoved a hand down her shirt, in between her breasts, and pulled out the sachet, holding it under her nose with both hands. Breathing deeply.

And slowly realized that other than looking like some kind of weirdo, she was just fine. Not passing out. Or losing her life.

It was all right there. Waiting for her to take control and move forward. From a bad moment to what came next. Knowing that if she just kept going, good would be there waiting.

Even if the relief just came from a whiff of lavender.

Mitchell's voice came back to her. "...out of an abundance of caution. There's no evidence to prove that Whaler, or a human being for that matter, was dragged."

Dove took it in, the deep timbre. The warmth. Along with the words. And drew in a full breath, too. "What's next? How can I help?"

"You keep your cell phone charged, and on your person, in case he tries to contact you."

Of course. A given. She nodded anyway. "What else?"

The look in Mitchell's eye brought another flash of fear for a second, but then all she saw was warmth, and she wondered if she'd imagined the fear. Or had projected her own terror onto his glance.

"We go to the grocery store," he told her, as though they'd already had the plan.

She was game. If there was something there, some camera, some person, that could give them information. When he didn't offer more, just counted out cash from his wallet, placing it with the bill on the table, she asked, "What are we doing there?"

"Buying groceries." His tone sounded so normal, she went with it for a second.

Until reality hit again, and with dread she asked, "To feed the search and rescue team?"

Mitchell stood, and so she followed suit. "No," he said. "You said you'd cook for your keep. Dinner's in just a few hours."

Oh. Well. Dove hurried after him out to the car. Thinking about what he'd said. Another few seconds of something to focus on other than what could be happening to Bob St. James.

Or what could already have…

No. It hadn't. She'd know.

The fates had strongly prompted her to seek out Mitchell Colton's help. She had to trust that he knew what he was doing. That whatever it was, and for whatever reason, she was meant to follow along. And so she asked, "Do you prefer your vegetables sautéed, boiled or baked?"

Because at the moment, the thought of planning anything more than the side dish was beyond her.

She'd be in better shape once they were actually at the

store. Walking the aisles. She'd find her strength. Come through.

She just had to trust. Trust herself.

Trust her father to stay alive.

And trust Mitchell Colton, too.

Chapter 8

Mitchell had had no intention of taking Dove up on her offer to cook for him. Didn't want to cross paths with her in his home at all, if he could avoid doing so.

But the whiteness around her lips had been so stark, the blank look in her eyes so acute, he'd seen an emotional break down looming and had felt compelled to distract her.

He'd blurted out shopping plans on the fly.

And had forestalled disaster once again.

Because that's who he was. The prevention guy. His whole life. While his brothers and cousins went brazenly about their lives, to face danger and win, not just against nature, but against odds, too, Mitchell was the one who watched out for them all. Looking for dangers that would beat them, and doing all he could to make sure that that didn't happen. Just as he did before and during every single time out he took for himself.

Maybe if someone had paid a little more attention to the guy Aunt Caroline had said was stalking her…

What the hell?

Pulling into the grocery store parking lot right behind Dove St. James, Mitchell put an immediate halt on his train of thought. He was the prevention guy because he liked the law. Liked facing cerebral dangers, pitting himself against them and winning.

Just as his family did with nature.

Nothing to do with an aunt he'd never met.

Two days with Dove St. James—three really, if you counted their initial meeting in his office—and he was starting to sound as flighty as she did.

It was one thing needing to put himself into a clients' mindset professionally in order to predict what might befall them, but quite another to adopt that mindset personally.

But then, Dove wasn't officially a client yet. And, if Mitchell had his way, she never would be. Whaler might be. Down the road.

They weren't down the road.

He was walking into the grocery store with the man's daughter. Preparing to buy food for her to prepare for him.

To keep her focused and as calm as possible while they waited to hear back from Kansas. And Welding. And Eli, who was reporting in on whoever was heading up the Fletcher part of things.

Because, until they knew the extent of the danger she could be facing, he'd opted to be the one to provide safer housing for her.

Right.

She chose interesting food items as she filled their cart. Other than her earlier query as to how he liked his vegetables cooked, she hadn't deferred to him even once.

About to question and give input, he stood back instead. Literally. Walked a step behind her as she made her way through the store. Curious to see what came next.

And later, after they got home.

If he didn't like dinner, he'd pull something out of the freezer. Order in. Fill up on trail food, for that matter.

Mostly, he didn't want to disturb her mojo. Whatever she had going on in that oddly captivating head of hers, it was working to her benefit. The color had returned to her face. Lines of strain were dissipating from her cheeks. Her shoulders had relaxed. He wasn't going to be the one to mess that up.

Not unless he had to. By way of preventing something worse.

Like the shopping cart that was suddenly flying down the aisle, coming right at the display of cans that... "Dove!" He hollered, and dived forward, catching her around the waist, throwing them both into a ground roll that took them to the end of the aisle.

A woman screamed, cans crashed. Mitchell saw a pair of black boat shoes fly by. Someone running away, not stopping to help.

In the next second Mitchell was only aware of the soft, womanly body clinging to his with both arms and legs wrapped around him.

And for the first time in his life worried about what in the hell he'd gotten himself into.

The screaming stopped.

"Dove! Are you okay?" Hearing the voice from far off, recognizing it but unable to place it, Dove loosened her death grip on the man who'd saved her and rolled off him and up onto her feet.

Recognizing the wide-eyed woman who'd approached, she immediately filled with a semblance of calm. "Cindy, yes! I'm fine," she said, brushing herself off.

Cindy Morrison had lost her husband and young son in a boating accident the year before and had been on the verge of a breakdown when she'd come to Dove's studio just after

Christmas. In the eight months they'd had together, Cindy had finally been able to allow herself to travel through the stages of grief. To begin the healing process. Letting go of the negative energy one breath at a time.

Seeing Dove hurt could set back that process. Not that Dove was some kind of guru protected by her angels, but because she was lending Cindy some of her own strength. Support from one human being to another. She didn't want Cindy to even entertain the idea that anyone else she leaned on or cared about would end up dead.

Store personnel came running up the aisle, darting around rolling cans, and as Mitchell approached one of them, Dove led Cindy around to the next aisle. Away from any hint of danger. To get herself out of the chaos and to tend to Cindy, too.

"That was wild," she said, breathing back a shudder and managing a ragged chuckle. "I'm guessing whoever stacked those cans is going to be getting a demerit today." Making light of the situation helped. Asking Cindy how she was doing helped more. Gave her mind focus while her body's physiological state righted itself.

When Mitchell and the store manager came around the end of the aisle to find her, she felt better equipped to make her statement. And insisted on finishing her shopping, albeit quickly.

"Dove." Mitchell called her gaze to him as the manager left them. "You should have let him call the police."

"I didn't stop him," she pointed out. "I just said I didn't feel a need to report the incident." She started to push their cart that another store employee had brought around to her—still bearing her beans, greens and natural proteins. All foods that enhanced intuitive abilities. She'd roast the raw cacao beans first chance she got.

Her mother's first go-to anytime things were out of whack.

Sticking to her side, Mitchell pulled out his phone. "I'm calling Eli."

"I expected you would," Dove told him, feeling oddly calm as she pushed the cart. "Which is why it made no sense to call in yet another police officer." She stopped and looked at him. "Unless you hurt something when you took the brunt of the fall for both of us?"

He shook his head as he lifted the phone to his ear and gave his brother an account of what had just transpired.

Hearing Mitchell describe the episode, the basket that came forcefully at her, seemingly out of nowhere, set to knock her into a display of cans that would send her into a fall that could easily break bones or inflict other bodily harm, the black boat shoes he'd seen fleeing the scene...

What?

She stopped. Watched a couple of other shoppers pass, who turned to look at her—because of the incident in the canned vegetable aisle, or just because she was her and she'd always been stared at, she didn't know. Didn't much care.

And pinned Mitchell with a stare the second he ended the call. "You think someone deliberately tried to hurt me?"

"I think it's way too much of a coincidence that that cart just happened to come out of nowhere, heading straight toward you, while you were standing directly beside that display."

Fresh fear sluiced through Dove, but she quashed it. Thought of Cindy. Of her mother's roasted cacao beans. And said, "It's called karma, Mitchell. It comes to pay back bad as well as good."

He stared at her. His eyes narrowing. "Which debt did you just pay?"

"Good," she said, needing to believe herself more than she ever had before. "I went to see you even when I so didn't want to. And ever since, you've been like my guardian angel. I don't know what's happening with my dad. But I do know that you were meant to come into our lives. That things are happening to show me that I need to trust you. And to believe that whatever the outcome, it was meant to be."

"You didn't want to come see me?"

"You think I didn't know how much you did not want to agree to help us?"

Mitchell started moving slowly up the deserted aisle in which they'd been standing, and Dove stayed right beside him.

Shoving the tips of his fingers into the front pockets of his jeans, he said, "It's not that I didn't want to help, Dove. It's that I didn't see much likelihood that my skill set would fit your needs."

He'd deftly owned his lack of enthusiasm to come to her aid. She gave him credit for not denying what she'd sensed. And all that mattered was that she'd sought him out against her own best wishes. And in spite of his doubts, he'd been fully present every time she'd needed him since.

Heading straight for the ground beef, and then to the pasta aisle, followed by the dairy, Dove gathered what she needed for dinner, trying not to notice how closely Mitchell stayed beside her. A reminder of the heat and strength of his body as he'd saved her from being scrunched between a runaway basket and the cans of diced tomatoes that, had she fallen into them, could have caused her serious harm.

"What's for dinner?" he asked then.

And she almost smiled as she said, "Lasagna."

He'd paused over the menu item at lunch, before he'd chosen the lighter, more lunchlike club sandwich.

"How do you know I even like lasagna?"

"My spirits told me," she replied, her tone purposefully serious as she kept a grin to herself. Sometimes being perceived as a little odd had its amusing moments.

And sometimes a woman had to grasp at every distraction she could in order to keep her head above water.

While the small bit of earth upon which she stood seemed to be crumbling beneath her.

He needed her to change out of the sexiest outfit he'd ever seen. The same one that had just appeared out there to him that morning. Flighty. Not funny how an incident on the tile floor of a public grocery store, with danger-induced adrenaline pounding through him, could completely reframe his perception of clothing choices.

Even less humorous was the way his mind seemed to be playing tricks on him where Dove St. James was concerned. Was she flighty? Or just playing with him?

While he'd have assumed the former two days before, he was leaning more toward the latter as he pulled into his three-car garage and saw her pull into the driveway behind him. He couldn't spend the rest of Saturday afternoon and evening alone with her in his home.

As big and stately as the place was, it afforded far too much privacy. Laying groundwork for things to happen that no one would need to know about.

Activities between consenting adults that happened on a casual basis, leaving both parties able to walk away without looking back.

With her father missing, able to do nothing but wait for

news, Dove needed activity. Just not the kind his body was suddenly fixating on.

Almost exclusively as he showed her to the guest suite downstairs, across the hall just inside the garage door.

Didn't seem to matter to his libido that his bedroom was across the three-thousand-square-foot home and up a winding flight of stairs. He could carry her up, no problem. Hell, they could do it on the stairs for all he cared.

Problem was, of course, the rational part of him did care. And that part was boss.

Always.

As he set Dove's suitcase and satchel in the middle of the floor of the room, he did a quick scan of the four-poster bed, nightstand, across to the couch and coffee table beneath the window, checking for security weaknesses.

Found none. Other than that, he'd like it better if the room was on the second floor. That window...there were security cameras, a state-of-the-art alarm system, steel window frames, bolting locks and the same kind of unbreakable glass found in high-rise hotel rooms.

"Do you really think that thing at the grocery store was on purpose?"

Dove's words expressed a sense of vulnerability—at least the way he heard them—and Mitchell immediately turned to her and said, "Logic is telling me that it's possible." Everything else seemed to point to that certainty, but he wasn't a man who allowed himself to dwell in places he couldn't prove existed.

She'd implied that she'd listened to one of her promptings to seek him out in the first place and was taking all of his attempts to help her as proof that her guidance had been spot-on.

But what if, instead, her karma was just playing a bad joke on both of them?

He needed his time-out. The weekend he'd had planned—the time away he protected diligently—to keep himself levelheaded. So that he could serve all of those who relied on him without fail.

Dove wasn't unpacking. She was just standing there, watching him. "To what end?" she asked. "How does someone benefit from trying to hurt me with a can attack in the grocery store?"

Relieved to finally be certain of a response, Mitchell replied immediately. "First, it's another bout of bad luck in a space in which you feel safe. Which adds pressure to the fear someone is trying to build within you. Second, if you're hurt, you're less likely to get in the way. Right as your father goes missing. All of which could be designed to weaken you. To make you doubt everything you know. Feeling threatened, overcome by fear, you'd be more likely to entertain the idea of convincing your father to sell the business."

"And if something's happened to him, to sell it myself and leave town," she said softly, her gaze clear as she stared at him. "You think my father's dead?"

He couldn't just put that one out there. He told her the less painful truth. "I don't know." He *didn't* know, but he did think the strong possibility was on the table.

Dove shook her head, her long amber waves falling over her shoulders in a confusing array. "It's not like my father's business is worth killing for," she said. "It's not a million-dollar outfit."

"No, but it could be, if expanded upon and run properly." According to what Eli had told him, Brad Fletcher had the funds to invest. He'd built a lodge at one of his marinas.

An upscale place that attracted wealthy clientele. The same could be done in Shelby.

A look of fear crossed Dove's face, but it was quickly gone. Replaced by an almost serene expression that seemed to bear a cloak of steel. "Which is why, as soon as he's home, the three of us are going to get to work implementing your plans for the place," she said and turned to lift her satchel onto the couch. "Which will also then ensure that you get ample compensation for your work."

She had it all figured out. As though, just like that, she sees and it becomes. Shaking his head, Mitchell had no immediate response coming to him. He didn't know what to do with her. How to interact.

With his own internal pressure building, he said, "Do you own jeans and hiking boots? If not, we can go buy some. I've got something to show you."

He just wasn't sure what it was yet.

There were a plethora of places he could take her, sights he could reveal that she never would have seen before, bounty that their homeland had to give that he'd discovered on his own over the years. By the time they headed out, he'd land on one of them.

"I live in Alaska," Dove said, reaching for her suitcase. "Of course I have jeans and hiking boots." He moved to grab her bag, to lift it to the bed for her, but she grabbed it and swung, almost hitting him in the process. "I also brought them with me," she said as she started to unzip the bag. "Just in case my dad…"

She didn't finish the sentence. And Mitchell left it hanging there. For a moment. "Meet me in the garage when you're ready," he said and took the stairs up two at a time so he could change and beat her there.

Patting himself on the back as he did so.

Getting her out of town would be the best way to protect her. And he, with his years of practice of disappearing into the ether, was the best man for the job. If someone thought to hunt for her in the mountains, or along the seashore, they'd follow trails. Shoreline. Even if they went off-trail, no one was as skilled as he was—except, perhaps Parker, Eli, Kansas and Spence, and probably their fathers—at taking on Alaska's challenging terrain.

Mastering it.

Most would more likely get hurt, possibly killed, if they tried.

Ironic, really, how his years of selfish pursuits were suddenly proving to be advantageous to someone in need.

Almost as though fate…

Mitchell stopped the thought before it completed itself.

No way was he going to start thinking that some kind spirits guided all for their own good. If that were the case, his grandparents and Aunt Caroline would still be alive.

Or, at the very least, they wouldn't have suffered such brutal deaths.

Chapter 9

"Wow, this is…" Leaning back against a tree, Dove couldn't finish the sentence as she slid down to the ground, staring out over the cliff face just feet away, to the Bering Sea beyond. Her gaze landing on the glaciers she'd been acquainted with her entire life, but never seen from that vantage point.

The climb had been hours long. Rigorous. Challenging to her toned muscles, but nothing she couldn't handle.

The bear that had been within yards of them, not so much. Mitchell had taken care of that one all on his own. Other than the noisemaker he'd handed her, something the kids in Shelby learned how to use during grade school. She'd done her part there.

He'd seen the tracks first, had heard the movement when she'd thought he was only listening to the breeze in the trees. He'd been conversational as he'd told her that it was a black bear—not saying how he'd known, and she hadn't asked. She'd been too busy glomming on other bear information she'd learned as a kid in school. Black bears were generally not aggressive.

She'd seen its back as Mitchell stood his ground and the animal had slowly ambled off in the opposite direction.

That had been an hour before. She'd been thinking ever since about the man's appearance in her life.

Leaning her head back against the tree's bark while Mitchell stood gazing at the horizon, Dove closed her eyes and took deep, pure breaths. All the way through her diaphragm and filling her stomach.

Over the course of the past hours, she'd found her way back to herself. To fully trusting. Against her own judgment, she'd followed her heart's missive to seek out her exact opposite, the practical and staid Mitchell Colton. And she'd most definitely been led to the place she'd needed to be in that space and time.

She didn't kid herself that there was any kind of future for them. Dove rarely thought about a future for herself that contained a husband. Or even a permanent male companion.

Most of the men she knew didn't understand her. Or believe in what she knew to be truth. And there was no way she could compromise her heart. Any relationship she attempted to have after that would fail. You couldn't love without heart.

She didn't question why she'd been given a deeper sense of the heart and soul, the spirits within and around her. Didn't ask why she had an understanding that never reached most people. But she knew that, above all else, she had to be true to that which she could feel but not see. Or even explain.

Finishing a litany of thanks, she opened her eyes to see Mitchell pulling out his phone.

"Is this a service point?" she asked, reaching for her own cell. They'd stopped at two others during the hours they'd been out. There'd been no news forthcoming at either of them.

But when she saw Mitchell nod as he tapped his phone screen, she tapped her own. Saw a new text message, and recognizing the number as one of her father's employees, Hal Billows, she tapped to read it immediately.

Dread flooded her being at the first few words. She finished reading and said, "Mitchell." He reached her in two strides, and she handed him her phone.

Saw the words in her mind's eye as he read them.

Tell your father I'm sorry, Dove, but I'm quitting St. James Boats as of today. I've been offered a position at another marina for a lot more money. And better chances of longevity. Keep my pay for the past week in lieu of my two weeks' notice.

There was no other marina in Shelby. And as Mitchell had pointed out recently, Brad Fletcher owned the marinas in the neighboring towns on both sides of them.

She could no longer turn a blind eye to the facts that were presenting at an alarming rate. Mitchell had been right. Someone was putting the squeeze on her and her father.

Someone with the power to offer a St. James employee a handsome raise at what was surely one of Brad Fletcher's marinas.

At the same time Brad Fletcher was being increasingly aggressive with her in his bids to buy her father's marina.

It didn't take a mathematician to put two and two together on that one.

Nor to see that if she didn't take Fletcher's offer, she and her father would be destitute. St. James Boats was no longer raking in the dough, but it was making enough to cover Whaler's minimal needs and alcohol with enough left over for the monthly installments on her mother's remaining medical bills.

Namaste kept her afloat. But with nothing to spare.

"I might have a solution for this one." Mitchell's words slowly got through the fog taking over her brain.

"For what? We can't offer Hal more money."

"No, but with your permission, I think I might be able to find someone who can take over his duties. The son of a buddy of mine from high school. Dete Littleton. Like your father, Dete's a sea captain, gone most of the time, but his son, Kirk, has been raised on boats since he was born. He's only twenty-one, just back from college graduation…"

A dream come true for St. James Boats. Even temporarily.

That math added up quickly, too. Glancing at Mitchell, accepting without question the good coming from him, through him, she said, "You have my permission" and sat calmly while he made the call.

Bad would come. It was a part of the learning experience. Her job was to trust. To know that, regardless of what happened, her spirit would be fine. She was loved.

To believe that answers would always be there.

And to keep firmly in mind at all times that Mitchell Colton was merely a conduit.

Not intended to be a personal part of her life.

Kirk was ecstatic at the idea of working at St. James Boats. He'd grown up with the marina in his backyard. Had hung out there as a high schooler, just to learn, to feel like he was closer to his father out at sea.

Unbeknownst to Dove, Whaler had let the kid tag along and help him out when he was working on the boats. And the others had, too.

"It's a blessing of fate," Dove told Mitchell as they headed back down to civilization to meet the young man at the marina. It would be getting dark by the time they arrived—would be nearly eleven at night—but Kirk wanted to be able to help on the docks in the morning, and Mitchell had to close the deal. Several of the boats had reservations on the books for the next day. Including Whaler's largest, most expensive boat in the fleet—the small trawler, *Wicked Winnings*.

"It's business, Dove. It's what I do. Put together people and products that mesh through fair contracts." It was clear, concise, logical business.

Something he'd done dozens of times during his nearly ten years since he'd opened Shelby Law Office.

Business. Not some kind of guided-by-invisible-powers miracle.

And because he was bothered by her comment, he had to bring the point home strong. "It's what you're paying me for," he said succinctly.

Something that wasn't yet technically true. There was still no official agreement between him and St. James Boats.

Nor was he planning to charge the business for hooking Kirk up with them. More like he was doing a favor for a friend—his high school buddy, not Dove St. James.

He would oversee the employment contract, however. And update the one Whaler had with his one remaining full-time employee, Wes Armstrong. And should get something in writing with Lyle Morris, the college kid who was helping out for the summer. For all he knew, Kirk and Lyle knew each other. Stood to reason since they were only a few years apart in age.

Something to keep in mind, to ask Kirk about when they

met up. If there was jealousy or any kind of bad blood between the two, he'd want to see that both men were able to get along at work before he suggested that Dove leave them alone on the dock with Wes. Whaler's senior employee did not need employee-relation problems on his hands.

Energized by the thoughts, back to doing what he did and did well—taking care of his clients' business interests and preventing disasters—Mitchell was almost eager to get off the mountain and back to town. He was back in control of his world, himself again.

Right up until at the marina where, after the grocery incident, they'd decided to store her car that afternoon before leaving on their hike, Dove got in the passenger seat of his vehicle to ride home with him.

"It's like a miracle," she said, beaming in her usual way. Something he hadn't seen since her father had gone missing. The glow hit him in the gut. Hard.

He knew it would fade. Kansas had called in again to let him know there were still no signs of Bob St. James, nor did they have any viable leads. Which meant they were forced to take each road, each trail, each overhang one at a time. Her team would be at it again at first light.

"Kirk is just what St. James Boats needed!" Dove continued to gush. "And the idea you two came up with, him captaining *Wicked Winnings* three times a week to bring in a serious catch to sell, providing fresh halibut and salmon for the grocery store and for The Cove, too, is brilliant. The cash flow from that alone will be a boon. Dad's only been in the boat rental business for others to fish for sport and recreation, but making fish a part of our business is just the step we need, and now with Kirk onboard, we can actually implement the idea."

"We still have to talk to the businesses to see if they'll

buy what *Wicked Winnings* brings in," he warned, trying to let her down easy before he got to the tough stuff.

"Even if they don't go for it, you know locals will come down to the dock to buy fresh catch less expensively, and it's pretty much a given, with the discount you suggested, that the grocery store and The Cove will be on board."

"There will be an initial investment," he warned as he turned to head them out of town. "More insurance, for one thing. And means and protocol for proper handling and storage of the fish. Pricing structures. Packaging."

Nodding, Dove turned to look at him. "What's bothering you?"

It was unsettling how much time the woman spent reading his moods. But in the moment, she helped him get where he had to go. "There's no sign of your father yet."

She nodded. "I figured. You got two calls while we were at the marina. If either of them had been good news, you'd have told me."

So...all her purported happiness about Kirk had just been...fake? Avoidance? A cover-up for what she didn't want to see?

"The second call was from Welding. Someone's been keeping an eye on your place today. Mrs. Bentley called in to report the same car parked down the street, saying she saw an individual wearing a baseball cap in the driver's seat with binoculars pointed toward your house. She didn't get a license plate, and by the time patrol got there, the car was gone."

Mrs. Bentley, the retired English teacher both Mitchell and Dove had had in high school. The longtime widow had been the only upper-class English teacher during the years both of them had been in school.

Dove's response was a little slower in coming. He was

prepared for tears again, when he got, "Which explains why I was guided to stay at your place." And then, "Or why you were prompted to invite me to stay."

"Dammit, Dove, this is serious." Mitchell calmed his tone, some, but not the frustration warring with compassion inside him. "Your life could be in danger. Judging from the break-in at Namaste, your property most definitely is. You can't just brush this all off and breeze by it, hoping it will go away."

He'd pulled into his driveway. Slid into the garage in total silence. Wishing he hadn't had to quiet her chatter but encouraged, too. He had to know that she was going to watch her back every second until the police found enough proof to be able to arrest Brad Fletcher.

When he put the car in Park and turned to look at her, she stared right back, saying, "You think that's what I'm doing? Running? Pretending? Avoiding?"

Softening his tone at the obvious disappointment in her eyes, he said, "Your father's missing, I'm telling you your house is a target, and all you want to talk about is spirit guides and their promptings. Where were they when your father either strayed off or was hauled off his path?"

The question seemed kind of cruel. Heartless. And yet, if it got her to take the situation more seriously and saved her life, then he'd appear to be as heartless as it took. No way he was going to stand by and watch the woman fall into more pain.

Her gaze didn't falter. Her hand seemed perfectly steady as she lifted it to push a lock of wavy hair over her shoulder. "I was talking about intuition, Mitchell. As in listening to it. Your brain, in conjunction with your heart, collaborating between what you know, what you believe and what you want, to best guide you."

He'd been put in his place. Succinctly. Firmly. Kindly.

By a petite yoga instructor who'd shown up that morning dressed like a sexy purple daffodil in revealing Lycra and some kind of netted long tutu thing.

A woman who solved her issues by sitting on the floor, closing her eyes and breathing deeply.

Not a solution that would work in court.

Mentally framing his sincere apology, Mitchell was interrupted when Dove said, "As for the rest of it… I can panic, shiver in fear, as I was doing earlier, my initial reaction to a change in my circumstances. And if I continue to do that, I play right into the hands and intentions of whoever is trying to inflict evil on me. My best shot at winning in this showdown is to remain calm. Lucid. And the way to do that is to not let the fear take hold. You prevent that from happening by focusing on good thoughts, which perpetuate good feeling, which lessens fear's ability to take you over. And for the science to back me up, since you seem to respond better to what you can have visible proof of, look up *serotonin*. See where that leads you."

Wow. The woman should be a prosecutor. A defense attorney. Or…just who she was.

"You've got some in your body, in case you didn't know."

His body. The words, coming at him in the dark, from the lips of the oddest and possibly the most fascinating creature he'd ever met, had a wrong effect on him.

Sending him into inappropriate waters.

Clinging to shore with everything he had, Mitchell said, "In the first place, I apologize. In the second, thank you."

She shook her head. "What are you thanking me for?"

"Setting me straight." That wasn't right. Wasn't enough. He revised with, "Reminding me that my perspective is not the only valid one on earth."

"You're more in tune than you think, Mitchell. I've been struggling to get out of the fear. I was failing, in spite of everything I know to do to help myself. But you knew what to do. Head away from the world, from the evil lurking around me, and up into nature."

For a second there, he wanted to be that guy. To live in a world where he could just escape all of the threatening possibilities lurking around the corner. But to do so, he'd have to give up his livelihood and walk away from what he was best at. Looking for the danger. And preventing it from happening to others where he could.

Using the skills he excelled at—analyzing, paying attention to detail, making judgments. Staying focused on the bad that had happened, and could happen, in order to find ways to avoid it whenever possible.

"Are we going in?" she asked, bringing his attention back to her face in the dimly lit garage.

"I wasn't sure you'd still want to stay." Though, he'd have done all he could to talk her out of not doing so, if she had made that choice.

"Of course I want to stay." Her vehemence surprised him. Gave him another stab of the desire he'd been trying so hard to pretend wasn't there. Until she said, "I was prompted to seek you out, and willingly, knowingly, or not, you've been my answer every step of the way. I might appear odd to many in this town, but I am not one to make foolish choices, Mitchell. Nor to turn my back on the opportunity that's been presented at a time when I most need it."

Well, there he had it. She wasn't into him. Personally. Wasn't maybe starting to trust him. She was relying on her inner guidance. And he just happened to be the means by which she reached her goal.

The thought should have eased much of the bizarre emotional tension that had been building within Mitchell.

Instead, her words left him unusually deflated.

And still tense.

Chapter 10

Dove went straight to her room. Alone time was critical to her well-being and, other than while using the restroom, she'd had none since early that morning.

More than that, she wanted to get out of Mitchell's hair. If he quit on her, she had no idea what she was going to do.

The answers would come. They always did. She knew that.

But she could also reach her demise in the process of finding them. While she was not one to argue with fate, she also understood that self-will had power of its own. And she wasn't ready to be done with her earthly life.

After a quick shower and then prayer time—focusing fully on her father being alive—her head hit the pillow just before one in the morning. And by four, she was lying there wide awake. With worry bugs starting to creep under her skin.

Throwing off the covers, she tried to meditate but was already too lost in subconscious musings to find her zen. At home, she'd turn up the music and clean.

But she figured Mitchell wouldn't appreciate the chaos at that early hour.

Opening her door slowly, she crept out into the hall enough to take in the quiet of the house. That's when guidance hit. The kitchen was the room closest to her but the far-thest from the staircase that led upstairs to Mitchell's suite.

And she had dinner to make. She'd given her word. Had no idea what the coming day was going to bring in terms of claims on her time.

She loved to cook. Found pleasure in the activity itself, the joining of various ingredients to make something that tasted better together than any of them did alone.

And while the sauce simmered, the ricotta mixture soft-ened enough for spreading, and the noodles cooled, she prepared cacao beans for roasting. And mixed up a bowl of fresh, finely cut cucumber, broccoli, kale spinach, and other mixed greens for breakfast. Her own.

Breakfast casserole was on the menu for Mitchell's.

Even if he liked the idea of salad in the morning, no way she was going to expose the man to her dietary habits. He'd just end up asking questions.

And she'd end up telling him that the foods promoted intuitive abilities...because she *knew* he'd go look up their benefits—and find them, too. Proving her right.

And while she was not going to change who she was or what she did, she didn't have to be in his face with her life-style, either. Especially as a guest in his home.

That would be just plain rude.

Adding some cheese to her greens for protein, and then, when they came out of the oven, the chopped beans, Dove moved on to the next project. Roasting salmon in the air fryer on the counter. She'd seen a friend of her mother's use one. Had always wanted to try one out.

With the lasagna in the oven—she'd waited to bake it be-cause it took longer, at a higher temperature than the twenty minutes total for the beans—she pulled out the salmon she'd put in marinade when she'd first come into the kitchen.

Reading the instructions on the front of the air fryer, she set the temperature and time before putting the smaller pan in the middle shelf and hitting Start.

From there, she moved immediately to the refrigerator for the sausage for Mitchell's breakfast casserole. Putting that on the stove on low, taking time to crumble it nicely, she was just finding a bowl big enough for the egg mixture when she heard footsteps on the stairs.

At five thirty in the morning.

And was filled with instant dread. An hour and a half of good feeling dried up as she waited for her host to make his far too early appearance.

While she was at his place, and with his family working her father's case, it stood to reason that bad news was going to come from him.

It would also be what would get him up out of bed so early in the morning after having gotten to bed late the night before.

That and the fact that he had an office to open that morning, the thought came to her. With clients that could have early appointments before their own businesses opened.

She'd been selfish. Making the world all about her...

And should have put on more than just the pajama pants and cutoff tie-dyed T-shirt she normally wore to bed—and for cooking. Like a bra.

And panties.

She couldn't very well make a run for it with sausage browning on the stove. Nor was she one to hide from trouble. Most particularly not that which sprang from her own actions.

And if it was bad news coming her way?

Half-frozen in indecision, Dove moved by rote, not thought. Reaching into the refrigerator for the food she knew would give her abilities an almost immediate boost, she grabbed a fork and was standing by the bowl of eggs, chewing, when Mitchell entered the room.

Not in a suit ready for work.

"Something smells good," he said, seemingly unfazed to walk into his kitchen in a pair of silk drawstring shorts and nothing else to find a woman standing there shoveling salad into her mouth.

"It's salmon," she told him, because the fish was the one project she was least confident about so was most on her mind. The whole air fryer thing being an unknown component.

"And lasagna," she added as he passed the oven on his way to…the coffee maker. She should have made coffee. Hated the stuff. Wasn't sure how to work the machine. But…

"I couldn't sleep," she admitted, as she quickly chewed and swallowed another bite. Nearly choking on a shard of bean.

With a few quick and impressively efficient moves, he had a cup on the plate of the coffee maker, had inserted a pod in the top and was moving over to the stove. "And the sausage?" he asked.

He'd been with her at the store when she'd purchased it—and pretty much everything else she was using that morning—and had tried to pay for it all.

"Breakfast casserole. I planned to have it ready by six. In time for you eat before you have to leave for work." And then, thinking she sounded presumptuous added, "And it keeps well, in the event you didn't need breakfast until seven. Or eight."

The man needed to go. Out of the kitchen. At the very least.

It wasn't like she'd never seen a bare-chested male in the kitchen before, but Mitchell—she'd never been around a guy who...exuded...on overload. Her nipples were hard and, other than putting her arms up over them to cover them—which would just draw attention to her inappropriate reaction to the man sent to help her through a horrible phase in her life—she couldn't do a thing about it.

Except stand there holding her bowl in front of her, take another bite and look at Mitchell's chest again.

To stave off what she knew was coming.

And she'd been so pompous in her self-assertion moments before that she didn't run from trouble.

Kansas had said she'd be back at it by daybreak. Dawn had hit almost an hour before. "Have you heard from Kansas?" she asked then. Ashamed that she'd tried to hide behind the sight of a chest, rather than face whatever the day was going to bring her.

Or was she hiding behind the day so she didn't have to deal with what the sight of that chest had done to her? Way more than what she'd felt in the studio the other day.

She could not be sexually drawn to Mitchell Colton. He was her complete opposite.

And she needed him.

Sex was messy. And after the initial pleasure wore off, relationships usually didn't end well. At least not in her experience.

Every time she'd had to break up with a guy, he'd given her the cold shoulder.

Maybe it was just her. Not knowing how to break up right...

"I'm waiting on a call back from her." Mitchell's words put an immediate halt to her mental throwing up. And drew her gaze up to his face.

"And you wanted to be down here when the call came in," she said slowly. Because the couple of days they'd spent together had been intense, and his body language was easy for her to read.

Or, more likely, she hadn't lost her ability to tune in and gain understanding, in spite of her extreme mental and emotional flux.

A fact for her thoughts only. As secret and sacred as the sexual ones she'd been having the past couple of days.

Not to be shared with Mitchell Colton.

Ever.

Mitchell pulled his cell phone out of the pocket of his loosely fitting shorts. Set it on the counter. Wishing, for the dozenth time since he'd come down, that he'd thrown on a T-shirt before leaving his room.

The shorts had seemed sufficient when he'd been thinking that he was pulling them on with the very small chance that he'd see Dove St. James when he went down to make his coffee—a task normally done in the nude, right after he slid out of bed and before he got in the shower.

He'd hoped to be showered, shaved and fully dressed before facing the woman who'd bombarded his life. She'd had a hard few days and had gotten to bed late.

No way he'd expected her to be superwoman in the kitchen, making multiple meals, before six in the morning.

By the time he'd registered the unusual scents wafting through the air, he'd already been detected and could hardly turn tail and run. The explaining that would have required was painful just to think about.

Stirring the sausage that was bordering on being more than merely browned, he turned down the heat and faced the woman who'd kept him up even after he'd closed his eyes the night before.

Standing up straight, holding her bowl like an iron shield in front of her, she asked, "What are we expecting to hear?"

And he gave it to her straight. "Kansas found Whaler's cap."

Her gaze widening, her mouth dropped open. No words came out.

"I was hoping to know more before I saw you," he told her the truth.

"How much do you know?"

"The cap was found half-buried in some leaves, not far from an overhang about five miles outside town."

"Where? Hanging over what?"

Wishing he was anywhere but where he stood, Mitchell had never felt so underprepared—and underdressed— in his life. "Three miles up the mountain, overhanging the Bering Sea." He gave it to her straight.

Whether she was ready for the truth or not, she'd made it clear the night before that she deserved his full respect. Which, in his world, meant his full disclosure.

"They think he went over."

He couldn't tell her that. Kansas had given facts. Not opinions. "They're thoroughly checking the area." And there was more. "It looks like there was a struggle nearby, like someone was lying down."

Her eyes narrowed, and she took another bite of what looked to be some kind of rabbit food. That needed a load of dressing—for starters. "Were there signs of anyone having been dragged?" she asked.

He shook his head. Knowing full well that the news didn't mean that no one had been hauled to the edge of the cliff. Only that if someone had been pulled across the ground, the dragger had cleaned up after himself.

Dove nodded, then, setting down her container, moved over to the sausage, stirring it, as she said, "If you don't mind, I'd like to hang close until that call comes in." And then added, "Unless you have to go up and get ready for work?"

"I've got my paralegal handling things at the office today."

It wasn't the first time. Or even the fiftieth. He'd always been hands-on when it came to his work. Meeting his clients in their territory, not his. It was the best way to see it all and therefore gave him his best shot at finding ways he could help.

Like the fishing idea he'd come with while talking to Kirk the night before. A way for St. James Boats to make additional revenue.

"Unless something else comes up, I'd like to spend some time at the marina this morning," he told Dove. "To get a better look at everything involved in getting it set up for commercial fishing and additions that will need to be added for the selling process." Standing there naked except for his shorts, he was still a lawyer. Had to stay focused on business, not on the far too sexy woman standing at his stove, giving him full view of the intriguing butt that her thin pants outlined.

Turning suddenly, as though she knew where his gaze had gotten stuck, she looked up at him, her expression eager. "You really think it's going to work, don't you?"

The fishing. Not the sex. "I think it can," he told her, choosing his words as carefully as always. "We can't do anything until Whaler's back to sign off on it."

Unless the older man was found deceased. His pause

seemed to relay the message to Dove, judging by the instant drop in her expression.

Which prompted him to say, "But I'd like to have as much of the logistics ready as possible so that it's something he can run with quickly, if he chooses to do so."

Her eyes filled with tears. Because her father was missing and might not make it back? Because she had new cause to hope that if her father returned, life would be better? Mitchell couldn't read her, which made him uncomfortable in a huge way.

In his own kitchen.

Before breakfast.

He had to stop her before she had a breakdown. Leaked out all over the place.

He had to comfort her before his compassion became more than that and his own heart started to bleed.

Reaching out, he pulled her against him. Just for a quick hug.

Lawyer to aching client.

A business move he'd never made before.

Performed in not-business clothes.

Her untethered breasts pushed against his unclothed chest, with only the thin piece of cotton she wore between them.

Which affected him down below, where he was not appropriately confined.

Made clearly obvious against the thin cotton of her pants.

About to escape from his shorts, Mitchell jerked back abruptly, turned his back and vacated the room.

Leaving his cell phone on the counter behind him.

Chapter 11

Turning off the heat on the sausage, Dove sank to the floor. Back against the cupboard, she crossed her legs in the lotus position, let her arms fall, palms facing upwards at her knees, closed her eyes and breathed.

Deeply. Raggedly.

Tears fell.

She didn't try to stop them. She sat with them. Living through them.

Being.

In the way back of her mind, an image lingered. Mitchell Colton had held her and gotten hard. Just as her breasts had become over sensitized against his chest.

She didn't dwell there. If sex happened between them, it did. She wasn't going to fight it. Didn't have the strength to go up against nature's call.

But only if he knew that sex didn't mean a relationship. Or commitment.

And she had no idea if he knew that.

Just like he had no idea if her father was alive or dead. *Daddy.*

The name of old came to her. Called out of her toward him. Pulling him out of an abyss and back to her. She was there. Present. Helping him save the business that he loved.

Hold on, Daddy.

The words came to her, and from her, followed by a flow of conviction, of strength, so powerful that the sorrow left her being. Only for a few seconds. But for that brief time, she'd felt peace.

Grasping hold of the memory, she opened her eyes. Wiped her cheeks. And slowly stood. Holding on to that last impression she'd had, she finished putting together the breakfast casserole. Took the salmon out of the air fryer, wrapping it tightly for future salad use. Washed dishes while she waited for the lasagna to finish baking so the casserole could go in.

And heard Mitchell's phone ring.

Snatching her hands from the soapy water, she grabbed a towel, dried them and grabbed up the phone. Saw Kansas's name on the screen.

Just that. *Kansas.*

She pushed to answer. It wasn't like she had time to run all the way upstairs before the call disconnected.

And he could be in the shower. She had no right to trespass there.

She said the first thing that came to mind. "Mitchell Colton's phone. This is Dove St. James speaking." She shivered, but remained otherwise calm.

"Dove? Where's Mitchell? Is he okay?"

"He's upstairs in the shower," she said. At least that was her summation. She wasn't going looking to find out.

"And he left his phone with you?"

"It's my father you're calling about, right? If not, I'll hang up and have Mitchell call you back." She'd just finished the sentence when she heard footsteps on the stairs. "Oh, hold on, he's coming down now," she said and held out the phone, impatient to give it to Mitchell so that she could hear whatever it was Kansas had called to say.

Life was hanging in the balance, and protocols still mattered. There was something comforting about that.

Expecting to see Mitchell dressed, she stared when he came down wearing a towel with a robe over it. "I heard you talking to someone," he said, his expression containing a question and a bit of alarm.

Warming at his concern—even if it was just because he was a good man caring about humankind in general—she handed him the phone. "It's Kansas."

His instant attention to detail, the way his gaze firmed and he grabbed the phone to his ear, warmed her more. A sensation she clung to as she heard him give a couple of affirmatives but nothing more.

Trying to read anything from him, she failed. The robe, the towel, his bent head, she just couldn't tell what was going through him. Tension, no doubt about that. Having her there at all was causing some of that.

With a "Thank you. Keep in touch," he hung up.

And Dove, while scared and shaky, also felt a bit of a smile start to emerge inside her. They wouldn't be keeping in touch if they'd found a body.

She didn't say a word. Just watched Mitchell. Giving him time to formulate whatever would be forthcoming. Because he needed that. She didn't.

"They found evidence of a skirmish just over the side of the cliff, on a fairly substantial-sized ledge. A couple of footprints, which the forensics team are on now. We'll need your father's shoe size, and as much as you can tell us about the footwear he had on the last time you saw him."

"But no body," she said. No body meant there was still hope.

"No body," he confirmed. Studying her so long she felt a squirm coming on. "A body could have gone over, Dove.

It wasn't visible from the top, but a search and rescue team has been dispatched to coordinates directly below."

She'd already accepted that a body could have gone over. Didn't mean it was her father's. It could be whoever he'd been fighting with. "Signs of a skirmish are a good thing," she said then. "My dad's one hell of a fighter. You might not think so, given the way he hasn't been taking care of himself since Mom died, but prior to that, for his entire life, he's been focused on keeping himself strong and in the best physical shape possible. His freedom to do what he wanted depended on it. He's still stronger than a lot of guys half his age." She might be exaggerating a tad. She hadn't actually seen her dad on a weight machine in over a year. But if she was off, it wasn't by much.

"Then, we'll continue forward with good thoughts for his return," Mitchell said, still standing there, seemingly assessing her. Whether he really believed Whaler was dead or alive didn't much matter to Dove. She needed him, his focus, on her, on St. James Boats, not on her father. She— and she was certain her mother's spirit—had that one covered.

But she was only human. She faltered and fell prey to humanity's greatest evil: fear.

Mitchell's presence was needed to cover her. To keep her afloat while she held her father up. She fully believed that. Had seen proof of why he was there over and over in the past few days.

"Uh, about that...what happened earlier..."

Pulling up an innocent look born of knowing neither of them did anything wrong, she said, "What happened?" He had absolutely nothing to castigate himself for. And she knew she'd done nothing requiring an apology.

At least not in the moment he was speaking about.

"I never should have hugged you. It was inappropriate. Something I've never done before. And I can assure you, it won't happen again."

"Don't make promises you can't possibly keep," her mother's words of old popped out of their own accord.

Frowning, Mitchell wrapped his dark blue robe about him further, tightening the knotted matching dark blue fabric belt holding it in place. "I keep my promises."

"I fully believe you intend to, Mitchell, but how can you possibly see forty years into the future, which could be when you retire, and know that you'll never have occasion to give a client a moment of comfort?"

He stared at her.

And she moved in a little closer. Not physically. But with the softening of her gaze. And the words she let out. "As for the rest…the perfectly normal bodily reactions that occurred when you reached out to offer me comfort…it's not fair to yourself to guarantee that it won't happen again. What if I was falling, and you reached out to catch me, and we ended up in a kiss?"

He scoffed. "You've watched too many Christmas movies."

Aha! That had to mean he'd seen at least one, right? Maybe with his mom or sister?

Could be he even tuned in to one on his own at some point. Or with a girlfriend.

The last thought not as pleasing as the others, she let them go. And grew completely serious.

"Sex has a power of its own, Mitchell. When two consenting adults are both consumed by that force at the same time, there's a good chance they'll come together physically." She was practically quoting her mother then—from her reaching-puberty talks—but with an experience Dove had gained on her own.

He leaned against the counter, suddenly seeming a little more amenable to staying a while, rather than hightailing it back up to his ablutions.

And getting himself all decently covered, tucked in and hidden away.

With a quirk of his head and narrowed blue eyes, he said, "You're telling me that you'd be consenting?"

Delicious flames shot down between her legs. She knew to welcome the release from the dread that had been closing in on her as she pictured her father on a cliff ledge fighting for his life.

"I'm assuming we'll have a talk about it first," she told him.

Was that the time to have it? Right then? Did they schedule a time? She'd never actually done it that way before. Generally she was out socially with the guy and they'd already established that they were just friends.

"What kind of talk?"

"The kind where we establish guidelines. So no one gets hurt."

His eyes narrowed again. Kind of deliciously. And she didn't bother to camouflage her glance down to his crotch. A look that lingered as the robe moved, seeming of its own accord. "Do we make an appointment for this conversation?" he asked.

How the hell did she know? Mitchell Colton had a whole hell of a lot more experience than she did in the mingling-with-the-opposite-sex department. But if he thought that was a good idea… "We can," she said. Then added, "But we better make it soon, just in case. The whole power thing—" she glanced down at his crotch again "—it seems to be gaining on us rather quickly."

She'd grown wet. Without panties on. It was kind of intoxicating. And a bit uncomfortable, too, considering she'd probably have to wear her pajama pants again before she moved home and could wash them.

The way he was watching her…as though she was a slice of double chocolate cake with rich icing…no man had ever looked at her like that before. "Let's say, over lunch," she blurted. They'd be at the marina. Or she would be, and he'd be on the phone. All classes at Namaste had had to be canceled until the negativity bombarding her life had been resolved. No way she could live with herself if her bad energy spilled over onto those who came to her for help with their inner healing.

She was pretty sure Mitchell was holding back a grin as he nodded. "Over lunch it is," he told her and turned and walked away.

Right as the timer on the lasagna buzzed. "Mitchell?" she called out. Saw him stop, start to turn, and she grabbed the hot pads, pulling open the oven as she said, "Breakfast casserole will be out in forty-five minutes. If that's too long, we can finish it off at the marina. Dad has a toaster oven there." It wouldn't be nearly as delicious that way, but she wasn't the one who would be eating it.

"That's fine," he told her. "It'll give you time to get showered. I can make a couple of calls here in my home office, and we can take it hot to share with Wes and the rest of the crew. It will be a good way to start what will be an unusual day for them."

Bringing good to overshadow the bad. She smiled. Nodded.

And slid the casserole into the oven to the sound of Mitchell's feet on the creaky stairs. Smiling. Thanking her stars for sending her the helpmate they had.

The man had a deeper understanding of life.

He just didn't know he had it.

And she was okay with that.

The morning kept Mitchell busy. Dove, he noticed, not so much. She tried engaging when something came up that could use her attention, or when someone directly approached her. But for the most part, she sat on the floor of her father's office—dressed in a long flowing burgundy, pink and white skirt, and a long-sleeved pink crop top—and made some phone calls.

She didn't go out on the docks at all.

Or interact with customers.

Mitchell didn't blame her. He actually admired her for being there at all. And appreciated her attention to detail when her focus was needed.

But while she didn't go outside, he, on the other hand, spent a good bit of his time on the docks. He'd dressed accordingly, in jeans and a flannel shirt, rather than the suit he'd worn his first day of lawyering at St. James Boats. Hard to believe that only a few days had passed since then.

In some ways he felt like a completely different man. Freer. Which made absolutely no sense, so he pushed the unusual contemplation aside. Disregarding it as woo-woo, a result of the company he'd been keeping, not based in his own reality.

He spent a couple of hours taking a much deeper look at Whaler's books—finding the accounting to be nothing like he'd seen before, but once he figured out the old sea captain's process, he found the entries to be in fairly good order. Consistent.

The business was dying a slow death. But a clearly delineated one. So seeing, he was quickly able to ascertain weaknesses and formulate possible solutions.

If Whaler made it back and got sober, he could have the place running a profit in very little time. Two very big *if*s.

Neither of which were looking to be likely possibilities.

The better bet would be to get the place in shape, to show its profitability and then put it up for sale. With the hope of finding a buyer who wouldn't be intimidated by Brad Fletcher. A conversation he intended to have with Dove over lunch.

Because there was long-term good news in there. And he was particularly eager to give it to her. The woman took on so much. Tried so hard.

And was holding on by a thread—made clear to him by the conversation she'd instigated after his apology in the kitchen that morning. Capitalizing on the change of topic from threats and possible death to a topic that often resulted in extreme pleasure.

Could be she'd been messing with him to cover up her embarrassment.

Or, more likely, she had been using the momentary, very unfortunate lapse of protocol between them as a distraction from the terrifying disappearance of her father.

Either way, it was up to him to make certain that he was never again in a position where he was turned on by her. And absolutely not when he was underdressed enough for her to pick up on that fact. He was the lawyer. The man she was in the process of hiring to help straighten out a very grim situation.

She was the victim.

He'd rather go off the grid and never have contact with another human being for the rest of his life than take advantage of a woman who'd come to him for help.

To further victimize Dove St. James in any way.

Stepping outside the office just after eleven to take a call from Stuart, his loyal and hardworking paralegal, he walked up to the parking lot in front of the marina so he could discuss other clients without being overheard.

And was just in time to see a man getting out of an expensive-looking sedan and then, glancing in Mitchell's direction, get right back in and pull off the lot. The man had been dressed in fishing gear.

It was possible he'd just forgotten something. Or suddenly taken ill.

Mitchell's mind was heading loudly in another direction. Telling Stuart he'd call him back, Mitchell pressed the contact icon on his screen for his brother and asked for an image of Brad Fletcher to be sent over to him. It arrived almost immediately, with Eli still on the line, and Mitchell was almost certain Brad was the man he'd seen.

The car had been at a wrong angle for him to have gotten a look at the license plate. He hadn't been thinking along those lines at the time, in any case.

"I'll get with Welding, find out what's going on with the team watching Fletcher," Eli said and then, telling Mitchell to stick close to Dove in case Fletcher tried to contact her again, he quickly rang off.

Eli had problems of his own, Mitchell knew. His cousin Spence and Hetty Amos, a sea pilot for the Colton family adventure business, had stumbled over a dead woman in the woods, only partially buried, with her hair and her left hand wearing a large diamond engagement ring still visible. Eli had been assigned the case, and so far, other than being certain the woman's death had been no accident, he had nothing substantial to help him solve the murder.

A mirror to Whaler's disappearance—no viable leads—

which Mitchell knew would be eating at his brother. Cases with no solid clues made investigators uneasy. Two of them happening around the same time—especially in their relatively quiet remote town—raised cause for alarm.

Mitchell kept an eye on the marina and watched the road as well while he completed his business with Stuart as expediently as possible, and then he headed straight for the small office not far from the docks.

Lunch in a neighboring town sounded like a good idea to him. Get Dove away from Shelby and all the heartache, intimidation and fear she'd been suffering over the weekend. Yet they'd still be within easy range in the event that Whaler was found alive. In a restaurant, conversation would more easily stay focused on the business he had to discuss with her, even with someone as intent on living through her inner voices as Dove was. So yeah, his reasoning was partly to ward off his own discomfort.

More than that, though, Brad Fletcher, or anyone he hired to keep digging at Dove, would not be looking for her in a dockside restaurant twenty miles down the road.

Calling ahead to the place—one of his regular eateries for business lunches with clients—Mitchell made the reservation. And walked into the office to see…

A card table set with a red-and-white checkered tablecloth, two big bowls from his kitchen, cutlery, napkins and glasses—and Dove on the floor behind it all.

She stood as he came in, saying nothing, and moved to the refrigerator Whaler kept stocked with beer.

No alcohol was his first thought. He'd made a list of guidelines to prevent him from repeating the morning's debacle with his body in the kitchen. Feeling attraction, as he had in the studio the other day was one thing: normal reaction. That morning in the kitchen…he'd made a wrong move and had caused himself to cross a line.

"I'm assuming there's been no word from Kansas?" she asked the same question she'd greeted him with every time he'd entered the small structure that morning.

Shaking his head, more at the table than anything, he said, "No." He wanted to tell her he was sorry but was too focused on the food she was pulling from the refrigerator.

Freshly roasted salmon. Greens. Dressing.

Not beer.

With tension filling him, Mitchell sent a quick text to cancel the lunch reservation he'd just made and went into the small bathroom to wash up. The sink, floors, stool and towels were all clean.

There'd been no cleaning service on the St. James Boat books.

Nor did Whaler seem to deal in cash. All transactions that he'd reviewed, both private and personal, had been completed by card. Even his bar tab.

Which had been astronomical.

Dove. He wasn't going to ask, but he knew the cleaning most likely had been done by her. The bucket of cleaning supplies on the corner bottom shelf—right next to extra toilet paper rolls—looked a lot like the one she'd pulled supplies out of to hand to him Sunday morning in her studio.

It had become pretty clear to Mitchell that Dove had been taking care of her father in all the ways she knew how—and could get away with.

She'd only come to him when she'd done all she could herself.

Some of the things she'd said to him over the past few days lined up in a row, replaying in his mind.

"How do you know I even like lasagna?"

"My spirits told me." The tone of voice she'd used—
she'd been playing with him. Letting him know that she
knew that he'd branded her as a bit out there, along with
much of the rest of the town. Just as they'd done her mother.

And then… *"No, Mitchell, I'm not calling you a liar. I'm
just paying attention to your posture, your tone of voice.
You're uncomfortable, which tells me that you know more
than you're saying."* He could clearly picture the smile that
had teased the corners of her mouth on that one. As though
she'd known he'd been uncomfortable—because he'd been
taken in by the rumors that she and her mother thought they
could read minds.

There were others.

In less than four days' time, he'd come to know her better than people he'd been acquainted with for years.

He could almost feel how difficult that had to have been
for her. To have to beg for help from someone she hardly
knew but was acquainted with enough to understand that
he'd judged her without having actually spent time in her
presence.

She'd walked into his office, head held high, knowing
that he thought her flighty.

The realization held him hostage there in that tiny space,
as his mind tried to unravel the implications. Leaving him
with the certainty that no matter what happened between
them, he couldn't turn his back on her and live with himself.

"Mitchell, you okay in there?"

He jerked as her voice came to him through the thin
walls and he was mentally transported back to that morning in his kitchen.

The room was closing in on him.

Pulling the door open he said, "Fine. Just had some boat

grease to get out from under my fingernails." True. But a task he'd completed minutes before.

Standing between him and the beyond, she glanced at his hands, while he took in her flat pink leather sandals with laces that climbed up her legs and under the hem of her skirt. When his gaze made it up to her eyes, he found her staring at him.

Without hesitation, she said, "And here I was thinking you were avoiding our prearranged lunchtime conversation."

About to start believing that her fates had it in for him, Mitchell would have bolted then and there, if she hadn't been blocking his way.

Instead, confident that what he had to discuss with her would override their earlier agreement, he said, "I'm eager for the upcoming conversation" and followed her to the table.

He couldn't walk away from her. But he could play her at her own game.

And win.

Chapter 12

Dove wasn't surprised when Mitchell took immediate control of their table conversation as he filled his bowl with salad, topping it with the ginger teriyaki dressing she'd made.

From a lawyerly point of view, it was the right thing to do. Keep things on the surface. Avoiding any detours into topics that could be considered inappropriate in the workplace.

She listened to what he had to say. Was somewhat surprised by how quickly an implementation of his ideas could make her father's relatively small boat-rental business into an entity worth a whole lot more money than Brad Fletcher had offered her even when he'd been acting decently. Enough, according to the numbers Mitchell slid in front of her, to pay off all of her mother's medical bills and still have a substantial sum left over.

More money than her family had probably ever had.

It was the stuff her dreams of a week ago had been made of.

"This is all great, Mitchell," she said, forcing herself to swallow bites of the food she knew would not only sustain her but strengthen her intuitive abilities as well. "Exactly what I originally came to see you about, and what we're going to be paying for. As soon as my father is back home, we'll be ready to hit the ground running." She took another bite, swallowed and said, "This should be enough to get his head and heart in gear—enough to motivate sobriety."

She didn't know if the latter was true. But she had to believe it was. And knew for certain that there was a good possibility.

"As for the rest, being able to find a buyer other than Fletcher, someone we could feel good about selling to, is a fine thought, but not one I'm interested in entertaining. You misunderstood if you thought my goal was to absolve financial obligations. I told you about my mother's bills so that you would understand how much of a profit we need to make. And to know that my father wasn't just throwing his current paychecks into the bottle. He pays my mother's bills first and foremost, every month. It's like an honor to him, to do that for her."

And would be for Dove, too, if she was ever required to take over the deed.

When his eyes lost some of their glow, she quickly added, "That's not to say that I'm not overjoyed by the work you've managed to do this morning. I cannot wait to get started on all of this. Just as soon as we find my dad."

Because, hello, that was the only thing on her mind at the moment.

Except thoughts of Mitchell. And possibly having sex with him. Every time she'd started to sink into an abyss of negativity that morning, thoughts of Mitchell and their upcoming conversation had pulled her right back out and into the moment—and task—at hand.

Staying positive long enough for Kansas and the SAR team to work their magic and find her dad.

It would happen in fate's time. Not her own.

The only say she had, the only control, the only choices she had in the meantime pertained to how she managed herself while she waited.

Did she stay strong? Vital? Present and able to hear the silent promptings within her?

Or did she fall into a hell from which she might never emerge?

Fantastical as it might sound to some, in Dove's mind, the answer lay in having the real conversation that lunch was about. She had no idea what the outcome would be.

Whether or not she'd ever have sex with Mitchell Colton.

The conversation wasn't about whether or not they were actually ever going to do it. Or even wanted to do so.

"So talk to me about your views on sexual activity," she said when he seemed to have no ready response to her replies regarding his business conversation.

They'd made an agreement to talk about it. She hadn't coerced him into doing so and felt strongly that if she didn't hold him to his word on the matter, something not good could result.

No clue what that something was or if it even pertained to her.

"I view all such action to be inappropriate in the workplace."

The response disappointed her, while at the same time she realized she should have expected it. Mitchell was Mitchell. Logical. Living fully in his head. Maybe even a little uptight.

"Well then, it's a good thing that St. James Boats hasn't actually hired you yet. No contracts delivered or signed. While I'm a signer on the business now, I'm not an employee. But I am a guest in your home. Where we ended up in the kitchen, outside of office hours, in less than professional attire."

She could go on. Would go on if he forced her to do so. She could be a whole lot blunter. But she stopped there, giving him a chance to own up to his own culpability in their need for the conversation.

And if he walked away? Told her he'd have her things delivered from his home?

Her guidance had clearly led her to him. Was she on the verge of making a personal choice that ruined the good she'd done by listening in the first place?

"I like sex." He looked her straight in the eye as he delivered the short sentence.

Swallowing, she pursed her lips. Then found enough voice to accept his challenge, maintaining eye contact as she said, "So do I." There were caveats to her proclamation. A lot of them. She wasn't sure why she held them back when he'd given her the perfect opportunity to get them out. She wasn't asking why.

"I don't have it with clients."

She'd figured as much. But just in case he hadn't yet discerned the same about her, she said, "Nor do I."

Forking a healthy bite of salad, he said, "So are we done here?" and filled his mouth with her bounty.

The delicious food she'd provided, she mentally corrected herself.

She took a bite of her own salad, suddenly unable to swallow without discomfort. "No."

He nodded, as though he'd expected the response. Almost as though he was enjoying their repartee.

She kind of was.

Except that she couldn't lose sight of the very real necessity for having the talk to begin with.

"There's a likely chance that what happened in the kitchen this morning will happen again."

"Not if we agree not to be in the kitchen at the same time."

His almost childish response had her gaping at him. It wasn't like they'd planned to be there that morning. Even less likely that they could time Kansas's phone calls to when they were in an office situation.

Chances were greater that the kind of call she was awaiting would come in the middle of the night. It just always seemed to happen that way. Evil at work in the dark.

Except...she pulled herself upright. Evil wouldn't be at work because her dad was going to be found alive.

Giving herself a mental smack for having fallen down the dark hole even while she was consciously working on staying out of it, Dove followed the self-directed negativity with a mental hug. An apology. And encouragement to herself for having seen what was happening and thus could prevent a permanent dive.

She didn't do that by playing around. Putting down her fork, folding her hands on the table in front of her, she said, "I'm not averse to having sex with you, Mitchell. I would never have expected to be attracted to you—business suits aren't my thing—but I am. A lot."

He adjusted his sitting posture, and she pictured him over there growing hard. The image, egged on by their early morning meetup, gave her plenty of impetus to continue.

"However, I cannot engage in the behavior unless you understand that it's strictly a mutual enjoyment of physical activity. No strings attached. No commitment of any kind to any future involvement between us—business or otherwise."

His fork stopped halfway to his mouth. "You're telling me that you no longer want me to work with St. James Boats?" His entire demeanor had turned into one big frown.

"Hell no!" she blurted loudly, as she'd heard her father do. And then covered her mouth with her hand. Shocked at herself. Embarrassed. And then, half behind her fingers, said, "I'm saying that the sex needs to have no effect on anything outside the physical act. If we work together, that's a separate thing. But..." she lowered her hand, leaned in and looked him straight in the eye "...if us having sex means you won't help my father with his business, then it's off the table."

His gaze lightened. He ate another big bite. Then after he'd swallowed and wiped his mouth, he said, "Then, it's off the table."

Damn. She'd given him a way out. But he had to know...

Staring at him, she held him to the only real fire she knew. The silent kind that couldn't lie.

"I don't want to have sex with you, Dove."

She continued to hold his gaze. Breathing easily.

"Okay, I do. Quite fiercely, apparently. But I can't take advantage of you that way. Or use you—"

"But it's okay if I take advantage of you? Use you?"

He took yet another bite. Chewed. Swallowed. Repeated. Holding her gaze in a way that felt...easy. And that's when she knew she had him. In a place of calm that one reaches through total honesty.

"Do we have a clear understanding that *if* it were to happen, there'd be no strings attached? No expectations? And nothing weird between us after it was over?" She wasn't going to let it go until she knew. Her own future depended on that one.

"We do," he said clearly, succinctly. Confidently. Looking her straight in the eye.

And Dove stood, cleared her things off the table, put the leftovers in her bowl in the trash and the dirty dishes into the bag she'd brought from Mitchell's house. She'd failed to bring dish detergent in with her that morning.

Mitchell emptied his bowl into his stomach. One bite at a time. Then stood and brought his bowl and fork to her. Holding it out but not letting go of it, he asked, "Are we on for tonight, then?"

And she dropped the bag she was holding.

Mitchell hadn't seriously been planning to have sex with her. At least, most of him wasn't. But if it did happen, which, given his behavior that morning along with her assertion of wanting him, was a good possibility, he was one hundred percent on board with her terms.

They were way too different to actually sustain a relationship. And he had zero desire to hurt her. But it made sense, her feeling as she did, given what he'd heard about her lifestyle. And had observed from afar himself.

So if they could give each other a little pleasure at some point, he saw no harm in that.

Kind of liking the way his uncharacteristic boldness had knocked her off her game enough for her to drop her bag, Mitchell had his mouth open, ready to tease her a bit more, when the stark fear in her suddenly widened eyes clued him in that she wasn't looking at him.

Swinging around, he turned in the direction she was looking to see his cousin approaching the office. Her head and shoulders were visible through the small window beside Whaler's desk. A window he'd known always to be covered with a drawn blind.

It hadn't even registered that Dove had opened it until that moment.

Kansas was on site at St. James Boats.

She hadn't called.

Dropping his lunch leftovers on the counter, Mitchell moved behind Dove. His hand at her back. Lightly. Professionally.

But most definitely there. They'd found Whaler.

And Kansas had shown up in person.

Without a smile, her step denoting purpose, she approached with tightly pulled back long dark hair behind firm shoulders, and a grim expression.

Clearly like the family notifications his cousin had shared with him over beer more times than either of them would have liked.

They took the wind out of his cousin every single time that Mitchell knew about.

"She was a year behind me in high school." Dove's words came at him out of nowhere. In that first instant, he was worried that he'd lost her. That she knew what was coming and had fallen into some kind of mental paralysis.

"I remember once when Jack Percy was giving me a hard time in the lunchroom. Kansas stepped right up to him and told him to back off."

He hadn't heard that story. But he wasn't surprised to hear that the Percy kid had been a bully. Or that his cousin had come to the aid of one being persecuted.

He also hadn't pegged Dove correctly. Rather than disappearing, she was finding something good to cling to in the face of gloom. How he knew that, he couldn't say. Keen observation over a very intense few days, most likely.

She didn't move toward the door. Didn't move at all, and so neither did he.

When the knock came, firmly and loudly, Dove called, "Come in" in an equally raised tone.

A friendly one.

His hand at her back was stronger then. More the support of a friend than a lawyer. He was briefly aware. Didn't care.

Even if what he suspected was true was about to unfold—Whaler had been found dead—Dove's trials had just begun. There'd be an investigation. Hope to God a quick one. With an equally rapid trial.

And a tie-in to the vandalism at Dove's studio.

Kansas had stepped fully into the room. Her blue eyes steady, and her fit, strong form seemed to dominate the space. "Good, I'm glad you're both here," she said. "We found Whaler." She stopped abruptly. Looked straight at Dove and said, "I'm sorry...*your father.* He's alive, Dove, but unconscious. An ambulance is on the way to the hospital with him, and I came to take you there myself. With sirens on."

Whaler was alive. Mitchell kept the thought firmly at the forefront of his mind as Dove turned to look, wide-eyed, up at him. And when she moved to grab her purse, he allowed the next thought full flight: Kansas didn't expect Whaler to be alive for long.

Following Dove as she ran after Kansas, he locked the door behind him and climbed into the back of Kansas's car just before it sped off.

He wasn't officially on the St. James clock.

But there was no way he was leaving his clients unprotected for a second.

Or so he tried to tell himself.

As though reading his mind, Dove turned then, meeting his gaze over the seat, her gaze filled with trepidation, but something warmer, too.

And he had to admit, at least to himself, that there was only one reason he was in that car.

To be present if and when Dove needed him.

The look in her eye seemed to tell him that she knew it, too.

Mitchell wanted that to be a good thing.

But knew that it wasn't.

Chapter 13

Bob St. James was alive. Dove heard the rest from Kansas during the ten-minute drive to the small hospital, medical and trauma center at the edge of town. And again when the trauma doctor met her in the hallway outside the unit where her father lay unconscious.

He was alive, but barely. They let her in to see him, but only for a few minutes that first time, as they were still tending to him. Doing all she could to fill the small emergency-room cubicle with positive energy, she kissed him on both cheeks, told him she loved him and had good news for him.

She was sobbing when she pushed through the emergency room doors, to the quiet hallway beyond. Releasing the fear that could disrupt her ability to help Whaler pull through.

She dropped down to the first chair along the deserted wall, needing to be right there in case they wanted her. And to know the second her father was being moved to one of the eleven inpatient rooms in the facility so that she could be with him.

Closing her eyes she sat back, lotus position with her skirt secured around her, her head against the wall, and let the tears continue to fall through the cracks in her lids.

Drawing on her inner strength in an attempt to have enough to share for as long as it took.

"He's still alive," Mitchell's voice came to her, moving closer with each word, his tone as though he was telling her something new. By the time he'd finished the sentence, he was sitting down beside her.

For a second there, she considered keeping her eyes closed. Blocking him out. Putting up a shield against everyone. But something inside her refused to capitulate to the escapism.

Wiping her tears away, she took a deep breath. Nodded. Then shuddered. "He's in terrible shape, Mitchell. Two days of most likely unintentional detoxing without medical assistance, which is stupefying enough by itself. He has a pretty good lump on the side of his head. A nasty gash in his side. They don't know about broken bones, yet, though there's nothing obvious there…"

"And his vitals?" Mitchell's question was firm. To the point.

"They're stabilizing."

"Good. That's good, Dove. And what you need to be focusing on. If they can keep him stable, the rest will heal. And…" He paused, as he was second-guessing whatever he'd been about to say.

Dove looked over at him, met his gaze and held on. "What were you going to say?"

He shrugged. "Maybe the detoxing…is the good that comes out of this."

Reaching over, Dove slid her hand inside of his, took hold of it and squeezed. He'd gotten her to the point she hadn't been able to see.

The good that was coming.

Which maybe should have surprised her, him being who and what he was. But it didn't. At all.

"I saw Kansas as she was leaving," he said, not pulling his hand from hers. "She said she and a member of her team found him just below a mountain hang outside of town. About half a mile from where they found his cap. She had his clothes in an evidence bag, had already asked Scott Montgomery, one of ABI's forensic scientists at the office here in town, to get on them ASAP. And was leaving here to go directly to him. If we're lucky, we might even get a viable fingerprint."

Heart lifting again, Dove looked over at Mitchell, thanking her lucky stars that they'd led her to him. And got the distinct impression that she needed to lighten up on him a little.

No more sex talk. Or anything else that made him uncomfortable. No challenging him to do better at anything.

The man was already pretty much the best anyone could be. Vastly different from her, but that was okay. To be celebrated, actually. He lived true to himself.

Life's greatest challenge. At least according to her mother. And now...according to her own heart, as well.

Mitchell—just as he was—was exactly what she needed for this period in her life.

So thinking, she smiled at him and as unobtrusively as possible slid her hand from his.

Local police were providing protection for Whaler at the hospital. Mitchell stayed with Dove until Whaler was moved to a room, and then, when she went to sit with her father, with the officer just outside the door, Mitchell left to head back to the marina. To make certain that Wes was handling things. And to be there in case of any problems that might develop.

The boat rental business was Brad Fletcher's ultimate goal. With Whaler out of commission, causing Dove to be by his side, Mitchell saw the window of opportunity for the shady businessman to move in. So thinking, he made an executive decision, financed out of his own pocket as he wasn't going to bother Dove with it, and had hidden security cameras installed at the docks. And up by the office, too. The fact that he wasn't, technically, an executive hired to watch out for the business yet was immaterial to him at that point.

Didn't matter to him whether he ever got paid. Nor was he worried that he was opening himself up to potential lawsuits if Dove or Whaler ever decided to come after him for the step he was taking.

Definitely a departure from any other choice he'd ever made—brushing aside potential blowback—but he did it anyway.

Because to leave St. James Boats vulnerable was much more of a risk. And just plain wrong in light of the threats, vandalism and assumed abduction that had all just taken place.

He hadn't forgotten the neighbor's call about someone suspected to have been watching Dove's place, either.

Whoever was out to get Dove and her father had started out tamely enough. But was clearly escalating to dangerous proportions.

A thought that was brought home to Mitchell most clearly when Eli called him midafternoon to suggest that St. James Boats might want to consider getting security cameras installed ASAP.

It was nice validation of Mitchell's decision to have already put that into motion. And good, too, as the least actively aggressive male in his family to be able to tell his older brother "Happening as we speak."

"I'm impressed," Eli said then, sounding tired, but with a note of older brother, egg-him-on punch, too. "It's not like you to get so hands-on involved."

And like the younger brother he was, he let Eli's words rankle. "I'm always hands-on. My job just requires less in-your-face presence."

"From what I hear, you've maybe got more than just your hands on this one." There was no mistaking the quiet humor in that one.

Mitchell tensed, in spite of himself. "You haven't learned by now not to believe everything you hear?"

"I believe Kansas. She tells me that Dove St. James answered your phone just after dawn. You were upstairs in the shower, she told Kansas. And then you came downstairs and took the call."

Damn Kansas.

And… Dove had said *that*?

Making it sound like…

"We are not sleeping together," he said, for the record, while a part of him noted that it was good to get the words out while they were still valid.

Because they most definitely were in question.

"After the break-in and her father's disappearance, it didn't seem prudent to have her in her small place alone. She's staying in my guest room. At the opposite end of the house from me, as you well know. I'd left my phone in the kitchen when I'd headed back upstairs from making coffee. She heard the phone ring and, seeing Kansas's name, knowing it was about her father, she answered it."

"And you're honestly going to tell me you haven't noticed how hot she is?"

He refused to validate the question with an answer.

"I'm just giving you a hard time," Eli said then, all notes of teasing gone from his voice. "Seriously, bro, you're a Colton, doing what any of the rest of us would in the same situation. You think she's going to be okay if Whaler doesn't make it?"

He was doing all he could not to ask himself that question. "She won't have much choice, will she?" he responded in the only way he knew how. Logically. And then asked, "Still nothing solid on Brad Fletcher?"

"Nothing we can pick him up for. Or even sufficient evidence to get a warrant for his phone records. Based on some of his known associations, it's likely that he hired someone to trash Dove's studio. Probably has someone watching her house, too. I know Kansas is looking at him seriously for Whaler's assault. Hope to God some prints show up on the clothes she brought in. In the meantime, I figure him for putting pressure on Dove within the next several hours. Fits the MO. The man is determined to take over Whaler's business."

Mitchell had already come to the same conclusion. "I've told her not to answer if he calls. To leave any text messages and voice mails for me to deal with," he said.

"Be extra diligent, Mitchell. This Fletcher guy…he doesn't need the income from Whaler's business. He's just a number one ass. It's all about him. Him getting what he wants. Anyone tries to tell him no or go against him, he makes them pay. Including the three ex-wives in his past, from what I've heard."

The news tightened the muscles in Mitchell's gut. And

honed his thinking to getting back to Dove—and not letting her out of his sight if he could help it.

Maybe a bit drastic. But there, just the same.

There was an off note in Eli's tone that got through to him, too. Enough so that before he ended the call he said, "You sound tired. Still nothing on the body that Hetty and Spence stumbled upon?"

"It's worse than that," Eli said, gaining Mitchell's full attention. Worse than an unidentified young female corpse half buried with her left hand—bearing a flashy engagement ring—sticking out of the ground?

"Two more bodies have shown up in the past twenty-four hours," Eli said. "Both found along the Muskee Glacier Pass. Both young women, both half-buried, left hands exposed. Haven't been able to identify either one of them. Coroner thinks they've both been dead about a year."

"Dear Lord," Mitchell hissed quietly. Implications quickly piling atop each other.

"It's looking like we've got a serial killer, Eli spoke aloud the conclusion Mitchell was reaching on his own, already grabbing his keys.

To hell with an officer outside Whaler's door. Mitchell was heading straight back to the hospital. A serial killer on the loose with victims getting closer to Shelby?

Dove, a young, gorgeous and sexy woman?

What if there was an explanation far more sinister than Brad Fletcher for the break-in at Dove's studio? And the subsequent possible stalker outside her house? What if her woes, and Whaler's, weren't related at all?

Telling his brother to keep him posted and to let him know if there was anything he could do to help, Mitchell was already in his car, engine started as he hung up.

A serial killer on the loose, and Dove vulnerable and

unprotected? With no family to check in on her? Protocol be damned.

Mitchell wasn't letting the woman out of his sight.

Whaler hadn't moved a muscle, other than to breathe. The fact that he was managing to do that on his own was cause for great thanks. Maybe even miracle level.

As were his vitals. Considering the way he'd abused his body over the past couple of years, sousing it in alcohol and failing to feed it healthy meals often enough, he was actually doing well. His blood pressure was a little high. His oxygen levels were good. Thank God he wasn't a smoker.

The biggest concern was the obvious trauma to his head. The fact that he hadn't shown a single sign of regaining consciousness was a huge concern. He was scheduled for more scanning later in the day or early the following morning. Until then, all anyone could tell Dove was that he was in a coma.

There was no prognosis.

Except to hope, every second, that it would be the one in which he woke up.

Hours of sitting in the chair by his bed, holding his hand, talking to him, while she hoped hard with every breath, was draining Dove of the very strength she needed to help keep her dad alive.

Slowly stealing her positive energy away in the process.

So when her friend and client Hetty Amos texted, saying that she was at the hospital for a checkup on the healing bullet wound she'd sustained in her leg and was available if Dove wanted to talk, Dove agreed to meet her at the coffee shop just down from the hospital.

The second she saw the twenty-eight-year-old pilot, she knew she'd made the right choice to be there. Hetty might still be figuring out how to tune in to her own inner voices, but as far as people went, she was as strong as they came. And, being a year older than Dove, she had been someone Dove had looked up to in high school.

When you lived in a small town your whole life, it always seemed to come down to that. Who was who, who they knew and who they hung with in high school. Hetty's light green eyes were troubled as she gazed into Dove's.

"There's lots of reason to hope," Dove blurted the first thing that came to her mind. And knew she was okay when the words sank in. She'd said what she'd needed to hear. It had just taken someone else needing to hear to get it firmly planted within and without her.

"I heard he's stable," Hetty said, without asking a single question about what had been going on in Dove's most recent past.

Hetty would have gotten the email that Dove had sent to all her clients that morning, letting them know that the studio would be closed for the next few days due to her father's disappearance. There'd been no reason to couch the news. People who knew would hear the truth from her—or the grapevine. She figured it had been better, less alarming, coming straight from her.

Still didn't say how the injured pilot had heard the most recent details.

"Spence told me," Hetty said before Dove had responded. And then the woman gave a somewhat sheepish grin. "Look at us," she said softly, as they sat sipping the coffee they'd ordered from the counter as they'd first come in. "Who'd have thought that I'd actually be dating Spence Colton, and you… I hear you're staying at Mitchell's place?"

She nodded. Met Hetty's gaze. And said, "It's mostly a business relationship," her truth ringing loud and clear.

"I mean, he's sexy and all, but we're so different. I'm sure the gossip is going to have us in a relationship, but I want you to hear it straight from me. Not happening." The words sounded so final, and not exactly accurate, so she added, "I think he might be a friend for life, though."

Warmth flooded her. As though a source higher than herself was confirming the accuracy of her proclamation. She sat back in possession of another huge reason to be thankful and listened while Hetty told her that her doctor had just said that her wound was almost completely healed and Hetty should be able to start back at Namaste as early as the following week.

Assuming classes were back in session.

As far as Dove knew, no one was aware of the vandalism that took place at Namaste other than two people from Repo, the police and her. It wasn't that she had any reason or desire to be duplicitous about the attack: she was just trying to protect her clients from any residual negative energy the mental picture would build to slow down their healing process if they knew the sacred space had been violated. She was about to tell Hetty, though, when Lakin Colton, Mitchell's adored adopted sister appeared, pushing in through the door and, seeing them, headed straight for their table.

While Dove had looked up to Hetty in high school, Lakin and Hetty had actually been close friends. How much of that was because they had crushes on each other's brothers, Dove didn't know. But she'd always wondered.

"I'm so sorry to hear about your father, Dove," Lakin said, her eyes wide with compassion. And warmth. "And I'm praying for him, too."

Kind of uncomfortable with the attention she'd been getting at the hospital…the reaching out to her as though she was a regular person, not just a flighty believer in things unseen… Dove nodded. "Thanks," she said. "He was found alive. The rest will come." She had to state intention.

No matter what others might think of her.

And the fact that she was staying with the woman's older brother? That might have put a bit of a defensive wall up inside Dove where Lakin was concerned. She didn't want to know what Mitchell's close-knit family would be saying to him about having the odd woman in town living with him. Didn't even want to think about them thinking it. Which was why she had to shield herself from Lakin.

Who'd turned to Hetty, anyway, letting Dove off the hook.

"Did you hear?" Lakin asked Hetty. "Troy's due back next week." And Dove had to smile as she heard the words. Troy was Hetty's brother, but Lakin as his girlfriend got the news.

Did that mean that as the one staying with Mitchell, she knew more about what was going on with him than his sister did? She could hope, couldn't she?

What other choice did she have? It wasn't like she'd be asking Lakin what Mitchell might have said about her.

At least she wanted to hope she wouldn't have been that weak, stooped that low, but was saved from finding out as Lakin, hearing the bell at the counter, glanced up and said, "That's my order, gotta go" as she left the table.

But as she collected her take-out drink holder, Lakin stopped back by the table, her glance specifically on Dove. "Seriously, you're in my thoughts. And I want you to know my brothers, my cousin Kansas, they'll get whoever did this. They won't stop until they do."

The promise broke through the defenses Dove had so quickly thrown up when Lakin had first appeared, and she was moved by the woman's sincerity. "Thank you," she said, almost tearing up. "That's just what I needed to hear."

Lakin had just confirmed, heart to heart, what Dove had known but apparently had needed to hear again.

She could lean on Mitchell, just as she'd thought she'd been meant to do. Not just with approval from her spirits but from his family as well.

But more importantly, she could trust him with her life.

Chapter 14

She wasn't there. Approaching Whaler's room, seeing in through the opened door before he arrived, he could see part of the man's body in the bed, but no sign of Dove. The chair pulled up to the bed was empty. Blowing right past the officer standing a couple of feet to the right of the door, he burst into the room, his gaze taking in every inch of floorboard around the room, expecting to see her sitting, back up to the wall, eyes closed. He saw nothing but floor. And molding.

No Dove.

Two strides took him back to the door, and a young officer he hadn't yet met. "Where's Dove?"

"She left twenty minutes ago, sir. Said she was going next door to meet a friend for coffee and would be back shortly."

"You let her go? You're supposed to be guarding her!" He swallowed as he heard the very clear reprimand in his raised tone. And then, lowering his voice and checking his attitude, he said, "Her life is in danger." A serial killer was on the loose and Dove could already be pegged as his next victim. All the victims were young, and Eli had just said that, so far, they all had long hair. Dove's long wavy amber waves were unforgettable…

The officer's face tensing, he said, "I'm sorry, sir. I didn't know. I just came on. I was told to guard the room. I thought that just meant the patient."

Turning, Mitchell sped off down the hall, hearing the concerned young man's addition, "She left her cell phone number with me in case anything changed with her father's condition…"

If there was more, he missed it. Whaler's was currently the only occupied room in the small unit. No one cared if a Colton on a mission stormed out.

However, he was saved making a further ass of himself when, just outside the unit door, he saw Dove, in that long billowy skirt and crop top, that long fiery hair, walking toward him.

Relief flooded through him washing away the haze of panic that had taken hold. Enough so that he was able to sound at least somewhat like his usual, practical self as he said, "Are you aware that there's a serial killer on the loose? And that his victims are about your age and all have long hair?"

He clenched his teeth shut the second he heard himself. Really heard himself. Looking around, he was immensely glad to see that there was no one else around to have heard the information that was not his to leak out. And took Dove's arm as he led her to a couple of armchairs set in an alcove. "I just talked to Eli," he said softly, slowly, but no less urgently. "This isn't information I should be spreading around town. The ABI will disseminate details as they feel is necessary to best protect the public, but the break-in at Namaste, someone watching your house, it could be him, Dove. Until we know more, I need you to promise me that you go nowhere alone. You've got police protection here at the hospital. And I'll escort you to and from. You've already got safe housing. Everything else we'll work out on a case by case basis."

The deflation, as he reached the end of his litany, almost left him weak. At the very least, strangely unsettled. Like he'd just given everything he had to prevent death and then…faced no immediate danger at all.

Dove was perfectly safe. She'd had coffee. And had returned to her vigil.

"You need to take a breath, Mitchell," the woman said to him, softly, calmly. More like his usual self than he was currently portraying. "Several of them," she added.

She was going to argue with him. He knew the wave was coming. And knew that there was no way he could vacillate on the issue. No matter how much inner truth she brought to the table.

But he would give her what he could. Breathing, his or hers, wasn't a deal-breaker, so he nodded, sat back and prepared to wait for however long it took her to determine he'd completed the task she'd given to him.

A minute passed. At least. Mitchell didn't much mind. Dove was safe. Where she wanted to be—within yards of getting to her father if need be.

Kirk had proven to be a legitimate asset during his first eight hours on the job.

Wes had reported an above-average day with no issues.

Stuart, the same.

Pretty much covered Mitchell's responsibilities for a very long Monday. With the night's duties still ahead.

Duty. One duty that night.

Keeping Dove safe while his family members did their jobs. Okay, two duties. He also had to keep his piece in his pants. Which would be most easily accomplished by forgoing his usual sleeping mode—in the nude—for one that included the pants.

Mental note made.

Not sure how much longer they were going to sit there—and pondering best solutions for dinner given the current circumstances—Mitchell leaned his head back against the wall.

Taking a deep breath, he sighed. Settling in.

"Wow, that took a while." Dove's voice, sounding loud to him in the silence, interrupted his reverie.

Straightening, he glanced over at her. "What did?"

"You getting to the point of taking a breath."

Shaking his head, he frowned. Not in the mood for funny stuff. Even as he knew he had to keep her as agreeable as he could. "I've been taking breaths the whole time. One after another. It's what people do to stay alive."

"That's breathing," she told him, quite congenially, but there was no humor that he could see in her expression. "Taking a breath is more. It's pulling air in purposefully, more deeply, than normal breathing. It helps the body to relax."

Mitchell wanted to roll his eyes. To tell her he didn't need her magical cures. Except that…once again…her words contained a certain practical sense.

"Noted," he told her. But had to add, "If you'd explained that ten minutes ago, your mission would have been accomplished that much sooner." Just for future reference—in the event she put him through any more of her life lessons during the time of their acquaintance.

One he'd thought would be miraculously short. He was starting to accept that it could turn out to be much longer than he'd expected.

As in, a regular workload for the time it took to get St.

James Boats back on its feet. Whether for Bob to run, or to sell. Either way, Mitchell's part came first.

He had another, much larger challenge facing him before he moved from the chair. She might think she'd distracted him with her breathing antics. But, "I need your promise, Dove. You go nowhere alone, you continue to stay at my place, until this serial killer is found or the police find proof that Fletcher or someone else vandalized Namaste and was watching your place."

"I promise."

With a sharp turn of his head, he stared into the eyes facing straight at him. "I mean it," he said. "No funny business."

"You mean like saying that an angel was with me so I wasn't alone? Or flew in my window and carried me out into the night?" She looked so innocent as she spoke.

Mitchell wasn't sure if she was being facetious, or if she knew what the town thought of her. He feared the latter.

And hated that he'd made her feel that way.

"I meant no making a promise and then finding a way around keeping it."

She continued to watch him—study him was more like it. Giving him nothing from within herself. "I can't tell if you're saying you don't trust me to keep a promise or just think I'm naive enough to not realize that, under no circumstances, am I to waver from the dictates you laid down."

When she put it like that...

Mitchell took another deep breath. "I'm sorry," he said. "I trust you to keep your promise. And I absolutely do not think you're naive." He meant to leave it there. And started talking again anyway. "But I also know that you're independent, headstrong and smart enough to find a way to manipulate a situation if you feel a need to go outside the boundaries I've set."

She smiled then. An expression that started in her eyes seconds before it landed on her mouth. "You might be right in other, less severe circumstances," she told him and then her expression turning serious in an instant said, "I know that my best chance at making it through this in as successful a way as possible is with you, Mitchell. The things you've already done for me, calling in the best of the best to help when, without you, my father more likely would have died out there before anyone found him. The safe place to sleep you're providing…until this is over, you're the boss. That's just the way it is."

A deluge of sweet relief hit him, wiped away in the next second when she added, "In terms of the guidelines you set out above, and for the stated purposes."

The woman just wasn't going to stop challenging his thinking every step of the way. "Mind expanding on that?" he asked. Not willing to risk another embarrassment by hazarding his own guess.

"Just that," she told him. "Speaking literally here, Mitchell, keep up."

Not hating their repartee as much as he'd have liked, he met her gaze full on. "Go on," he told her. More out of curiosity than anything else.

"I still have autonomy over all of my choices that don't involve keeping me safe from the bad guys."

Here it came. The out he'd been expecting from the beginning. "Such as?"

"Such as a choice I could make to…accept physical activities while in your care." She didn't even blink as she said the words. Her gaze locked on his the entire time. "Were something to arise in that area, I do not want to hear anything about you taking advantage because I'm in your care or beside myself with fear or worry or grief. Nor will I accept that my concurrence with your stipulations put us in a situation that opens the door to concerns about sex in the workplace, or any other possible moral or legal consequence you could see possibly arising in the future as a result of the…activity…while I am under this safety agreement with you."

No smile cracking on that one. Not even a hint.

She was dead serious.

And the only response Mitchell could conjure up was…

A very slow nod.

Whaler hadn't given even a hint of waking by nine that evening when the small ward went into lockdown for the night. Two nurses, an orderly and a police officer were all there just to watch over her father, and Dove had to be content with that.

A trauma doctor was on duty in the urgent care portion of the facility and would be checking in on their one in-patient. He assured Dove, just before she left with Mitchell, that he expected her father to rest peacefully through the night.

And that they'd call the second there was any change in his condition or hint of him waking up.

Knowing that she would be no good to her dad if she didn't get some rest—most particularly after her mostly sleepless hours the night before—she gave him kisses on both cheeks. Told him she loved him. That she'd see him in the morning.

And then, with tears in her eyes, walked beside Mitchell out to his car.

"His vitals are good," he said more as a reminder to her, she figured, than anything else.

"I know."

"Tonight is better than last night. We know he's alive. We know where he is. We know that he's safe."

She nodded. Taking in every practical, logical word.

Just as she'd forced herself to eat and swallow most of the salad he'd ordered in and had delivered from The Cove for dinner.

He wasn't her mother. Or a guide. But he was doing a pretty impressive job of reminding her how to keep her head out of the sewer of fear trying to suck the life out of her.

But she was tired.

Had never felt so alone.

And needed to know, "Why are you doing this?"

"Walking you to my car? You know why."

While, in a better state, she might have teased him about focusing so much on the literal, or in a worse one thought he was playing with her, Dove didn't have the energy to engage in light conversation.

"I mean giving up your own schedule, your regularly scheduled life, to babysit me."

They'd reached his car, and when she would have left his side to go to her door, while he opened his he grabbed her elbow lightly, shook his head, and said, "You get in with me."

Without missing a beat, she did so, sliding over on the seat to allow him access behind the wheel, buckled herself in and prepared to sit through the ten-minute drive to his place in silence.

She'd asked a question that wasn't factually based. He wasn't going to answer. And she didn't have the energy to fight him on it.

It wasn't like his reasoning mattered all that much. He'd insisted on his role. She'd agreed to it. Case closed, Counselor.

Keeping her secure between his body and the car door, he'd checked the back seat before nudging her to get in. And gave the same kind of intent concentration on watching all around them as he pulled out of the parking lot and headed down toward Main Street. From there, a short jog west would take them out to his place.

Clint's bar had the door open, with people milling inside. Dove saw Oscar, sitting on his usual stool, and wondered if he'd heard about Whaler yet. Mitchell had told her that the police were keeping things quiet, that the employees at St. James Boats had all been asked not to say anything until the police knew more.

Still, she almost asked Mitchell to stop long enough for her to have a word with her father's young friend. Until she realized that maybe her need to connect with Oscar was more for her sake than his and reconsidered. Oscar had enough problems of his own.

And better that there were answers—and that Whaler was conscious with a good prognosis—before Oscar found out what had happened to him.

No way did she want to be responsible for driving the man to further drink.

Mitchell made the turn toward his place, keeping his eye on the rearview mirror as much as the windshield, and then seemed to relax.

She actually saw him settle back in the seat, his shoulders visibly relaxing.

And she knew. "You were afraid we were going to be followed."

She should have figured that one out for herself.

"*Afraid*, no," he said. "*Aware of the possibility*, absolutely."

Which made her think of something else. "Let me guess, you have a pistol in the glove box." They lived in rugged territory. There were a lot of nonhuman predators that could appear at any moment, making a gun the only difference between life and death.

Her mother had refused to learn to shoot.

As had Dove. She could be struck by lightning or drown in the sea. If nature was going to take her, it would find a way to do so.

"I do," he told her. "And one in the house, too. You get your pick of which one you want to take to bed with you."

She shook her head. "Neither."

"One or the other, Dove…" His tone had grown all boss-like.

"Neither, Mitchell." Suddenly filled with a surge of energy, she sat up straighter. "You're crossing into my autonomy here…" She started in with the fight. And then, just as quickly depleted, told him, "I'm safer without a gun. I've never held one in my life, nor have I ever so much as pulled the trigger on a plastic squirt gun."

When he said nothing, she added, "Or on the handle of an arcade game."

No shooting. None. Period. Her spirit spoke silently inside her, and Dove welcomed the communication. Wanting to hold it within her.

Needing to be hugged.

"You think I'm weird," she said, for no good reason, which meant she should have held her tongue.

"I'm thinking I'd feel a hell of a lot better if you knew how to shoot a gun."

She believed him. The response was so Mitchell. Practical. Logical.

The thought left enough of a positive tail that she asked again what she really wanted to know. "Why have you put your own life on hold to watch over me?"

She didn't really expect an answer. But she deserved the chance to pose the question. To try to find understanding about something that pertained to her directly.

She knew full well why she was trusting him.

But…what was in it for him?

Sex?

She'd already intimated that he could probably get that just by asking.

It certainly wasn't the money. There wasn't going to be much anytime soon.

"You remind me of someone." His words fell softly into the darkness. Startling her. And ringing with a truth, a depth, she hadn't expected.

"An ex-girlfriend?" He'd never been married that she knew of.

"No," he told her, then, as though making up his mind that telling her was better than not, he sighed and said, "My aunt."

"Spence's mom?" She didn't get the likeness. Not even a little bit.

He shook his head. "My dad's and uncle's younger sister."

The words carried a wealth of grief. It came to her slowly. Heavily. And stifled any question she might have asked. He pulled into his garage. Turned off the engine. Pushed the button for the door to shut behind them and sat there with both hands on the wheel.

"Eli met her. Parker, too, though he probably doesn't remember. I never did. She was killed before I was born."

Her sharp intake of breath had been completely involuntary. She stared through the garage's dim light, wishing for the glorious sunset that had just been beginning to appear outside to infiltrate their midst.

If he opened his car door, she'd follow him inside and never speak of the topic again. But she'd remember, for the rest of her days, the grief she'd felt emanating from him.

A man who'd always seemed so...emotionally sedentary.

"She was seventeen. My grandparents were upstairs in bed. She was found on the couch with her stalker..."

Suffused with a sudden urge to cover her ears, Dove physically forced herself to remain open by sliding her hands beneath her thighs. Sitting on them.

"Eli was around five at the time. He and our dad came in and found them there, both dead. The killer had never actually met her in person prior to that night, but thought of himself as her boyfriend. He killed her and then himself."

"What about your grandparents?"

"They were murdered, too. Probably before Caroline was."

With tears running down her cheeks, Dove looked over at him through their blur and asked, "Her name was Caroline?"

He nodded.

"My mother's was, too."

He nodded again. "I know."

And she knew, too, right then and there, without a doubt, that she and Mitchell had been meant to connect, for however long either of them needed, and that no matter what happened between them, they'd remain deep, abiding friends for their earthly lifespan—and beyond.

For whatever reason, this uptight man who was nothing at all like her, was a soul mate.

Which meant, to her, he was sacred.

And when the day came that her father got old and passed, she wouldn't be alone on earth.

Chapter 15

What in the hell was this woman doing to him?

Had he pissed off her angels somehow? Failed to see someone in need, to meet their need, and this was their way of getting even with him?

He'd heard Lakin talk about karma once. Some force of nature that supposedly acted as some kind of supernatural adding machine—keeping track of the good and bad you'd done, and dumping your fullest account on you. If you did good, you got good. If not, then watch out.

Not even wanting to get his temporary housemate started on that one, he kept the fact that he knew the term to himself as he led them both into the house.

But was starting to sweat a little as he was running through a tally of his good deeds and bad as he followed her down the hall to the kitchen.

He hadn't made it past the time, in third grade, when he'd accidentally knocked a kid's tooth out with a wildly thrown pitch and then laughed.

He hadn't known yet that the kid was hurt. Hadn't thought he'd thrown it that hard.

Third grade and he was already seeing how his account was going to look.

Dove had emptied the bag from lunch that she'd brought in with her and was rinsing the dirty bowls and silverware.

"I'll get that," he told her. Expecting an argument. Not sure he'd fight her on it, though he deeply needed his space to himself for the few minutes he was going to get that night.

Which was really why he was sweating.

It was going to be a *long* six or eight hours.

"You go do whatever it is you do to get ready for bed, dress in whatever you have that is the most comfortable and nonrevealing, and we can head upstairs."

Spinning so quickly she splashed water all over the floor, Mitchell had the inane thought that maybe the action was going to be a sin she'd need to pay for, too. "Upstairs?" she asked. And before he could explain added, "This is your way of saying you want to have sex?"

"Hell no!" He spoke with such force he almost spit. "You don't know how to shoot. I do. There's a serial killer on the loose. I'm charged with protecting you. You do the math."

He had math on the brain. Karma addition.

Reasoning calculations.

"You want us to sleep in the same room."

At least he knew she was good at adding things up. "Yes."

She turned back to the dishes. Making quick work of them. Not arguing.

He was reassessing his karma situation—only slightly, but the lack of argument was a good thing—when she said, "You have condoms up there, just in case?"

He wanted to tell her no. To put her on the spot and ask her if she'd brought any. Somehow getting to a place where, if she hadn't brought any, there couldn't be any activity that would require a need of them. But couldn't lie to her. "Yes."

She nodded.

He started to get hard. And blurted, "But I'm tired, Dove. And so are you. We have no idea what tomorrow is going to bring, or even if we'll be woken up with an emergency in the night…"

Turning off the water, she turned around, wiping her hands on the kitchen towel she'd pulled from the oven door. "I know," she told him. Then looked him in the eye and said, "But I got your mind on something besides death and grief there for a second."

It wasn't a question.

Didn't require an answer.

And he didn't give her one.

Instead, he stood there with a brand-new awareness of what sex could do…

If someone was in need of relief from the demons that seemed to be hunting them.

Or her.

Dove didn't look at the room. Much. Enough to get her bearings. To know what would be causing any shadows lurking when darkness fell completely. There were no curtains on the two big windows overlooking—from what she could see—a whole lot of nature and nothing else.

With the quilt from her bed downstairs hanging over her shoulder, and a bottle of lavender clutched in her palm— just in case she needed a quick inhale that wouldn't suffuse the other occupant in the room with the scent—she was ready for bed.

Mitchell had already been up to thoroughly check the second floor. He'd said he'd be a few minutes, giving her time to get settled. He'd had something to do in his office. More like he was avoiding them going to bed together.

He could try to prevent any further closeness from happening between them. She knew they were already as close as any two humans could ever get.

Physical stuff was momentary. Or, in some cases, lifelong, but in one life only. Soul couplings were forever. In the pajamas she'd had on that morning, she quickly arranged her quilt on top of the spread on the left side of Mitchell's king-size bed. Left was farthest from the door, and the nightstand on the right had his phone charger on it. Pulling her own phone out of her pocket, she grabbed the charging cord from the elastic waistband of her pants, plugged it in, connected the device and was...done. Ready for bed.

Except that she wasn't. At all.

She needed to be. She'd only had those few hours of sleep the night before. Fear had much greater opportunity to invade her system when she was tired. And she'd be up at dawn. It was just a thing. Dawn came, she woke up. Nature telling her good morning. A gift she welcomed.

The reminder got her butt to the bed, under the covers. She'd left on the light in Mitchell's adjoining bathroom, having completed her own ablutions downstairs. Turning to face the wall across from her side of the bed, she closed her eyes. And when her mind reacted to the darkness with a vision of her father's lifeless body lying helplessly in a hospital bed, she immediately opened them again.

To reset. Focus. The threes. Three things for which to be grateful. Three things about which she'd been critical replaced by three positive thoughts. Three people other than herself.

Starting with the last, because thinking about others was the best way to stop magnifying her own circumstances and to build her heart cells. Hetty. First, she and Spence had finally been able to see what had been obvious for a long time. They belonged together. Second, her bullet wound was almost completely healed with no permanent damage. She'd be returning to yoga classes soon, but…stop…that was about Dove, too, so probably shouldn't…stop. No criticism of any kind allowed in the sacred moments. Wasn't that criticism? To criticize the thought she'd just had?

And why was self-affirmation wrong? It wasn't. Maybe there should be more than three? Should there be a fourth? Self-affirmation?

Maybe. But not when thinking of others. Stick to the plan. It's there for a reason. It's healthy. Scientifically proven. Not that science had to matter in the larger, non-earthly scheme of things. But they mattered to Mitchell.

Mitchell. He was another. No. Wait. She hadn't done Hetty's third yet. Third. Troy was coming home! That was good for Hetty and Lakin. Double dose of good.

Lakin. Mitchell's sister. His bed. He would be coming up soon. Getting into bed with her. Maybe she shouldn't be thinking about Mitchell.

Back to the threes. Stick to the threes. And no Mitchell. For the moment, anyway. If she said *no Mitchell*, that fostered negativity. And she most definitely did not want… Okay, Mitchell. Three things. He'd been sent to her for her good, but for his own, too. She hadn't quite worked it all out. But she knew. Caroline. Her heart flooded with all-consuming emotion again, just remembering Mitchell saying the word. Second, he'd been able to help his friend's son, Kirk. Which helped his friend, too, which could be a third, but no, she'd lump those two together. Third, he had condoms.

Quick, who else? Her dad. He'd been found alive. Second, with the new initiatives being discussed, his business was going to rebound. Third...

He just missed her mother so much. It was like she was calling him to her every single day. Or like he thought she was. Love was meant to uplift. To strengthen. Not be a downfall.

Maybe not her father. Okay, who else?

Footsteps on the stairs. No matter how she tried to get herself into an unconscious state, Dove was fully present as she listened to the creaks on the stairs, telling her that Mitchell was entering her space.

His space, too. First. Most. Condoms there.

"Dove?"

His almost-professional tone of voice yanked her back to full reality. Whatever he had to say, she had to hear. Turning onto her back, she looked at him standing in the doorway to his room. Still in jeans and the flannel shirt he'd had on all day.

"Kansas just called," he told her. And the breath she hadn't known she'd been holding released. She let it go. Pulled in a long breath of fresh air. Kansas. Not the hospital.

Sitting up, she prompted, "And?"

"Scott Montgomery was able to pull some evidence off from Whaler's shirt. Saliva."

Heart pounding, she sat up. "Someone bit him?"

Mitchell shook his head, opened his mouth, but before he could say anything else she threw out, "What, kissed him? Someone thought he was dead and kissed him goodbye?"

Who would that possibly have been?

She hadn't yet conjured a single possibility when Mitchell said, "It's spit."

A wave of horror swept through her. "Someone spit on him?" Eyes wide she stared at Mitchell, needing to hold onto him.

He nodded. And before their eye contact could get broken, she asked, "Who?"

Stepping farther into the room, closer to the bed, to her, his words fell over her softly. "They don't know yet. There were no matches in the system. But they have something to test against as soon as a suspect is brought in."

"Brad Fletcher. There's got to be a way to get a DNA sample from him."

"Legally," Mitchell said, just standing there. He'd come close. Then abruptly stopped. As though he'd read a sign that said *no closer*. "It has to be obtained legally or it doesn't stand up in court and he walks free."

Nodding, Dove lay back down. Pulled the quilt up over her tie-dyed T-shirt, the sliver of skin it left atop the elastic waistband of her pajama pants. "Scott Montgomery," she said. He could be her third. Except…he'd found evidence, but she was drawing a complete blank on two other good things…

Because Mitchell wasn't exiting the premises. He was ruffling through a drawer in the dresser farthest away from her. As though looking for something he hadn't seen in a while.

When she saw the black pajama pants he eventually came up with, she turned back to face the wall. Mitchell. He could be her third. Because even in the midst of hell, he could make her smile.

Which made it about her. But about him, too.

He really was a genuinely nice guy.

With a beautiful soul inside that gorgeously masculine body.

Dove appeared to be asleep when Mitchell came out of the bathroom, freshly showered, and in the brand-new pajama pants and shirt his aunt had purchased for him a decade or so before. Lucky for him, they'd been big at the time, so they fit now.

Whether his bedmate was truly out or not, he was going with a big *yes*. Had no intention of doing anything to find out differently.

Her safety was his business. Her sleeping state, or lack thereof, was not.

Checking to make certain his gun was loaded, safety off, he plugged in his phone, walked back to turn off the bathroom light, pulled down his covers, got into bed and smelled...lavender.

Holy hell. Had she brought the stuff to bed with her? Drifted petals on the sheets? He was too far in to look. Would have to sit up, pull the covers away...

Closing his eyes Mitchell did the only thing he could do—he shut down.

Turned off life's challenges, trials and temptations until morning, and with a last thought about the gun lodged between the bed rail and the mattress, drifted into sleep mode...until he wasn't asleep.

Fully alert suddenly, he lay there, assessing his situation. How long had he been out? Had he heard something? Or was he just so on edge he hadn't fallen fully asleep as he did every single night the minute his head hit the pillow?

Dove hadn't moved. He wasn't looking at her— purposely—but could see the shadow of her quilt-covered shoulder in his peripheral vision. Just as it had been when he'd closed his eyes. Just to be sure, though, he turned his head.

And noticed three things. She was lying on top of his bedspread, the quilt her only source of warmth. She was shivering. And based on the time glowing at him from the phone she'd set up on the nightstand over there, he'd been out for almost five hours.

Her shivering must have awoken him.

Figuring the best, easiest and least obtrusive way to ease her discomfort from the night's chill was to just pull up the spread from his side of the bed and lay it over her, he did so. Slowly. Gently. Careful not to actually touch any part of her with any part of him.

And leaving himself with only a sheet for a cover.

On his back, he checked on the gun, closed his eyes, figuring he could get another three or four hours in and, instead, lay there in the darkness, trying to convince himself that Dove was sound asleep. He'd seen the slight jerk when he'd dropped the last corner of the spread to her shoulder.

And suddenly couldn't clear his mind of images of her. That morning in his kitchen. In those thin pants and ridiculous, half shirt thing. What was it with the woman and leaving a strip of her belly bare? Didn't she get that she lived in Alaska? One of the coldest states in the nation?

Flash-forward. The stark fear in her eyes when she'd first walked into the hospital, seconds away from seeing her father.

The saucy grin she got on her face when she was messing with him.

He heard a sniffle. Tried to pretend that he hadn't. For all she knew he'd fallen back to sleep. Normally he would have done. Should have done. Wished he had.

And might have actually done, if she didn't start to move, turning slowly to a flat position and then scooting toward her edge of the mattress.

Keeping his eyes closed until she was off the mattress, he glanced to see her back as she tiptoed across his carpet. Ready to snap his eyes shut if she started to turn back. Instead, he watched her head not to the adjoining bathroom, as he'd expected but to the bedroom door.

Without moving anything but his mouth he said, "Sorry, that's a breach of protocol."

In the moonlit shadows he could make out her shape. Her nod. He couldn't read her expression as she glanced toward the bed. "I didn't want to bother you with my tears. I'll be right back. Just let me—"

"I'm bothering you by requiring you to remain in my presence. You have a right to bother me back. Please get in the bed. If you go, I have to get up and follow you."

She could ask under whose orders he was working. But what would be the point? They both knew the score. She was free to go at any time.

But she needed his help, and his connections too, probably. And he needed to keep her safe.

Deal or no deal. Up to her.

Spinning on her heel, she faced the bathroom. Then said, "You want to check in there first, to make sure no one's lurking?" He wanted to hear snarkiness in her tone but didn't. He heard compliance.

"No," he told her. He could see the security camera blinking over his bedroom door. And would have had a phone alert if the room had been breached. Same for the alarms on both windows. They were lit, signaling working order.

But he lay alert, staring at the ceiling until he heard the bathroom door open. And then, eyes closed, waited for the dip in the mattress to signal that she was back in bed. Relaxing, he told himself he'd be back to sleep in no time.

"Thank you, Mitchell." The nearly whispered words drifted over him.

"You okay?" he asked then, instead of issuing the *you're welcome* that would have been more his style.

"Yeah. Crying is healthy, you know. Helps release the toxins that build up with stress and grief. You might try it sometime."

He'd take her word for that one. But didn't bother to share the news. "Get some rest," he said instead and, closing his eyes, ordered himself back to sleep.

Chapter 16

Tuesday passed with no new fears hitting Dove in the face. Her father was still showing little sign of waking up, but his vitals were okay. He seemed to be resting peacefully. And most incredible to her was that his brain scans, while showing some swelling beneath the gash to his skull, showed no sign of malfunction or permanent damage.

Mitchell asked about the scans the second he returned to the hospital room where he'd left her under the care of the changing guard outside the door, with a promise from her to order in, not go out.

In the suit and tie he'd donned that morning for a half day in the office, he pulled a chair in from the hallway to sit beside her.

"The doctor said he'll wake up when he's ready," she relayed the prognosis last. Leaving off the last line the woman had issued with clear warning. *Or he won't.*

Leaning forward, his elbows on his knees, Mitchell's gaze was pointed at Whaler. As though he could get answers from the older man. Or somehow telepathically send her father the assurance that he'd be there to help when he woke up.

She was being fanciful on that last bit, she knew but allowed herself the luxury. Hours alone in a mostly deserted facility made it a challenge to keep the demons at bay. Thoughts of Mitchell had helped.

"She said that his continued unconscious state could be a result of the swelling on his brain. Or it could be psychological." That was the part that was getting to her the most. The idea that Bob St. James would actually make the choice to die and join his wife than stay around to be a part of their daughter's life.

She had to be okay with it. To honor whatever choice he made without resentment. She just wasn't ready to let go. Didn't feel as though it was time to do so.

And so she stayed, holding on. To her fortitude, and to him, much of the time, too. Interlocking her fingers through his. Brushing hair back from his forehead. Washing his face. Rubbing his arm. Talking to him of the life they had waiting. The plans for St. James Boats, his lifeblood.

Kirk, the new hire.

But she had no way of knowing if any of it was getting through. Maybe she was just helping herself, maintain her vigil as she was, but if so, then so be it. As long as there was a chance that her father would fully rejoin the living, she had to be ready to be everything he needed as he got back on his feet.

To make life so good he wouldn't reach for the bottle again.

Her job, while Bob finished detoxing and rested, was to keep herself positive. Finding the good. Feeling it all the way to her soul.

So when the time was right, she could share it with him. Like an IV straight from her heart to his.

To that end, she asked Mitchell, "How are things going at the docks?" More to allow her father to listen to the conversation if he cared to than because she had any concerns.

Mitchell had said when he'd dropped her off that morning that he'd be checking in with Wes and the others throughout the day.

"A couple of newlyweds, first time to Alaska, stiffed Kirk out of nearly fifty dollars in fuel charges," he said.

And she shook her head. Not the type of conversation she'd been seeking.

Mitchell didn't seem to get the message as he continued with, "Wes rented the boat to them, and they'd said they'd pay for the fuel they used on their return, and when Kirk checked them back in, he told them they were good to go. They didn't tell him that they owed money. He said he'd pay for it himself."

Did her father's finger just twitch?

Dove had been staring for any signs of coming back to life all day. Looking for any movement at all that couldn't just be a process of breathing.

Just in case Whaler had an opinion about the incident involving his newest employee—a young man she'd told him all about, including that his father was out to sea most of the time—she quickly, and more loudly than necessary, said, "Please let him know that won't be necessary. It's our fault for not having a line item on the rental agreement for fuel, just as you already pointed out," she said, watching that finger the whole time. "I'm sure Wes had expected to check the boat back in, and he'd have known about the fuel."

There was no movement. No matter how hard she stared. She glanced over at Mitchell, to see if maybe he'd noticed something she had not.

He was looking at her as though he half suspected she'd spent the afternoon with a bottle herself.

"The doctor said he can most likely hear our conversation. I…thought I saw a finger move when you mentioned Kirk paying for his mistake."

Warmth flashed in the blue eyes gazing back at her. She wanted to believe it was born of admiration. Or comradery, at least.

But feared it had been nothing but a surge of pity.

She didn't need his pity.

She just needed him to believe, as she did, that Whaler was going to wake up.

Or…she just needed him.

Mitchell didn't stay long at the hospital. He'd stopped in on his way to the docks. He'd promised Dove he'd keep an eye on things for her, and he intended to do so. Everyone had already left for the day. Their last rental had come in just past two. But he wanted to go over the day's receipts. To take a look at the boats needed for the morning's reservations. And get a start on some of the paperwork he'd said he'd help Dove overhaul. Beginning with the rental agreement.

She opted to remain with her father. And while he didn't think the choice a healthy one—her sitting there all alone, for so many hours, watching a man either sleep or slowly die, he respected that she had to be where she felt the most needed. She clearly felt as though she could have the greatest impact by Whaler's side.

He just didn't like the idea of her being in the room all alone when Whaler took his last breath. *If* he took his last breath, he amended.

In Whaler's office, changing from his suit to the clean jeans and flannel shirt he'd thrown in the car that morning, he kept picturing Dove, sitting there in her spaghetti-strap tie-dyed caftan thing. Draped in darker colors, browns, reds, burgundies with patches of gold, he wondered what her choice of the day's attire stood for.

And, realizing what he was doing, justified the thought by the fact that he knew she chose her clothes for purposes other than looks. Maybe the day's dress had been something her mother made. Or had even been her mother's.

Maybe it was just comfortable.

Maybe if he was a better friend, he'd have stayed at the hospital with her. Or asked why she chose the dress and flip-flops she'd come out to the kitchen wearing not long after dawn that morning.

Her long hair flowing like gentle flames all over her.

His cousin Kansas had hair as long as Dove's. But she kept it tied back most of the time. Dove didn't restrict her locks.

Mitchell liked that about her.

Giving himself a serious shake, he headed out to the docks with purposeful strides, getting himself back to the mindset he'd slipped into the second he walked into his office that morning. His natural self.

Not the mucked-up version that time spent in Dove St. James's company seemed to be bringing out in him.

He'd taken half a dozen steps before he started to run. *What the hell...*

Ladybird wasn't in her usual slip. Jumping into Bob's runabout, he grabbed the keys from the slot in the bottom of the seat where Dove had told him her father kept them and was on the water within a minute. And had Wes and then Kirk on the phone—together, a conference call if ever there was one—seconds later. Both men swore the boat was moored as usual before they left the dock.

While *Ladybird* wasn't their most expensive boat, she was one of their highest earners with tourists because of how easy she was to take out—even on the sea. And because of the larger number of passengers she could carry.

"I check every single boat myself," Wes said. "Have been doing so since Oscar left. Whaler don't need any more problems."

"I, uh…" Kirk started and then stopped. And Mitchell's heart sank, even as his gaze remained focused intently on every inch of shoreline he was slowly cruising.

"You what?" he asked his buddy's son, knowing without doubt that if he'd made a mistake in recommending Kirk, he'd do what he had to do to make things right.

"I checked them after Wes did," he said. "My dad taught me to use a double bowline, and… I did." The young man paused and then said, "No offense to you, Wes, I just—"

"No offense taken, kid," Wes cut in. "Double bowline it'll be from now on."

Which was fine, except it didn't help him where *Ladybird* was concerned.

"I'm on my way," Wes continued. "About five minutes out."

"I'm seven," Kirk piped in.

The three of them talked about shoreline coordinates and divvying up areas, but Mitchell cut the conversation short. "I've got her," he said. "She's bobbing in the water twenty-five yards out from Bone's Cove."

An inlet that local fishermen had unofficially named.

Both men met him there, in one boat, with Wes jumping aboard *Ladybird* to drive her back to shore.

All three checked her over. Found nothing damaged.

Except the mooring rope.

It was missing altogether.

"It's my mother's boat. And one of our highest, most consistent earners." Dove paced Mitchell's kitchen floor, needing to expend the negative energy that had been building within her all day.

He'd waited until they'd arrived back at his place to tell her about the mishap at the marina. Whether he'd purposely made the choice because he'd known that the tension the news would have brought in Whaler's presence could mean the difference between her father choosing to come back to them or not, she didn't know.

Didn't really care. He'd been led, whether he got it or not.

Believing that gave her the strength she needed to keep looking forward. When all she wanted to do was crawl in a hole, cover her head and wait for the storm to pass.

She wasn't alone. She had her spirits, angels around her and souls up in heaven guiding her. And on earth, she'd been led to a man she'd never in a million years have sought out herself. Just as she knew, without a doubt, he'd never have initiated contact with her.

Her job was to trust. To keep her mind and heart focused and healthy. And to live by the inner promptings that, as long as she was in a good place, would never lead her wrong.

Engulfed in a myriad of emotions that swirled around her in a pool of anxiety, she had no promptings. Just the solid floor beneath her feet. And awareness of the man who leaned against the counter, silently watching her march to no drumbeat at all.

She glanced at him as she passed by. "If you hadn't stopped by after business hours..."

Whaler was the only one who ever did that, and whoever was out to get them would know that her dad was out of commission. They would have lost one of the boats upon which all of their future hopes were based.

"But I did stop by." Mitchell's words were truth. His

tone so completely practical that it jolted through the storm raging inside her.

He did stop by. Disaster had been averted.

Halting midstride, she spun to face him. Staring. As her mind slowed and she regained a semblance of her sense of self. Mitchell had said something the night before about having a security system installed at St. James Boats. "Did the security cameras catch anything?" she asked, the question that should have come from her several minutes before. The second he'd told her about the vandalism. No way two ropes, two sailor's knots, tied by an experienced boatman, just unraveled and disappeared on their own.

Missing ropes, no evidence. Except for…

Mitchell was shaking his head. "The camera was angled to cover the entire fleet on that side of the marina. It catches *Ladybird*, all but a couple of feet, including the mooring."

"What about people? Surely whoever did this was seen coming or going."

"Peter Welding has the recordings. They're going over them now. Wes, Kirk and I have already watched them and didn't see anything, or anyone, who looked suspicious. Everyone on tape had cause to be there. And no one is seen after Wes and Kirk left for the day, until I arrived."

"He had to have swum up to the dock!" The answer was obvious to Dove. Maybe because… "I did that once, to trick my dad. There's a cement base under it that forms a platform with a place to stand. Something there from before Shelby was a real town. Anyway, I stood on it, hiding, until he got on his boat. That was back when only his personal boat was tied up there. Before St. James Boats." She stopped, a smile forming but fading before she remembered the rest. "I was banned from reading books for a week." The memory of Whaler's very real anger engulfed her. The danger she'd put herself in, swimming in those waters alone, with no one aware she'd even gone in...

"Banned you from reading for a week?" Mitchell's tone drew her gaze up to his confused looking frown.

"It was the worst punishment they could give me," she said, shrugging. "From prekindergarten, I was always drawn to books. Spent most days after school reading. That was the loneliest, longest week of my life."

Nodding, eyes wide with something...positive, Mitchell asked, "Did it happen often, this punishment?"

Oddly distracted by his interest in a younger her, Dove said, "Just that once." Pursing her lips she nodded. Then seeing his smile, felt a lightening in her heart and said, "I was a quick learner."

"A smart girl who grew into an intelligent woman."

Dove stared at the man who'd just uttered words that changed her world in the space of the second it took him to say them. A minimal change, perhaps, but there.

"Most people just think I'm a kook," she said, knowing that he'd been one of them. And maybe still was.

"I'm guessing you don't give many people the chance to really know you."

Feeling as though she'd always been open to others, she couldn't answer to that. But found his take on the situation curious.

And not nearly as important as, "You want to call Peter Welding, or should I? Someone needs to be checking shoreline, looking for any sign of entry...and do a thorough search of the water around that platform."

The sun had already set. "Best wait until morning," she revised her thought. Glad to have had it though. To be back in a right mode.

Finding herself.

And saw Mitchell pull out his phone. "It won't hurt to give him a heads-up so he can have someone out there at sunrise."

Before the small St. James Boats marina was open for business.

The dawn of a new day. Shining light on what she'd taken as bad news: *Ladybird* having been left to float until she crashed. When, instead, she should have focused her thoughts on the positive that could come from the way the situation had turned out.

One of her father's biggest assets had been saved—with absolutely no harm done to it—and the police had a chance to find evidence to bring in the man who was hell-bent on ruining the St. Jameses' lives.

A new day, filled with possibility, would be arriving in hours. There was every chance her father would wake up. Their stalker would be caught. And with the start of Whaler's drying out already happening and the new outlook for St. James Boats, she and her father could finally start to live again, to find true happiness—carrying her mother's memory with them into a new future.

Feeling a full-out smile inside her for the first time in many, many hours, Dove looked over at Mitchell. "You ready for bed?" she asked.

When what she'd wanted to do was tell him he was good for her. His practical way of viewing the world, while not her way at all, had a place and a time. And the ability, apparently, to pull her out of negative energy, too.

Something to ponder.

In the new future.

Once they got through the present trials and had returned to their individual and very separate lives.

With differences. They'd say hello when they saw each

other out and about. Maybe exchange a *How are you doing?* now and then. And if either one of them was ever in serious need—the other would be there.

He might not get that part.

But she did.

And was content to hold that truth sacred for both of them.

Chapter 17

As he had the night before, Mitchell gave Dove time to get settled in upstairs before taking himself to bed. He'd talked to Peter Welding. But something wasn't sitting right with him. How would Brad Fletcher have known about that underwater platform at the front edge of the dock?

He'd had Dove draw him a rough likeness of the docks, to take a picture of and send to Welding, and he and the local police officer could both see exactly what she meant by someone being able to get to the ropes that moored *Ladybird* from in the water.

Overnight, the sea's constant movement would have taken her from there. She could have crashed into the other boats. Floated for miles. Hit a glacier. Or another boat, potentially taking lives. More likely, she'd have crashed into any of the jutting pieces of land that were an integral part of the landscape in their portion of the world.

What if it wasn't Brad Fletcher they were after?

Could it be Wes? Even as he had the thought, Mitchell shook it away. He'd known the man most of his life. Not closely but he was good people. Happily married, came from a good family, was raising one of his own.

And he was watching his livelihood sink into the sea

because of Whaler's inability to get control of his grief and quit drinking.

Hating the heartache such news would bring to Dove— and the potential harm that would come to St. James Boats if they were down their only experienced employee—he decided to keep his suspicions to himself until he knew more. He could be way off base. And didn't want to hurt Wes's reputation, either, simply due to a logical supposition. But he'd keep a closer watch on the docks, until he knew more.

Decision in place, he made quick work of his nightly routine, set his phone where he could see it, checked the gun he'd carried with him that day and lodged it between bed frame and mattress. Dove had covered herself with the same quilt she'd used before. Her choice to not get under the covers had been a wise one, but she needed her sleep. Needed to be comfortable. About to get another blanket to lay over her, he stopped.

She was a grown woman with the right to make her own choices. For all he knew, she'd put on warmer clothes—a wise decision all the way around.

Either way, not his business.

And if she was asleep, he most definitely did not want to risk waking her.

Careful to make as little movement as possible, he slid under the covers and lowered himself to the mattress.

As he had the night before, he closed his eyes, turned off the day and willed himself to a good night's sleep.

Except that there was a woman lying a foot or so away from him, not quite hugging her side of the bed...and he smelled lavender again. A woman who'd suffered enough.

Who had to have some good coming her way. If there was any truth at all to the karma she believed in.

And… Wes had dropped everything to come help secure *Ladybird*. Would a man who'd meant to harm her do that?

He'd come after Mitchell had already found her.

A man trying to avoid suspicion would do that. He'd been around his brother enough to know that perps often insinuated themselves into crime scenes. And investigations, too.

Had he told Wes anything about their suspicions regarding Brad Fletcher? He didn't think so. But couldn't speak for Dove. She'd known the man much more closely than Mitchell had—over a good period of years. It was feasible that she'd said something.

Welding already believed that Fletcher had been instrumental—had instigated, even—Hal Billows's surprise departure that week. It stood to good reason that the businessman had approached Wes as well…

"What's the matter?" Dove's voice, floating softly to him, carried caution. And hit him like a fist to the gut. He was sleeping alone—not with someone.

They were two individuals in the same bed.

They weren't together.

"Nothing," he told her. His train of thought made sense in the dark of the night after a difficult day. He wasn't going to be an alarmist, and possibly irreparably damage relationships, until he'd entertained them in the light of day.

And had done a little preliminary digging.

"Go to sleep," he added, as though talking to a child. Hearing himself, too late, he wished he'd just left it at *nothing*.

Because, other than the current problems in Dove's life, there was nothing. Could be nothing. Between them.

"That's the third big sigh you've made since you got into bed."

He didn't turn his head to see if she was still facing

the wall beside her, but neither had he felt her move. Taking that as a good sign he said, "My mind's on a situation I'm dealing with for a client," he told her in absolute truth. "Nothing I can discuss."

"Attorney–client privilege," she said, helping him out of his mess.

He didn't say yes. Technically, he'd be lying. Because when the client with whom he was speaking was the one whose case he was pondering, privilege was moot.

But he took care to put work out of his mind. Or to put the client who was consuming him on the back burner. To, at the very least, ensure that he kept his breathing even.

And, in doing so, felt himself relax enough to sleep.

Skin against skin. Brought to a semiconscious state, Dove registered the sensation. Human warmth against her arm. She'd been in a boat on a river in the dark, rowing so she didn't make any sound and bring danger upon her. Her arms were growing weary.

And there was warmth. She wasn't alone.

Lying still, she wavered between sleep and consciousness, relaxed and dropped off again. Until movement woke her completely. Then she froze.

She was lying on her back, not on her side as she'd fallen asleep. And not on the edge of the bed, either. Her arm had most definitely met human flesh. Mitchell's back. A bare portion of it.

And it felt…so incredibly good to be touching him.

Their time together—with no breaks—seemed like weeks, not days, and yet, other than the hug he'd given her the other morning, and the time she'd slid her hand into his at the hospital, they'd never touched.

As though doing so was off-limits.

How could something that brought so much comfort, even just an arm to a back in the night, be wrong?

She wanted to move until her hand was touching him, too. Just to lay her palm against him and go back to sleep, but didn't want to wake him.

Didn't want to spoil the moment.

But the more she lay there, wide awake, the more she wanted. Which led to thoughts of how he'd wanted her, too, the other morning.

And the more she thought, the more consumed she became with knowing how it felt to have her hand flat against his back. To absorb the sense of life emanating from his skin. To feel his essence in a physical sense.

Could her touch help him? Maybe instill some positive energy within him? She'd never practiced touch therapy before, but knew others who had. For healing purposes.

But what about just for…comfort? The word came again. Pushing at her. And Dove capitulated. Because…what if she denied herself and lost an opportunity she'd been given? Keeping her movements as imperceptible as possible, she slowly put her hand where her arm had been.

Just lay it there. And smiled. Never in her life had she taken such a large dose of positive energy from another human being. Maybe she hadn't been as open to doing so.

Or hadn't needed it so urgently.

Closing her eyes, she lay there, not holding Mitchell, just…feeling him…and drifted back to sleep.

Mitchell awoke abruptly. From an erotic dream that had left him hard as hell, a hand to his penis. A dream that didn't end with consciousness.

He was hard, all right. And holding a feminine hand that

contained the fingers actually covering a part of himself that hadn't known feminine company in months.

He worked to get his mind in gear. Came up with two things. He'd figured out how Dove had handled her getting-cold-in-the-night situation. She was under the covers with him.

And the second was just more of a wondering. Was she conscious?

Followed by a third. Did he want her to be?

Oh, God help him, he did.

He was about to explode, and she wasn't even doing anything. Well, she had her hand…there. With his on top of it.

Knowing that embarrassing himself was imminent, he gave an involuntary push against himself, adding pressure to her hand on him, but managed to hold on long enough for the immediate moment to pass. And breathed a sigh of relief with the victory. Never in his life had he lost control without his own consent.

All that was left was to extricate himself. Preferably without waking her up.

Unless…very softly he whispered, "You awake?"

The clasp of her fingers around him, a very definite sign of consciousness was his response. And made his exit not so clear-cut.

Most particularly when, of its own accord, his body pressed itself into her palm as a reaction to her hold on it.

Rolling to his back, Mitchell turned his head, meeting her wide-open gaze in the darkness. Pinpricks of light to pinpricks of light.

He thought her head started to move toward him. Knew his head started to move toward her. He was going to kiss her. Just fact.

And when he did, other facts hit home as well.

The woman kissed like a temptress.

And there was no option but to accept that they were going to have sex.

Dove had been dreaming. There'd been clouds. Pleasure.

How her hand had slid from Mitchell's back to his hard-on beneath the waistband of his silky pajama pants, she had no idea. Didn't figure it mattered. His hand over hers, holding her there, was all the impetus she needed to hold on. And to open her lips to his when he turned to her.

Nature had her way of directing her course.

Dove's choice was to follow it.

His pathway was an intoxicating surprise. Precise, as purposeful as he was. But so much more. He took his time to explore her mouth, allowing her to get to know his. Lips soft and gentle, and then more demanding, he took her more deeply into him, somehow, than she'd known a mere kiss could do.

So much so that her hand left his lower region as she had to plant both palms on his cheeks, to be there completely with him.

And when his pelvis pushed against hers, lighting a fire within her that would singe her without him, that was right, too.

She didn't speak. Didn't need words from him.

They'd have been superfluous. Interrupting the communication that mattered.

With her eyes wide open, she drew her palms up his sides as he sat up to remove the shirt that had ridden up on him during the night. And then, lying half on top of him as he rested back against his pillow, she watched as she let her hands get to know every inch of his chest. His shoulders. His stomach.

And squealed when he suddenly rose up and over, lowering her to her back after stripping off her half shirt. Her breasts tight, nipples hard, she lay there a willing and eager captive, delighting in the almost reverent look in his eyes as he cupped and caressed, teasing her nipples with his fingers and then his tongue. Before his mouth suckled in the age-old ways of time.

Just as she was losing herself to that pleasure, liquid seared through her, pooling in her crotch, and as though he'd known the second it happened, he slid on top of her, straight legs to straight legs, teasing her as he moved himself up and down in the crevice between her thighs.

Holding her knees together, she let her clothed thighs caress his hardness, reaching higher and higher as, with each pass, he pressed at the nub of her.

And when she was going to fly off without him, she rolled them to their sides. He reached for her pajama bottoms, got his own bottoms off and, kissing her, showed her another layer of hunger as he taunted and played with her, allowing her to explore him more completely than she'd ever known a man's body.

More than she'd ever before had a curiosity to know one. But, in those moments, couldn't know enough.

And then, somehow timing her need perfectly, he was just there, half on top of her, and she spread her legs wide open, inviting him in.

His initial entry after condom duty was slow, as though he was taking his time to say hello, to know her, in particular, before he danced with her.

She accepted his presence inside her with pure joy, welcoming his size, his strength, his need.

And when it was time to fly, she was there with him,

too. Her body moving as urgently as his did, their need to reach the sky seemingly the same.

Until, in one breath, they cried out, her body convulsing around his as his pulsed within her.

There'd never been a more perfect dance.

A purer joy.

And minutes later, with her naked body beside his under the covers, lightly touching his, she fell back to sleep.

Mitchell slept, and when consciousness returned, he was wide awake. Forget-falling-back-to-sleep awake.

What in the hell had he done?

Allowed her to do?

Encouraged her to do?

Checking for the blinking lights of the alarm sensors that greeted him every morning, he left his bed in spite of the fact that dawn had not yet made its appearance. Taking his phone into the bathroom with him. A quick look at the downstairs cameras, verifying that there'd been no breaches during the night, he went straight for the shower. A cold one.

And returning five minutes later to his room fully clothed in the blue jeans and shirt he'd put in the hamper the night before, he wasn't at all surprised to find Dove gone.

He had to shave. To grab clean clothes and get into them.

But first, he made a trek down to the kitchen. To get his coffee.

And to make certain that no unseen danger lurked in Dove's midst. Standing outside the bathroom door between her room and the kitchen, he heard the shower running. Took a peek in her room just to assure himself that everything looked normal, and conceded that he was being a little paranoid.

Most particularly when he was relieved to find that she hadn't packed her bags.

The fact that they'd had sex didn't change the circumstances that were keeping them together. He had to make certain that she shared his understanding on that point.

Which was why, fifteen minutes later, when she came out dressed in a gauzy orange flowing skirt with yellow flowers, another long-sleeved cropped shirt in green silk and sandals with ties that ran up to her knees, he was standing barefoot and unshaven in his kitchen, still wearing yesterday's clothes and sipping coffee.

The peaceful expression she'd been wearing as she'd entered the room disappeared the second she saw him. "What's wrong?"

"Nothing," he told her. Except that change, the second she saw him, gave lie to his words.

"Someone called. Who? Kansas? Welding? Your brother?" And then with a deep breath, "The hospital?"

The stiffness in her shoulders propelled him toward her, to reach for her. Except that he had a cup of hot coffee in his hand.

And they weren't…a couple.

"No one called. I just…needed to make certain that things were okay. Between us."

The immediate softening of her features eased his tension immensely. Until she frowned. "Why? Aren't you okay?"

Thinking of the night before, the incredible pleasure they'd made together, he said, "I am."

She nodded then. "You just thought I wouldn't be."

With a nod he shrugged. Guilty as charged.

"No strings attached. No commitment of any kind to any future involvement between us," she said, her gaze clear as she looked straight at him. Repeating what she'd said after the first time the subject had come up right there in his kitchen. "You think I was just kidding about that?"

Another shrug was all he had to give her. He wasn't even sure why. It wasn't like any of the women he'd been with had come after him wanting a wedding ring after one night together.

"Sex is a part of nature, Mitchell," she said then, moving to the refrigerator to pull out the container housing her bizarre grasslike breakfast. "Our bodies are designed to need it. Just like they require—" she held up the container "—food."

He should have been elated by her response. Instead, while he was pleased that she was in a good mood, he felt a little deflated.

Grabbing a fork, she stood there and took a bite of the same unusual meal she'd had the other two mornings they'd spent together. Then, swallowing, she glanced up at him, with an almost otherworldly smile on her face, like she had some kind of great secret. "But we did it in a pretty phenomenal way, huh?"

To which Mitchell said, "We sure did," and hightailed it out of there.

Before he was tempted to throw caution to the wind and ask her for a repeat performance on the kitchen floor.

Chapter 18

She wanted him again. And again. And again.

More so, and much worse, she didn't want him to leave his house. Ever. Didn't want him out there in the world where other women could ogle him. And want him, too.

Which made her the absolute worst human being on earth. A failure on all spiritual levels.

Selfish to the core.

A fraud.

Eating her greens—still holding out hope that their intuitive properties would help her right herself—Dove paced the kitchen, waiting for Mitchell to finish his shower and get her out of there.

Away from infernal temptation.

Him in the shower…water sluicing all over every inch of the body that she hadn't had nearly enough time with… a specimen of nature's ability to create perfection in male form…

She shoved two forkfuls in her mouth at once. Forcing herself to chew with her mouth open. Breaking her mother's heart, she was sure.

"Always chew with your mouth closed, Dove."

"But, Momma, I can do a better job at chewing with my mouth open. Then my cheeks don't get in the way so much."

"But then you take away the appetite of others who are eating with you. Which is the better choice? Chewing for your own comfort? Or making a choice that benefits others?"

Technically, she wasn't hurting anyone else with her current chewing choice.

So…perhaps she was still in her mother's good graces.

With the exception of the whole wanting-to-keep-Mitchell-locked-up-for-the-rest-of-their-lives thing. No, not locked up. It would be a sacrilege to cage the magnificent animal that he was.

Just…just…what?

She wanted the world to know he was hers and respect that choice? To have him tell her that she was the only woman he wanted to be with, would be with, no matter what?

Then she could trust him to go into the world and not be affected by what other women wanted. Like her mother had trusted her father all the months he was out at sea for all those years.

And what about her dad? Had he trusted her mother, too? Had he given any thought to what he was leaving behind?

Or had he taken her mother for granted?

Thoughts she should have had before. Long before. She'd just never looked at her parents from the partner perspective before. How horribly…lacking…of her.

And now? When Whaler looked at all the months, all the years that he'd lost? Thinking that he'd have a lifetime of years with his love when he retired from the sea? Only to have her get sick less than a decade afterward?

An onslaught of regret hit her so hard she slid down to the floor and adopted the lotus position just to get through it. And was hit with another bit of understanding.

The bottle. She didn't condone Whaler's drinking. It was

killing him. But it suddenly made more sense to her. It wasn't just grief sending her father to seek constant oblivion.

It was the sense that his life choices hadn't lived up to expectation. A lesson learned too late to avert the consequence.

How did a powerful man like her father live with the negative impact from a situation he'd created and couldn't fix?

How did Dove help him find a way? When she didn't know the way herself? Her mother had never taught her the lesson—not in words.

And not really in action, either. While she was absolutely certain her parents had adored each other, that her mother had loved her father and Dove, too, with her whole heart, she had no idea if they'd had an open marriage or not. If her mother had taken lovers while her father was away, Dove had certainly never known about it.

Nor could she come up with a single male figure in her mother's life who might have been more than just a casual acquaintance.

The sound of Mitchell's shoes on the creaking stairs had Dove scrambling to her feet. Putting the lid on her greens and shoving the container back into the refrigerator.

Feeling as though she'd had a good morning session, even though she hadn't technically been in a meditative state.

Her incredibly odd reaction to sex with Mitchell hadn't been about her. It had been a way for her to gain understanding of her father's struggles. To be able to find a way to help him, where in the past she'd failed.

A new perspective with which to greet him when he awoke.

She didn't have all the answers yet. But with her new understanding, she was finally on her way to finding them.

And knowing the reason behind her uncharacteristically territorial reaction to the previous night's activities meant that she'd just freed herself up to have sex with Mitchell again.

A thought that brought enough of a flood of good feeling to drown out the pricks of fear as she headed out with him and into her day.

Or would have if he hadn't come into the kitchen with tight lips and lines marring his forehead.

"What?" she asked, when his gaze sought her out and held on.

"There's no sign of *Ladybird*'s mooring ropes, but they found evidence on the cement pad to indicate that someone had been standing on it within the last day. Not a footprint, but a lack of sea debris and algae growth, side by side, in the size of feet."

Picking up the bag she'd packed for the hospital when she'd first come down that morning, she slung it over her shoulder and headed for the door. "So we know that someone tampered with the boat, but we have no way of finding out who."

He was right behind her. Which just plain felt good. "Yep." He didn't sound at all happy about that fact.

"But we know who it is," she reminded him. "It just means we still don't have the proof we need to have him stopped."

"It means he's getting bolder," Mitchell told her as he slid into the car seat beside her. They pulled their doors closed at the same time.

In unison.

As though their sex dance had somehow put them in sync. The thought filled her with pleasure. She clung to it as she asked something that had been toying at the edge of her brain. Something she hadn't wanted to think about. "How would Brad Fletcher know about that cement platform? He's not from Shelby, nor has he ever, that we know of, spent any time at St. James Boats. I didn't even know about it until my dad bought the place and I started fooling around in the water. That was a few years before he'd retired, so before his fleet of boats were in. My folks would let me jump off the dock and swim, as long as one of them— Mom—was around to keep an eye on me."

She was jabbering. Had her parents—their relationship—on her mind. They'd had a good plan for their future together. Her mother had seemed really happy about it. Eager to spend time at the marina. She'd been a huge help in getting the business up and running...

"Same way he got your studio vandalized," Mitchell's words cut into her remunerations. "Hired someone local."

Maybe. Most likely. But... "Why go to all the trouble to swim in to get the job done when he could have just done the job from the docks?" With new horror shuddering through her, she turned to look at him. "Unless he knew about the newly installed cameras."

The way Mitchell's jaw tensed was his giveaway. "You already figured all this out," she said to him. "And you have a suspect. Kirk? You think Fletcher hired him?"

Mitchell's glance over at her as he paused at the end of his driveway held...speculation. Not confirmation. "It's possible Kirk told Fletcher about the platform," sounding... different. Tense, but not as...uptight.

"You suspected someone else."

Pulling out onto the street that would take them into town, he gave her another, easier glance. "Not *suspected*," he told her. "Just wondered about. Not because he's given me any reason to doubt him, personally, at all."

There was only one person left that she knew of that fit the bill. "Wes?" she asked him, incredulous. "Wes would no more sabotage my father's business than cut his own feet off. It's not about the money for him," she said. "It's about family. Loyalty. Keeping businesses local. The man is Shelby golden to the core."

Odd how Mitchell remained silent after her tirade, where normally he'd quietly lay out logical points as he saw them. And, not liking that he hadn't done so—worried that his not doing so had something to do with the sex they'd had, as it was the only thing that had changed between them—she said, "The facts point to him."

When he continued to face straight ahead, not acknowledging that he'd heard her, she pushed harder. "And you didn't want to tell me until you had proof because you knew it would upset me."

Nice. But…she couldn't go there. Most particularly not with him.

But really, not with anyone. She might need his help and physical protection against an attacker at the moment, but that didn't make her any less capable of handling the crappy challenges that life dumped on her. It was all part of the journey. Even if it meant she made mistakes. She had to be allowed to fail.

She'd asked for the help she needed.

He continued to drive. She continued to stare at him. Hard. "You didn't tell me because you're getting all manly on me, thinking I need protecting from emotional pain, rather than seeing me as an equal work mate," she accused.

And Mitchell nodded.

There was no point in avoiding the truth. A fact Mitchell had learned probably from birth. And while he did not like, or want, his newfound awareness where Dove was concerned, he knew better than to avoid it.

Most of the problems his clients—and his family members—brought to him were the result of avoidance. Not wanting to deal with something. Hoping it would go away.

Many things did work out as one hoped. There were times when possible problems didn't materialize. But that didn't mean you didn't prepare for them just in case.

And in his case, avoidance wasn't really even a choice. He was in the middle of a huge pile of muck. He wanted a woman he had nothing in common with.

To the point that he'd allowed her to convince him that sex was only body parts. He'd known better than that. A man didn't get a law degree—with a required class in family law—without gaining an understanding of two major truths. Emotions were a huge factor in problems between family members. And emotions were unpredictable. One couldn't see into the future.

Couldn't predict that a young love could turn so deadly.

Or that someone who adored another one year decided five years later that they no longer did. Nor could one predict how one would feel if they found out a spouse had cheated on them.

And how did it all pertain to him?

He'd known the messiest emotions of all stemmed from sex. Often even when one didn't want, or expect, them to do so.

Because sex was the ultimate form of physical expression. And if it was great sex, it often created a new awareness of that person. Which then, due to the way human beings reacted to needs within themselves by seeking to fill that need, created a need for more sex with them. Which led to an emotional bond between them. A bond that—due to a human being's ability to reason, to realize that the other's well-being directly affected their own emotional state— spilled out of the bedroom and into their lives.

He didn't make the rules. He just lived by them.

All of which flew out of his brain when, at Dove's request, he made a stop at the marina before taking her to the hospital to sit with her father. She'd called in. Bob St. James had not yet regained consciousness but had taken no turn for the worse. And she'd wanted to see for herself that *Ladybird* was okay. To look at the area. And check the office, too.

If anything was out of place—if Wes Armstrong had messed with anything Mitchell took that to mean—she'd be the most likely one to be able to tell.

They didn't make it to the office. Though it was only six in the morning when they pulled in, the sun was already shining, and his brain was just registering the sight before him when he heard Dove's sharp intake of breath. Followed by "Oh my God!"

She had her door open before he'd come to a full stop in the drive, but he was right beside her as she ran down to the docks.

He'd been looking at *Ladybird* as he'd first pulled forward, and supposed she had been, too. *Wicked Winnings* had been moored beside her.

The trawler's radar station and pilothouse were intact, but the forward hull, starting with the gunwale, were splintered, bashed in, as though someone had taken a sledgehammer to her. Or had had her out for a joyride and crashed. All of the damage they could see was out of the water, but that didn't mean the immersed portion of the hull wasn't also damaged.

Racing in front of Dove, maybe to get there first, to

somehow protect her from the horror she had to be experiencing, he said, "If she's taking in water, she'll sink."

He was already on the trawler by the time she'd caught up with him. And while he wanted to stop her from climbing aboard—even just to ask her to please let him get a look around first—he didn't do so. She'd made her point quite clear in the car. The fact that they'd had sex gave him no further influence over her. She would not tolerate him trying to take her autonomy from her.

He made a quick check of all at-risk areas, ending up in the pilothouse. She was sitting at the helm, staring out at the trashed hull in front of her. "She was our greatest hope," she said to him. "Our way to make enough money to keep the business going."

"She still can be," he said, words pouring out of him almost faster than he was thinking them. "There's no water coming in, Dove. While the damage is extensive, it's not as bad as it looks."

"Doesn't matter," she said, placing both of her hands on the wheel. "We can't afford the repairs."

His lawyer brain was in full gear. "You might not have to," he told her, placing himself so that she could just as easily see him as the damage in front of her. Wanting her to focus on him.

Not the destruction.

"This is clearly destruction of property," he told her, talking way too fast but feeling as though he couldn't get the words out rapidly enough. "A deliberate destruction. If someone had been joyriding and crashed, then based on the breakage we can see, there'd also have been extensive damage to the keel. The lower hull. There'd be water coming in."

Her face turned slowly, her gaze brushing up against

his. And then connecting. "You think we can prove sabotage?" she asked him.

Breathing a tad more easily, Mitchell said, "Yes." And then moved closer to her, taking her hands off the wheel and turning her to face him. Without forethought. Just doing it. Looking her right in the eye, he reminded her, "If this was done without taking her out, we'll have it on video, Dove."

He saw the focus, the strength, the…hope return to her gaze. So quickly the glow coming from her eyes was almost a physical touch to him. Jumping up, she moved toward the dock, stepping around debris as if it wasn't even there. "Should we call the police before we access the cameras?" she asked. "I don't want there to be any chance that anyone can say we tampered with evidence."

Mitchell didn't have the heart to tell her the trial, which wouldn't happen for months, was not her first concern by any means. But because he'd used the end in mind to help her fight back, he could hardly point that out. He had her back. For the moment that was all that mattered.

The rest, like the fact that she mattered more than anything else going on in his life, was just going to have to wait.

Chapter 19

They had him! Standing in her father's office with Peter Welding and Mitchell, Dove wanted to throw her arms around the attorney's neck, hug him and never let go.

She didn't, of course. But she was smiling from ear to ear as Welding took possession of the security-camera memory card that showed Brad Fletcher himself using some kind of gun that shot what looked to be electrical current onto the deck of *Wicked Winnings*. There'd be no fingerprints, no bullets that could be identified by striations. If not for the cameras that Mitchell had had installed, it could have been near to impossible to prove who'd done the damage.

Welding, as an extra precaution, sent a digital copy of the footage to his secure email at the station, and after Mitchell inserted a new memory card into the camera's mainframe, the officer walked with Mitchell and her to Mitchell's car.

Mitchell had an early appointment and needed to drop her off at the hospital first.

"I can take her," Welding offered, looking from Mitchell to Dove. "It's only a mile out of my way." Two for Mitchell, and Welding had no urgent business.

So as disappointed as Dove was not to have those minutes alone with Mitchell, to celebrate the victory in private conversation and ask him the next steps as far as St. James

Boats was concerned, she said, "I'm good with that," and before Mitchell could argue, grabbed her bag out of the back seat of his vehicle.

She'd never met Peter in person until that week and enjoyed his conversation as they drove across their small town. She watched as they passed Repo and Namaste, longing for her peaceful space, for her clients, but knew that she carried too much risk of passing her negative energy to them while she still felt...hunted.

Soon, she told herself, feeling as though the universe backed up her silent promise. With Brad Fletcher's arrest imminent, and so clearly, provably guilty, she could be back in her studio as early as that afternoon.

The thought filling her with happiness, she smiled when Peter mentioned that maybe they could get a cup of coffee sometime. And shrugged. Not a *no*. Not a *yes*.

Not an admission that she couldn't stand the stuff.

He didn't push. She didn't reject him. And she gave him an extra warm smile as he pulled up in front of the medical center's main building. "This where you need to be?" he asked, and she nodded.

"Thank you so much," she told him. "You have no idea how much this means to my father and me. We are most certainly in your debt. Maybe, once he's home, we can have you over to dinner. To thank you?"

Let him make what he would of that. He was a nice man. She liked his company.

And had zero desire to lead him on with an acceptance of what could only be considered a predate invite.

"I'd like that," he said, smiling in a nice way as she hopped out and shut the door quickly behind her, turning to wave and watch him drive off.

More because she didn't want him to see her walk from

the front of the building over to the inpatient wing that was attached to the separate, urgent care portion of the medical complex, rather than the doctors' and imaging offices where he'd left her.

The man didn't do anything for her in that department. He might have done. If she'd met him at an earlier time. And maybe, at some future point?

She wasn't closing the door on the idea. But wasn't alluding to it, either.

And he wasn't leaving. Reminding her of Mitchell for a second there. Until she reminded herself he was a good cop and doing his job. He needed to see her enter the building.

And so she did. Waiting around for several minutes, before she headed back out to get over to her father. And then, just to be safe, went out the back way, through the playground and park area set up for lunches or kids who had long wait times between procedures. As she walked, her mind filled with the future's possibilities.

The early morning chill seemed to lift her to a higher wakefulness, while the sun filled her with the serotonin that fed her intuitive abilities with its added ability to access good feelings.

She had so much to tell her dad. Now that they had Brad, it would be all systems go with the plans to get the boat rental business back to earning good money. Yes, they'd have a bit of a delay while *Wicked* was fixed, but with Brad Fletcher's money, it shouldn't be hard to at least force the man to pay that bill immediately...

Ugh!

A sudden blow to her back knocked the wind out of Dove, would have thrown her to the ground if she hadn't been honing her body since she was old enough to walk.

She saw the cloth coming around the side of her face,

toward her mouth, in the split second before it stunted her breathing abilities, and threw an elbow straight to the side of her face. Knocking the hand behind the cloth just as she kicked one leg straight up behind her. Landing in a squat facing behind her, knees bent, apart, hand on the ground to steady her, preparing for a throw of her palm to a nose with enough of a lunge to knock her attacker to his back.

Except…no face was there. Winded, stunned, Dove looked up to see an average-size figure dressed all in blue, or black…a hood running around the corner of a wing of the building and disappearing out of sight.

She ran then, too. At a pace fast enough to win races on the high school track field, and hurriedly, with shaking fingers, pushed in the code she'd been given to access the private inpatient wing. Fumbling once. Forcing herself to focus and push again.

Once inside, she walked at a rapid pace past the chairs she and Mitchell had occupied the other day, into the waiting area in view of the nurses' station.

Seeing two uniformed women and one man behind the desk, all of whom she recognized, she waved and pulled out her phone.

With her finger on the icon she'd set up for Mitchell, she remembered he was in an appointment and, as reality hit, went straight to the officer standing watch outside her father's door. Someone new, a woman she'd never met before.

Angela Waites her badge read. A first-year officer who called Peter Welding the second she heard about the near attack.

Apparently, Brad Fletcher hadn't been satisfied with damage to the St. James Boats ability to earn an income. Or threats. He was hiring thugs to make certain that she didn't get in the way of his goal.

"I don't think he was going to hurt me," she told Peter when, in short order, he was sitting with her in the same seats she and Mitchell had used out in the hallway between the trauma and inpatient units. She'd given him all the details, the minimal description she had, and had answered his questions mostly with *I don't know* or *I didn't notice*. "He was definitely planning to knock me out, though," she added after her last useless response. "Probably just to scare me. A warning to sell my father's business since, without *Wicked Winnings*, I can no longer afford to keep the place."

Peter's frown didn't slow her down at all. Not even when he asked, "That doesn't make a lot of sense," he said. "He's going to abduct you, get you to sign, and then think he can just walk away?"

He was right. Didn't make sense. Fear shot through her. A stab at a time. Growing more electrifying with each stab. "He was going to make me sign and then dispose of me, wasn't he? Just like he tried to dispose of my dad?" And then, before giving him a chance to reply, she said, "Or..." eyes wide with horror, she stared at him "...the serial killer..." She swallowed. Hard.

Struggled to draw in air.

The uniformed officer's gaze was kind as he looked at her, shrugged and said, "We can only speculate at this point, but I hope you've taken your last walk alone until this is resolved?"

He didn't call her on letting him drop her off at the wrong spot. He'd only been in town a short while, having applied for and taken the job, leaving a smaller force he'd worked for upstate. But he didn't know she knew that. She wouldn't have, hadn't, until Mitchell had mentioned it when the man had first been assigned to check out Brad Fletcher.

One of Brad's boat rental businesses was located in the small seaside town where Peter had last been employed.

Peter likely knew Brad. Maybe even well.

Filling with horror chills again, Dove wondered if she'd just walked into her own demise—leaving the unit to sit out there alone with Welding. Was he on Fletcher's payroll, too? Like the thug who'd just tried to kidnap her?

And the guy who'd been watching her house?

And had debased the sacredness of her studio?

Glancing at the door into the unit and feeling for her phone in her bag, she was trying to determine her best course of action against an armed and well-trained police officer when Mitchell barged through the door at the opposite end of the hall and came toward her.

Weak with relief, she felt tears fill her eyes.

But didn't take her gaze off him.

Not even when she saw the flare of his nostrils, the anger glaring from those blue eyes.

He'd come.

His anger didn't bother her. It was a natural reaction. What mattered was that he'd somehow known she was still in trouble.

And he'd shown up.

And...was shaking Peter's hand like they were friends.

Mitchell was in on it, then? He was...

The thought hit but only lasted for the split second it took her to slap down the fear that was trying to rob her of her senses.

Mitchell was there to help her. She had to believe that.

And if she was wrong? The insidiousness of negative energy wasn't letting go easily.

But she had an answer for it.

If she couldn't trust Mitchell, she'd just as soon be dead.

* * *

Mitchell sat with Dove after Welding left. Several minutes passed before the glaze left her eyes. The woman was a complete enigma to him. And if he didn't get some kind of protocol for himself where she was concerned, she might just be his downfall, too.

There was no future for the two of them. He saw it clearly. What's more, he was certain that she saw it, too.

So why her circumstances were affecting him so intrinsically he didn't know.

The situation didn't bode well.

Mitchell did not like things going on in his life that he couldn't explain rationally and logically. Which was why he was living the staid life he'd chosen to live. With all adventure happening between him and nature, period. No other humans around.

Until the past week.

He'd excused himself from an important merger meeting between two medical practices—joining two independent DOs into one practice—as soon as he'd seen Welding's name on his phone screen. Expecting to hear that Fletcher was in custody, he'd stepped outside just long enough to get the good news.

And never stepped back in. With a quick call to Stuart and then texts to his clients, he had his paralegal collect preliminary signatures and reschedule the meeting for later that afternoon.

Unprofessional, at best. Something else completely new and inexplicable to him.

Welding had already suggested that Dove get checked out over at the clinic. She'd insisted she was fine. The guy who'd tried to abduct her might not be, however. Welding had all clinics and urgent cares in Shelby and surrounding cities being checked out for any recent nose injuries.

"I wanted to believe there was no chance it was the serial killer after me." Dove's soft words were loud in the deserted hallway. Breaking a silence that had lasted several minutes.

He wasn't going anywhere until he knew that Fletcher was in custody. At the very least.

"We don't know it's him, Dove. To the contrary, there's no indication that women who reported being vandalized or stalked have gone missing."

When her head swung in his direction, mouth open, eyes wide, he quickly added, "I spoke with Eli on my way here from the office." There was more. He didn't want to tell her. To add to her burden. And yet…it wasn't up to him to determine what she could and could not handle. If she were a man, he'd tell her. Or another lawyer.

But because she was so sensitive…was no reason to undermine her.

The woman had taken out a would-be kidnapper with no warning, and it sounded like impressive precision. He'd been picturing the scenario that had been laid out for him over and over in his mind. Just…having a hard time digesting…so much.

"It's also less likely that it was the serial killer because another woman has just gone missing," he told her. Without giving the name, the details, that Eli had given him. Dawn Ellis. From Wasilla.

"Oh my god!" Dove's gaze wide-eyed again but filled with compassion as she looked over at him. "When?"

He shook his head. "I honestly don't know for sure. She was just reported missing." And fit the MO. "Even if I did know more, I'm not at liberty to tell you."

He wasn't free to take her into his arms, either, which

was all he'd really wanted to do since he'd seen the look of relief, and what appeared to be gratitude, that had entered her eyes when he'd come walking down the hallway toward her.

Pulling her sandal-strapped lower legs up to her chair, she wrapped her arms around her shins.

Noting, with relief, that she had Lycra shorts on under the skirt, Mitchell resisted the urge to wrap an arm around her and pull her against him. Feeling a bit powerless sitting there.

But equally unwilling to leave. At least until she was ready to go sit in her father's room. She'd said she didn't want to take her negative energy in there. That as long as she was close, in case there was any change, she'd prefer to stay outside his space until she had her breathing, her tension, under control.

The woman was an enigma, to be sure. Soft and needy, and yet, in some ways, he was beginning to think she was stronger than he was.

He controlled his environment. She kept hers wide open.

Thinking of the way she'd put herself in harm's way by walking unescorted, he figured maybe hers was too open.

"I shouldn't have been in the outdoor break area alone," she said, as though she'd read his thoughts. More like the incident that had taken place was replaying itself over and over again in both of their minds.

He didn't bother commenting on the obvious. She'd paid a heavy price for her choice.

"I just thought…within the complex I'd be safe. And mostly, because I felt safe here, my own physical safety wasn't at the forefront of my mind."

He had to bite back the words that came to him first. That her physical safety should always be at the forefront of her mind. But that wasn't his call to make. "We'd just got the proof we've been seeking on Brad Fletcher," he said instead. "It's understandable, with all that's gone on, your father lying in there...that getting the man in custody would be consuming you." Which was why he'd told Welding to make sure he saw her into the building.

Which the detective had.

Mitchell just hadn't imagined that Dove would head in the wrong door.

"Actually," she said, turning her head on her knees to look at him, "Fletcher wasn't the one affecting my thinking right then."

The way she said the words, as though she was telling him something she wasn't sure she should, treading in unsure waters, had him watching her intently.

She'd been thinking about him? Maybe about the fact that, with Fletcher's arrest, and the warrants they could then compel, they might soon be able to prove conclusively that all the destructive things happening to her stemmed from the shady businessman's attempt to pressure her into selling her father's business. Which meant that her time as a guest in his home was at an end.

They'd had their one night together.

And it was done.

"When Detective Welding pulled up to the wrong part of the medical complex, he was asking me out."

Mitchell's gaze swung back to her, more intently than it should have done. He managed to keep his mouth shut, however.

If Dove wanted to date, that was her business. They'd had sex. No commitment. No expectations.

"I didn't want to embarrass him, but at the same time I just had no interest. Except to be noncommittal and get out of the car before he could press for more. I didn't want to risk the chance that he'd hang around for a minute or two, to make sure things were good, and so I went out the back way."

Reeling with the words, he continued to stare at her. The idea that Welding had expressed an interest in Dove wasn't as fantastical as Mitchell's immediate reaction to the man for having done so. He'd have liked to punch the man in the face.

Which was better than the gun he'd have taken to her assailant had he been present during that travesty.

Still, he had no right to any opinion about Dove's love life.

Nor any reason to feel like strutting around like a golden rooster at her response to Welding's invitation.

She'd had no interest.

Which factored in not at all.

It was about the attack she'd endured. And her dealing with it. Getting by it as best she could. That was all that mattered.

About the fact that her would-be abductor was still out there. On the loose. Possibly planning to try again. Unless Welding and his team could get a look at Fletcher's phone records, his finances. Then figure out who was on his payroll and stop them.

Or it was until the door into the ward opened suddenly, with a nurse standing there.

Her expression—not grim—the uniformed woman said, "Your father's awake. The doctor's on her way."

And Dove was gone.

Chapter 20

Spirits soaring, Dove practically flew into her father's room, only just realizing, when she heard Mitchell's soft tones behind her speaking to the nurse, that she'd just left him sitting out there.

A part of her was stronger, knowing he was there, but she was fully focused on her father.

And stopped, not far inside his door when she saw the anger glaring at her from his older blue eyes. "What's going on?" he demanded in a tone she hadn't heard directed at her...ever. "Why am I here? Did you have me committed? Because I can tell you..." He started to throw off his covers and sit up.

"Dad, no!" she said, hurrying over to him, both arms reaching out to his chest. Not to push him back but to hold on. He didn't hug her back but had stopped moving forward, and tears burst out of her. "You were hurt," she told him, sobbing. "Please lie back down. At least until the doctor can look in your eyes and make sure you're okay to get up."

The words seemed to placate him. She felt his body relax against her arms, and helped ease him back to the bed.

Sorry to have to let him go, she sat on the edge of the bed beside him, needing to ask him what seemed like a million questions, but completely stupefied and a bit frightened of the uncharacteristic anger he'd spewed at her, she was afraid to say much or do anything until the doctor arrived.

"She's been called," she said then, wiping her tears, but feeling the residual of the storm inside her in the trembling of her lips. "The doctor. She'll be here momentarily, I promise."

With a wary look in her direction, he nodded. Then slid his fingers in between hers on the hand closest to him and held on.

Her daddy, again.

His grip strong enough to feel healthy, but not at all hurtful. And...shaky. His eyes seemed lucid, though he appeared a bit lost. And the vitals she'd been reading for two days on the machine beside his bed were the best they'd been. His pulse ran fast on and off, and she'd been told that was to be expected with the detoxing.

She wasn't a doctor. But she clung tightly to the hope in front of her.

Along with a possible boatload of anger, anxiety or resentment. She hadn't needed the doctor to tell her that part. Just as serotonin was a basis of happiness, the liver was a base for the more negative emotions.

A first-year intern had put a call into Peter Welding as soon as Whaler awoke, and he arrived right alongside the doctor before Dove had a chance for any further conversation with her father. The younger employee shooed her out while the doctor examined him and supervised Welding's questioning.

"It's a good sign that he was angry," Mitchell said the second she stood beside him in the hallway. "He's fighting."

Nodding, she watched the closed door. The anger had bothered her. But not nearly as much as the accusation had done. But she'd read up on detoxification. Hallucinations were sometimes a part of the process. Most particularly when the person was a heavy drinker.

Her father qualified as that. She couldn't take his first reaction to seeing her in a personal way. He was conscious. He wasn't himself.

One step at a time. She knew this stuff. Things were coming to a close. With Fletcher's arrest in the works, and her father awake, life could turn the corner toward the future. One where St. James Boats was fluid again.

Her father healthy.

Her studio thriving.

And her no longer feeling like Mitchell was her lifeblood to strength and endurance. No longer needing him. Or anyone but herself.

Standing against the wall, she hardly took her gaze off the door. And jumped when it opened five minutes later. As if by choreographed dance or staging, Welding went straight to Mitchell as the doctor came to her.

"He doesn't remember anything from the time he saw you in his office on Saturday until now," the doctor said softly, her gaze compassionate.

Dove didn't need compassion. Couldn't allow herself the weakness of leaning on yet another human being. "His memories of his time with you are fuzzy, but I understand he was pretty intoxicated then?"

She nodded. Hating hearing her father's situation being discussed so…realistically. Yeah, he'd been pretty drunk. More like totally wasted.

She just hadn't wanted to accept that she was losing him one sip, one bottle at a time.

"His pupil response is good," the doctor continued, talking about running another scan, some more lab work, before she could give Dove any idea as to when Whaler would be able to go home.

Warning that he was already asking for his bottle. Threatening to leave if someone didn't bring it to him. And then telling her that he'd already fallen back to sleep and could be expected to remain that way for a good part of the day. If he was up and alert by nighttime, they could start him on some solid foods. And maybe, depending on test results and his ability to tolerate food, get him off the IV in another twenty-four hours or so.

Dove nodded. Reminded herself that Fletcher was exposed, with or without her father's testimony. And that in spite of the lack of any sign that he was glad to have rejoined the living, her dad had the best chance ahead of him than he'd had since her mother died.

If he'd cooperate. Or even try to.

If he wanted to stick around to share life with her for a few years, a few decades, longer.

If they got through the next few days, she amended the earlier thought a couple of hours later when Mitchell, who'd been in and out, bringing her snacks and conversation in between his appointments, arrived in Whaler's room with a grim look on his face.

"Fletcher was taken into custody," his gaze, his tone, didn't reflect the good news at all, and she braced herself. "He admits to vandalizing the boat, hoping, since you've been completely ignoring him, to get your attention and convince you to agree to sell the place with your dad out of commission. He also admitted to the shady but not illegal way he'd convinced Hal to leave St. James Boats. But he adamantly swears he had nothing to do with your father's disappearance. Or any harm that's come to you. He has solid alibis to back up his claims—he was out deep sea fishing this morning—and his phone and financial records show no evidence at all that he's been hiring anyone else to create havoc in Shelby."

Her stomach a knot of lead, standing at the end of her father's bed in conversation with Mitchell, she stared up at his suit jacket and tie, looking all official and distant from her. "You're telling me no charges are being filed?"

He shook his head. "He'll face property damage charges. Has already agreed to have *Wicked Winnings* fixed, immediately, at his expense." He paused, and then said, "And based on signed statements, and no law allowing them to hold him in custody, his lawyer forced the department to let him go."

"What about the spit on my father's clothes? Did they get a DNA sample from him? Couldn't they hold him until they get those results?"

Mitchell just looked at her. Deeply. And she felt the crush of a hopeful day gone bad. "The ABI forensics lab ran a fast DNA test while he was in custody. It wasn't a match."

Feeling sick, wishing she hadn't eaten the tuna he'd brought her at lunch time, she said, "So he's paying cash and using prepaid phones to hire whoever is helping him."

"It looks that way."

Mitchell pulled a chair in from the hall and moved hers over next to it. Sat down. Clearly intending to sit with her. Seemingly for as long as she needed.

Dove slid down to the floor, with her back to the wall, legs in the lotus position, and closed her eyes.

If ever there was a time she needed an awareness of her spirits, of her inner ability to maintain ownership of herself and give her strength, it was then.

Because all she really wanted to do was crawl onto Mitchell's lap, feel his arms holding her close and cry.

* * *

Mitchell had Dove for another night. She'd eaten at the hospital, having ordered in, and he'd had dinner with Eli. Mostly to get his head on straight.

Older brothers had a way of homing in on any nonsense in kid brothers and knocking it right out of them.

They'd met at The Cove, mainly because Mitchell was at St. James Boats after finishing the merger paperwork with his physician clients and intended to return there after dinner as well, until Dove was ready to head home. And The Cove was close.

It was also quiet. Something he needed at the moment. The quiet. A lack of noise in his head so he could find the logic in his current situation.

That's where he'd expected Eli to come in, but the major-case lieutenant had been oddly moot on any mention of Dove St. James other than to mention how impressive her defense against her attacker had been that morning. And to ask how she was doing.

No ribbing Mitchell. And worse, no asking him what in the hell he thought he was doing with Dove St. James. Not even a mention of how out of character it was for Mitchell to be staying so closely involved with the case.

Not that he blamed his brother. With Dawn Ellis now missing, in addition to the three unidentified female bodies on slabs, Eli would be fully engrossed in the case and beating himself up to catch the killer before anyone else got hurt.

Dove had called not long after he'd left Eli and had talked about her father all the way home. Almost as though she couldn't allow a moment for any other conversation to happen between them. Because she was avoiding the possibility of more bad news?

Or didn't want to talk about whether or not they'd have sex again that night?

He studied her face when he stopped at a light, trying to figure out where she was at, but read nothing at all. Her expression was blank.

So he asked questions. Found out that Whaler had woken once before dinner. Had eaten the soft foods given to him, bitching about them the entire time, and then yelled at the game show he'd watched on the television.

Sensing there was so much more, hating that the woman was so used to dealing with every part of life alone— picturing his huge family, all leaning on each other, to the point of irritation sometimes—and wanted to bring Dove in. To let her know that she didn't have to carry the weight on her shoulders by herself.

To that end, as they neared his house, he asked, "How many times did he unload on you?"

He'd heard the abrasive greeting with which Whaler had greeted her the first time that day. Had witnessed the way she'd just taken it and then held his hand, without a single word to let him know that he'd been out of line. And had been wondering ever since if she'd grown up with that kind of verbal abuse.

If so, his respect for and good opinion of Bob St. James had just gone down the toilet.

"I didn't count," she told him, not even sending him a brief glance. Nor was she watching the world passing around them. Just kept staring out the front window. With the sun already set but dusk not fully settled in, there was still a lot to see out there.

Clearly her mind was focused elsewhere.

And he was guessing it wasn't on sex again. Not that he

blamed her for that. To the contrary, he was a little sickened by himself going there, under the current circumstances.

But eased his conscience a little bit with the knowledge that he wasn't just thinking about his own pleasure, or lack thereof. He knew he could bring the woman a good deal of pleasure—with sex. And have a chance to hold her, too, without her feeling as though she was seeking comfort from anyone.

Like doing so was some kind of mortal sin.

Her comments about sex, with her including no commitment and no expectations, were starting to sound loudly in his ears. She hadn't just been talking about sex.

Dove St. James had been talking about a way of life.

In her studio, she helped others deeply but from a distance. And seemed to live all of her life in the same fashion.

And why that should bother him, he couldn't explain. He'd tried. On and off all day. Kept coming up blank.

"He's angry with me for not bringing him a bottle." Her words fell without emotion as he pulled into his driveway.

Stopping to wait while the electric door lifted, he turned to her. "He does know that it's against hospital protocol, right?"

She glanced at him then. Seemed to focus for a moment but then looked away. "He's not in a place where he'd care even if he did know," she told him.

For a second there, as he watched the nearly comatose form sitting next to him, thinking about the way Dove normally effervesced with life, he was pretty pissed off himself.

Not at her. But at all of the forces stealing from her. Including her father.

"It's part of detoxifying," she said. "Rage, anxiety. It's what the liver sends out when it's uncomfortable."

That sounded more like her. In one sentence, she'd eased his concern about her. Some.

There was no teasing, no egging him on, not even any questions about his day or how everyone had done at St. James Boats that day. Or any conversation at all.

She hadn't even asked if Wes had been able to rent a trawler in order to fill the reservations that had already been on the books that day, and over the next month, for *Wicked Winnings*. Wes had arranged to get the boat fixed. Mitchell had paid for it, intending to add the cost to his St. James expense account when they got around to getting him officially on board.

As soon as they were home, she went to her room. He heard the bathroom door close while he was in his office. Five minutes later, heard the stairs creak as she went up. Unlike their previous nights together, he followed her up almost immediately after.

Dove was already in the bed. Her back turned toward him when he entered the room. If not for the very real threat of someone having tried to abduct her that morning, he might have convinced himself to take one of the spare rooms down the hall.

But while the police were thinking that there'd be no more harm coming against her now that Brad Fletcher had been caught—and put on warning—Mitchell wasn't so sure. Just because the man had been able to put on a convincing show for the police—and maybe his own attorney—it just didn't ring true that someone would go so far as to abduct a man, leave him for dead and then go after his daughter, and when he got a slap on the wrist, just walk away.

He wouldn't. He'd get more cunning.

Mitchell made quick work of getting himself ready for

bed. And double-checked the gun he'd had strapped at his waist, under his suit coat, all day long before lodging it between the bed frame and mattress. He took one last look at the huddled form beneath the covers on Dove's side of the bed before turning out the bathroom light and heading over to join her.

It was possible that she'd fallen asleep. She'd had an incredibly draining day. He sure wouldn't blame her for wanting to check out and escape from it all. Now that she was safe, lying beside him, he had plans to turn off himself, immediately. To get much-needed rest so that he'd be fully charged to take on whatever the next day or two was going to bring.

Lying on his back, he closed his eyes. Wiped his mind clean. And listened for her breathing. Until he realized what he was doing and stopped that, too. Wondering what he could do to help her. Not financially, or legally, but one human being to another. To give her some of the same sense of support he got from his family.

He'd come up with nothing, except another reminder to himself that he wasn't sleeping, when he felt the mattress move beside him. And a very definitely feminine hand landed on top of his penis, in perfect alignment. Gently holding him while he grew beneath her palm.

He didn't speak. Didn't even turn his head. As he had the night before, he covered her hand with his own. And then found her other one, sliding his hand underneath it, the back of his hand to her palm and lifted them, together, to her breast, his palm first.

It was like a scene from some karate movie, the way their arms were at angles, crossing their bodies top and bottom. It was almost soothing. To be sharing intimacies quietly in the dark.

And it was mesmerizing, too. He didn't stop growing at merely ready. Her nipple was rock hard, and he moved to the other one, sliding under her half shirt to do so. No longer content just to linger.

As his fingers touched her bare nipple, her hand slid inside the silk of his pajama pants, and Mitchell lost track of all thought.

They joined as they had the night before, and it was all different, too. More. Bolder. Three times instead of twice.

She only looked at him as he entered her, keeping her gaze locked with his as they rode together, and then her gaze was shut off to him.

All three times. She never spoke, so he respected her need for silence and said nothing.

When it was over, he returned to lying on his back, expecting her to turn toward the wall. She leaned over him instead, kissing him softly.

A caress which he answered with more than just his body. He wanted her to know she wasn't alone.

Lifting her lips from his she said, "Thank you, Mitchell," and then turned to her side, facing the wall.

He'd have felt used, except that he didn't.

Instead, he understood. Was glad that he'd been there for her.

And went to sleep.

Chapter 21

In a complete reversal of how she'd felt when she'd gone to bed the night before, Dove woke up Thursday morning with a sense of hope. She didn't work at accessing it, it was just there as she slid into consciousness. A positive anticipation of what was to come. With opportunities for happiness on the horizon.

Surprised to hear the shower running, she turned her head to see that Mitchell was already up. And when she made it downstairs, saw that he'd been there, too. A fresh coffee pod was in the trash. Figuring he had an early appointment, she got herself ready in record time. Pulling on the last clean outfit she had. A long green flowing skirt, topped with a tie-dyed tank top in all the colors of the rainbow with lace along the collar, and rhinestone-studded pink flip-flops. She was either going to have to go home for more clothes or do some laundry. Not having any idea what she was getting into when she'd packed to leave her home, she'd thrown in a bunch of stuff and left the rest. At the time, she hadn't been in a state of mind to plan.

She'd woken with a mind full of plans that morning, though. Brad Fletcher had been put on notice. Hopefully that bought law enforcement enough time to find their missing pieces. The man was sharp. But so was Peter Welding and his local team. With the experts at the ABI involved, the shady businessman had met his match.

And her father...she asked Mitchell to stop in town so she could grab a six-pack of warm and gooey cinnamon rolls on the way to the hospital. Her father's favorites. The doctor had warned her to expect more anger than not over the next days, but Dove knew that feeling good was a winning adversary over rage, and those rolls always made Whaler smile.

She offered one to Mitchell, a thank-you for stopping, and he smiled, too. Meeting her gaze as he helped himself to a napkin from the box, he said, "You seem better today."

In a knowing way. As though he had the secret behind her healed spirits.

Which, of course, he did. In part. The friend he'd been to her the night before...offering himself up as the source of good feeling, seemingly the only source in the world that would work for her right then, she was never going to forget.

"I am better," she said. And then, once again, said, "Thank you."

His response was a healthy bite into his roll, before heading back out into traffic. He'd dressed in jeans and a blue-checked flannel shirt that morning. "You're not going into the office this morning?" she asked.

He shook his head. "They're coming to work on *Wicked Winnings*, and Wes and Kirk are going to be involved with customers."

For a second, her spirits dimmed. On his behalf. "You don't have to give up your life for us, Mitchell," she told him. "Your work has to come first."

He nodded. "As it has a few times this week. Things are slow for me right now," he added, finishing off his roll and licking his fingers. "Might even be fate, huh?" he asked, smiling over at her.

She knew he was teasing her. Making light of the incredible amount of time he was investing in a new client who hadn't even yet signed a contract.

Her heart open wide and with an intensity she couldn't stop, she said, "I will always be here for you, Mitchell. No matter what or when."

He glanced her way, nodded.

And pulled into the medical center parking lot.

That last look had been brief, but Dove felt it to her core.

It was like he'd just returned the vow. Silently.

But she'd heard loud and clear.

It was as she'd known.

They were soul mates.

"Damn, girl, are you *ever* going to get it in your head that you aren't the boss of me?"

Mitchell paused just outside the door of Whaler's hospital room, just after nine on Thursday night, sharing a concerned glance with the officer outside his door—a young man he'd seen around town but never met.

"I'm just asking you to consider rehab, Dad. And to, maybe, talk to someone who's been through what you have, you know, just talk to them."

"You want me to go to one of those damned groups where everybody sits around and confesses and whines, and there ain't no way…"

Silence fell, and Mitchell was about to go in when he heard "I'm telling you, young woman, if you don't stop… you got no right, and I ain't gonna put up with none of your fairy crap. I've had enough, you hear? Enough!"

Mitchell had to take a moment to calm his own anger,

hearing Dove belittled that way. And by the one person in the world he was certain she loved. "Has it been like this all day?" he shared another glance with the uniformed officer, who nodded.

"She just keeps talking calmly," the man said, "cheerful and upbeat. I don't know how she does it."

Mitchell had nothing to say to that but thought of the police officer's words again a little over an hour later as he readied for bed. Dove had chattered all the way home about how much stronger and more alert her father had been that day. He'd eaten three meals, had been awake for several hours, his scans and blood work had come back better than expected, and the doctor had said that as long as he made it through the night with no trouble he could be released as soon as the next afternoon.

There'd been no further developments in their case. Mitchell had spoken to both Peter and Eli several times that day. Both of them were concerned about Whaler being on his own, prey to whoever had tried to kill him but hadn't finished the job. The man was not only refusing Dove's urgings to enter an abstinence-based program but even to go to rehab for a few days while he got more of his strength back.

She hadn't discussed any of that with Mitchell. Nor had she asked if he'd spoken to anyone. He knew she'd been getting reports, though. Peter Welding had told him that much.

He'd also heard that she'd been submissive, almost to the point of paranoid where her own safety guidelines were concerned.

With good reason. They weren't up against any deadbeat or deranged criminal here. They were dealing with a powerful, moneyed man who had connections. And above-average intelligence. At Peter's invitation, he'd watched the interview with Brad Fletcher from the day before. The man had been properly contrite at appropriate times—like when he'd been shocked to find out that Bob St. James had security cameras—but mostly he'd appeared cocky, sure of himself and not the least bit concerned. Mitchell's take-away had been that in Fletcher's mind, it wasn't a matter of *if* he'd get St. James Boats but *when*.

Glad that he had Dove safely with him one more night—knowing that he had to come up with some kind of plan in the event of Whaler's release the next day, like moving the older man in with him, too—he donned his pajama pants, leaving off the shirt, and headed into his room.

Wondering if Dove would be wearing the same light-weight pants to sleep in that she'd had on every other night in his bed. She'd asked him to stop by her place on the way home that night so she could pick up a few more things.

While he'd only seen the satchel she'd carried out of her room, he'd found himself entertaining thoughts about its potential contents. Mostly pertaining to sexy sleepwear.

The sun had set, dusk had come and gone, leaving the room in darkness broken only by the beam of moonlight coming through the window. One last check that his gun was in place as he'd left it moments before, he checked his phone and climbed into bed.

He wasn't going to reach for her. The call was hers. But he knew it was coming. She hadn't sent any sex signals. There'd been no come-on or tantalizing looks. They weren't Dove's way.

Nor his, either, he realized. He got the looks often enough from women who made it clear they were open to his attentions. And found them to be turnoffs.

Wide awake, anticipating, he lay there…for all of twenty seconds. He felt the mattress move. Waited for her touch on his already hard penis—eagerly—and felt her naked leg slide over his silk-clothed one instead.

Dove was the aggressor during that first encounter. Full of confidence that took him to a whole new level of hard with desire, she stripped his pants and played with him, sitting astride him, completely naked. Her exploration took them places he'd never visited. And the culmination was out-of-this-world incredible.

The second time was his turn. He didn't stop until she was writhing, begging and then crying out for release.

After they'd shared a third orgasm, he lay back, replete. For the moment. Heard her sigh, flat on her back next to him, and expected her to turn her face to the wall and go to sleep.

Wondering if he'd get a goodnight kiss as he had the night before.

Wanting it almost as much as he'd wanted the sex.

Neither happened. She didn't kiss him. Neither did she roll away.

Then he heard "We need to talk" come softly from beside him.

And Mitchell's heart sank.

The future was at hand. Her father was going to be released from the hospital. She'd need to stay with him; that was a given. And, until the situation was resolved with St. James Boats, which somehow meant getting Brad Fletcher permanently away from them, they were going to need some kind of protection.

All of which Mitchell would be sure to have suggestions to deal with, she was sure. And things they could talk about in the morning. Or afternoon. With Whaler present. Or not.

She had something more pressing on her mind. An important something that could help sustain her—and please him—during some potentially challenging days ahead.

"I don't want to be done with our sex, yet."

His head turned sharply, and though she couldn't make out much of his expression, she saw the glints in his eyes pinging on her. Felt them as though he'd touched her, but not with warmth. Or cold. Just...there.

"Unless of course you want to be," she clarified. No way did she want pity. Or any kind of a one-way street.

He didn't turn away. Wasn't saying anything. So she waited. Mitchell had to choose his words. And when he did, he spoke the truth. She wanted that, his truth. No matter what it was.

"What exactly are you proposing?"

A question. With no hint to his truth. Taking a breath, she said, "That we decide, both of us together, whether or not we're done with the sex." And then, in case he needed reassurance, she said, "No commitments, other than that. No expectations. Just...we're not done yet if we both don't want to be done. And if we're together on that, then maybe some kind of arrangement whereby we actually have sex," she said. "Since, after this, we won't be meeting up in your bed at night."

Maybe she'd read him wrong. Their joining that night had been so much more than before, and she hadn't thought that possible. But maybe, what to her had been perfection, a call for more, to him had been...goodbye?

Was that what had made it so powerful? And so sweet, too? He'd been kissing her goodbye?

"No expectation, no commitment." His words, slow in coming, had her heart pounding. "How does monogamy play into that? It definitely speaks commitment. And expectation, too."

So…he wanted to have sex with her and be free to sleep with other women, too? Could she be good with that? "I've never actually considered the point before," she told him honestly. She'd never wanted enough sex repeats for the situation to arise. "So maybe we *are* done." The words sent a sliver of fear through her. But she had to say what was in her heart. What she knew to be true. "I don't think I'd be okay knowing that you're sleeping with other women at the same time we're coming together. I apologize for leading you on. I just… In my mind, sex is sacred to the moment. For however long the moment lasts."

Instead of turning his head back on the pillow to go to sleep as she'd expected, Mitchell raised up on his elbow, hand bracing his head. "I don't know about the sacred part," he said. "Can't say I'm briefed on the matter, but I agree with monogamy. It's smart. Practical. You can't control how others feel, and if another partner outside the twosome has jealousy issues or expectations, they can then become a part of your situation as well."

"The case that was just in the news about the jealous cop who killed her lover after she saw him having dinner with another woman?" It had happened a couple of towns over but had reverberated through their part of the state.

She hadn't seen a discussion of current events being a part of that particular conversation, but the fact that he was still engaged in the topic at all was filling her with joy.

He nodded, so close, his head just above hers. Making her feel, in those seconds, as though she was his whole world.

Giving herself an inner mental shake, Dove smiled up at him. Not her whole world, just a lovely portion of her current one. A gift given to her precisely when she'd needed it.

Life at its best.

"I guess, before I can answer your initial question, I need to know a little bit more about what you're envisioning." Mitchell's words cut into her celebration.

She reached up, touched his cheek. "I'm not good at planning the future in detail," she told him. "Which is why I came to you in the first place, if you remember. A business needs that kind of skill. I'm more day-to-day, going where life takes me."

As soon as she said the words, she felt his withdrawal. Or thought he withdrew. At the moment she wasn't sure which part of herself she was accessing. Mind or senses. A state of affairs that didn't sit well with her.

"Let me ask you this," he said then, his tone more one of curiosity than interview, and relaxing, she nodded.

"Do you ever see yourself getting married?"

Eyes wide she stared at him. Surely he wasn't…no. The easy look on his face, that tone—a getting-to-know-you, not something more personal—relaxed her. "Not really," she told him. "My life, being kind of an outcast in a small town, based on my own choices—choices I'm good with— just didn't lead to me seeing someone wanting to take that on. Nor could I see me giving up what I know, what I believe, how I feel and think, in order to have someone share my life with me."

When he didn't back away or show any sign of disappointment, she said, "I wasn't raised like you were, Mitchell." He was a scholarly man. Looking to understand something he hadn't yet come across. And she was suddenly eager to fill him in.

"I grew up in an essentially single-parent family, with my dad, my mom's husband, sharing time with us whenever he was around. Their marriage was untraditional, my upbringing wasn't like any of my friends'. And certainly nothing like yours. I didn't have two parents, let alone an aunt and uncle, siblings and cousins. I just had me. And I've always, for the most part, been happy. But I don't fit the socially accepted, traditional lifestyle."

He sighed. Kind of smiled. And Dove was left strangely...letdown. "How about you?" she asked then, to let him know that her differences didn't have to change anything between them. His beliefs, goals, life plans were as important as hers. She wanted to know them and would accept them without question.

"I think you already know the answer to that," he told her. "I'm more of a traditional kind of guy."

She nodded. They were opposites. They'd both known that long before they'd formally met. But, "How does that fit with us having more time together?" she asked, the question consuming her.

He leaned down and kissed her. Softly. But with hunger, too. "I'm traditional," he said, "but I'm not a fool. As long as it's working for both of us, we'll be having sex."

With that he lay down, closed his eyes and in less than two minutes was breathing deeply.

A man right with his conscience could fall asleep that easily.

With a smile on her face, Dove closed her eyes and was right behind him.

Chapter 22

He didn't have a plan.

Not nearly enough of one, at any rate. Dove was capable of flying in the wind and landing on her feet. Mitchell, not so much. He didn't take off without the flight plan firmly mapped out, recorded and called in with responding verification of receipt.

Aviation laws were in place for good reason. Without them there would be plane crashes, with untold number of deaths, on a regular basis.

He could do the sex part. All day long. And night, too. He just needed the plan.

Pulling up outside the medical center the next afternoon, Mitchell was as tense as he ever got, due to the lack of firmly considered next steps.

Starting with Whaler's homecoming.

He'd offered his home to the old sea captain and had been turned down. Not all that kindly. The man damn well didn't need charity.

So Mitchell had paid for private security—all off-duty law enforcement—at least for the first twenty-four hours. Dove, who'd be staying at Whaler's place, knew the officers would be inconspicuously watching her father's property. Whaler did not.

She also had the head of command's cell phone on speed dial—a phone that would be on-property at all times, held by whoever was in charge any given hour. Had promised to push the speed dial icon every hour if need be. She was to report every single creak she heard in the floorboards. Even if it was because she was walking on it at the time.

Mitchell hadn't yet decided where he'd be staying. Close, he knew that much. Probably sleeping in his car. No way he was going to his place outside of town—too far away.

And there was little likelihood that Whaler was going to stay home. The man was headed straight for a bottle. Probably starting with glasses of amber liquid poured from one for him while he sat on the stool that was as much home to him as his own bed.

Dove didn't think so. She'd been adamant—with Mitchell during a phone call, and, according to her, with her father—that he was not leaving the house.

Nor was she going to let him undo the healing his body had worked so hard to do over the past week. Another couple of days and his liver would be completely detoxed. The rest, the mental and emotional healing, would take a lifetime.

She wasn't looking that far ahead yet.

Which was why she couldn't see what Mitchell already knew. Whaler had no desire to stay sober. Which meant she'd lost the battle before she'd even started to wage the war.

Seeing Whaler's truck already in the parking lot, with Welding just climbing out of it, Mitchell parked and joined the detective. As already laid out, Welding would be catching a ride back to his own car with the officer currently on duty outside Whaler's hospital room. After they led Whaler and Dove home, with Mitchell right behind the truck.

It wasn't a great plan. Or even a good one. But it was the best they could do after Whaler's very loud assertion that he had the right to make his own choices and he was damned well going home in his own truck.

How the man could be so confident that he'd be okay when he'd just spent days in the hospital after having been abducted and left for dead, Mitchell couldn't even begin to understand.

The only thing that made sense was that Whaler just plain didn't care if he lived or died. But he'd allowed the fact—mostly because it was the only way the doctor would release him, which was required in order for insurance to pay his medical bills—that he probably shouldn't drive. Dove would be in the truck with him.

She'd readily agreed to the proposed entourage.

And didn't yet know that Mitchell was financing all of the extra security. When she'd come to his office to hire him, she'd said she'd pay his bill, no matter the cost, on installments. There'd been no stipulations as to getting costs approved first. And it was up to him what line items he chose to include on that bill. As were any discounts he chose to offer.

If she thought the city was financing the locally employed police officers outside her father's home, he could choose to just leave it that way, too.

All smaller aspects of the lack of solid planning that was making him so uneasy.

While Welding waited outside, watching the area, Mitchell went in to let Dove know that her father's old truck was there and ready to go.

He walked up just in time to hear, "This is garbage! You're nothing but a whiner. Always have been. I said I want you to drop me at the bar, and that's exactly what you're going to do."

Dove had told him that the anger was to be expected. As heavy a drinker as Whaler had been, he'd be going through serious withdrawal. But hearing anyone talk to her as her father had just done...he had to make a conscientious effort to unclench his fist.

She'd told him during one of their conversations that her father had never spoken harshly to her growing up—except the time she'd been in the water without permission. And that she'd never heard him speak to her mother that way, either. Didn't mean he hadn't done. Only that he'd never verbally attacked his wife in front of their daughter.

Mitchell took a deep breath, trusting her version—that Whaler was in the throes of a medical situation and couldn't be held accountable for his rage. And put a smile on his face as he played his part in getting all of them out of there.

Whaler followed instructions, keeping himself glued to his daughter, and climbed immediately into the passenger seat of his truck, allowing Welding to help him up.

And then, looking between Welding and Mitchell, who'd seen Dove to the driver's seat, he said, "Thank you both. I'm sorry for being so much trouble."

Mitchell nodded. Glanced at Dove in time to see tears brimming in her eyes, and as he was closing the truck door heard "I'm most sorry to you, my girl. I'm not myself."

As he moved quickly to get into his own car and be ready to follow closely behind when Dove hit the gas, Mitchell was glad he hadn't decked Bob St. James back in the hospital.

Once again, Dove had called the situation better than he had.

Because she was far better at winging through life than he was.

Not a bad thing. Just a fact of life.

She'd made it all so clear the night before. They were night and day. And both were equally necessary and valuable.

They made it through the winding drive and out to the thoroughfare that would lead them to Main Street without issue. Mitchell was on complete alert. Calculating turns, counting down streets, until they got to Whaler's place, where his security detail was already in place.

A few more minutes, five to seven at most and…

Mitchell heard the loud crash before his eyes had even registered what had happened. Heart pounding, he slammed on his brakes in time to see Whaler's truck, with Dove and Whaler belted inside, rolling over an embankment. They'd been hit broadside. By a truck that had come out of a parking lot, plowing through a median and straight into them.

Adrenaline and fear pumping through him, Mitchell was out of his car and running full speed down the embankment before he heard sirens coming from above.

Dove. He had to get to Dove.

The truck lay at an angle, passenger side down. The bed was half-separated from the cab.

"Help!" Dove's scream, unrecognizable to him, but for the fact that it was feminine not masculine, propelling him through the weeds and fallen trees between him and the vehicle. Two feet away, he could see her head clearly enough to know that she was conscious. Rocking forward and backward.

He was there almost instantly, finding the roof so smashed there was no way Mitchell could get the one door accessible to him open. But the window had broken out, and he could reach in to cup Dove's face. "I'm here," he told her. "Help's on the way, and I'm going to stay right here with you until it gets here."

"Daddy," she said, tears streaming down her face. "Get to Daddy, first."

Mitchell had already taken the only glance he needed to toward what had once been the passenger side of Whaler's old truck. Thankfully, the seat was pushed back so far that Dove, trapped by her seat belt, couldn't see. The man's injuries were something that would have haunted her for the rest of her life. Whaler was clearly dead, but Mitchell didn't say so.

Holding her head with one hand, just supporting it, not moving it, he positioned himself so that she could look him in the eye. "Stay with me, baby," he said. "Help is on the way."

"Mitchell? I'm okay, get to my dad."

"It's best that I don't move either one of you," he said, finding words out of nowhere. "Just until the paramedics get here and make sure you're okay."

She nodded. Started to cry but didn't take her eyes away from him. "I can't get my door to open." She hadn't tried since he'd been there. Wasn't sure if she'd already discovered that the door was jammed shut, or was just talking off the top of her head. Heart thrumming through his body, his ears, he focused on her. Her face. Making sure that she got from him whatever she needed most.

Smiling he said, "That's because I'm leaning against it." He was hardly touching the vehicle for fear of dislodging it.

Her eyes seemed well focused. Her words were slow and shaky but clear.

And where in the hell were the…

"I'm glad you're here." Her eyes were still holding his gaze. And he smiled, blinking back tears. "I'm glad I'm here, too," he said.

And heard voices calling just before multiple sets of boots trampled in the dirt behind him.

"The paramedics are here," he told her, pulling his hand gently away from her head.

A hand splattered with blood came up to grip his arm as panic filled her eyes. "Don't leave me," she cried.

"I'm not going anywhere, Dove. I promise. I'll be right here."

The last was said as first responders, equipped with metal cutters, pushed him aside.

And two minutes later he heard Dove scream his name.

The little room was cold. Dove didn't much care. Cold was real.

And all she had left.

As soon as she had the all clear from the trauma doctor, she'd be free to go home. Or…just go. No place felt like home to her.

Not one that existed anymore.

Not in the future.

Her father was dead. She'd known the second she'd been freed from the locked-up seat belt and could turn around.

She'd called for Mitchell. He might have been there. She hadn't seen him. She'd been surrounded by emergency personnel scooting her onto and then strapping her down to a stretcher that had been solid, excruciating wood. A spine board, she'd later found out. In case she'd suffered potentially paralyzing spine or neck damage in the crash. At the time all she'd known was that she'd gone from one hellish situation of being held prisoner into another, worse one.

Daddy was dead.

All the energy…all the hope…all for nothing.

Her bold last-ditch effort to save St. James Boats—

to give her father a reason to live—had been a waste. A prompting, she'd believed.

Fantasy cooked up by a desperate mind, more like.

It would have been better for all concerned if she'd just kept out of it. Gone on teaching her little classes, believing that there was actually a way for human beings to have a choice in whether to be happy, ways to get rid of the negative energy if one was willing to work at it.

She'd really believed that the inner spirit could get messages if one could keep one's heart open to accessing them.

Right. That's why she'd just seen her father's mangled body in a vision she was never going to forget. No matter how many times anyone tried to cleanse her aura.

The kids at school, so many of the people in Shelby who'd looked at her askance had been right all along. The joke was on her.

She'd laugh if she had any humor left inside her.

The doctor had proclaimed her a miracle. Other than the obvious soreness she'd be experiencing over the next days, even into a week or two, she was fine. Cuts and scrapes, but nothing that needed stitches. No broken bones.

She'd been incredibly lucky. Escaping from the horrific accident unscathed.

Physically.

In reality, the body the doctor had been concerned about was all she had left. Her father—and the spirit through which she'd believed she lived—had both been fatalities.

At least one good thing had come of it all—she gave a brief, distorted chuckle at the fact that her poor behind-the-times brain was still trying to combat evil with anything that felt positive—at least her future was clear to her.

Something she'd never had before. The ability to look ahead with a set of clear plans from which she wouldn't sway. Within the next hour she'd take the police escort she'd been told was waiting for her to the small house she'd purchased not far from the marina, back when she had the power to make good things come to her. She was going to start packing immediately. Put the house up for sale. Cancel the lease on her studio. And let Brad Fletcher have St. James Boats.

He'd won.

She was leaving. No way she could continue to live in a town where she'd established a life that couldn't possibly sustain her. That was just plain stupid.

Coasting on hope was a pipe dream.

Mitchell had been right all along. Logic, practicality, they were all that mattered in life.

So, lesson learned. A real one, not some make-believe fairy tale.

He was there, at the medical center. Asking to see her.

She'd refused to see him. There was no point. She wasn't who she'd thought she'd been. Wasn't who he'd thought he'd known.

There were others there, too, she'd been told, but she'd waved away the nurse's words before she could tell her more. It was probably Peter Welding.

And maybe a client or two. Hetty Amos.

All of whom believed she was something she was not. They'd find out soon enough it had all been a lie.

She'd do what she could to make it up to them. Find a job and slowly begin to return all the client fees she'd collected over the years. She'd pay Mitchell, too, when she could.

It was the practical thing to do. That or face lawsuits and risk damages being awarded in amounts far greater than those she'd collected. Money to compensate for any pain and suffering she'd caused.

She'd pay that too, if she could...

But she was getting ahead of herself. First release papers. Then ride to the house she owned.

And from there, make short order of cleaning up and finding the quickest way out of town.

It was the only option she could see.

So the only one she believed in.

At least she had that. Something to believe in. Count on. That which she could see.

It wasn't a lot.

But it was going to have to do.

It was all that she had left.

All that she'd ever had.

She just hadn't seen it.

Chapter 23

No way was Mitchell going to just walk away to leave Dove to grieve alone. He got why she'd felt like she had to make that choice. In some ways, she'd been alone since the day she was born. Her mother and father had had their bond, before her and through her, too.

And when she'd grown up, been old enough to forge her own relationships, she'd been—due to the way she'd been raised—an outcast in her own society.

The woman had understanding beyond anything Mitchell was ever going to know, but he knew one thing. In order to heal, she needed family. Lots of it.

She also needed the news he had to give her. Maybe more than the rest.

It was that with which he was armed, just before sunset that night. He'd read the note she'd had Welding give to him after she'd insisted on leaving the hospital—through a back door—on her own. The detective had already dropped her off at home before driving back to the hospital to deliver her short missive to Mitchell.

Our time is through, Mitchell. I'm not who I thought I was, nor one who, with eyes opened wide, can continue to pretend. Please believe that while most of what I said wasn't real, my gratitude to you was, is and always will be. I wish you the best life has to offer. Dove.

Whether Welding had read the note scribbled on that back of a blank hospital prescription sheet, he didn't know. Didn't care. Peter was a good man. Had done his job with professionalism, compassion and seriously impressive skill.

Mitchell could hardly blame the guy for being attracted to Dove.

In jeans, a button-up long-sleeved shirt and boat shoes, he presented himself at her front door with her container of leftover greens in one hand, and her satchel over his shoulder. Her suitcase was in his car, too, if things digressed rapidly to the point of her asking for it.

Neither bag was packed. He hadn't been able to look at her things, not without tears shed. And he wasn't comfortable yet being that kind of guy. Even knowing he could be was taking some getting used to.

She looked out the window before opening the door to him. Applauding her caution—she didn't yet know the security detail that was supposed to have been switched from her father's house to her own had been dismissed— he was also patting himself on the back for thinking of the satchel and greens as a way to get her to give him a second of her time.

The things themselves wouldn't matter to her. Burdening someone else with her mess would.

She'd taught him more than she'd probably ever know during her time with him.

Without looking at him directly, she took the bowl from his hand saying, "I'll wash this and get it back to you" and then reached for the satchel.

He didn't give that up as easily as he had the container that he only wanted back if he had her to go with it.

"They found a match for the spit on your father's shirt," he said baldly, completely unlike himself, and yet seemingly right, too. He'd rather have had his speech all thought-out, but with Dove, planning didn't work.

Living authentically did. And while he had no idea how to do that, he at least got that he had to just let it all come out of him as it willed, with no forethought.

The way her hand reaching for the strap of the satchel faltered gave him hope. The first bit he'd had since he'd seen her pulled out of the totaled truck earlier that day and had been told she'd be okay.

"With enough evidence to prove that Fletcher hired him?" she asked, not meeting his gaze, but not shutting the door in his face, either.

"No," Mitchell said and, seeing her shoulders close in, quickly added, "Because Fletcher didn't do it. Not your studio. Not untying *Ladybird*, or watching your house. He wasn't the one who took your father, leaving him out on the embankment, nor was he responsible for your near abduction." He had no idea why he was listing it all out. He just felt a need to do so.

A need driven by her. By her reactions to his words. The more he said, the more she seemed to be listening. To be taking it in.

And if there was one thing he knew about Dove St. James it was that what she took in came out right.

"Who was it?" she asked, when he sensed that he needed to fall silent. "Why?"

He didn't answer. Just watched her. And, eventually, she met his gaze. Holding on long enough to ask again, "Who? Why?"

That's when he knew what he had to say. "Can I come in, please? It's going to look odd to your neighbor staring at us from her porch down there if I stand here much longer."

Such a Mitchell thing, concerning himself with every

aspect of a situation, looking for negative consequences. And yet, fitting that him doing so got him exactly what he needed from Dove in that moment.

"Please," she said, "come in." There was no... Dove in her tone. Just propriety. He took note.

Followed her into the room just off the door. A living space with a couch, a chair. A table with a small television set. And a full wall of bookcases that had books lining it, books on the shelves in front of other books, books sideways on the edges of shelves. Books stacked in rows on both sides of it.

He wanted to smile. But couldn't. Not without Dove sharing the moment with him.

So he sat on the chair, lowering her satchel to the wood floor by his feet. She sat, too. On the end of the couch closest to him. He took that as a good sign.

"It was Oscar Earnhardt, Dove," he told her. And then, as quickly as he could, he got the rest out there for her to access it all when she was ready.

"Once I knew you were okay, I was sitting in the waiting room until I could see you, and Eli started asking me about everything I could remember from the crash."

He stopped, watching to make sure she was up to hearing such details, and saw her watching him with an intentness he hadn't seen from her before. "Eli was at the trauma center?" she asked.

"Of course." The answer rote to him. But to someone like Dove, who didn't know that family came running in times of tragedy... "He was there, first to see how you were and—" he added something he never would have admitted before Dove, or to anyone but her "—to see how I was holding up...then to get all the details he could. The entire local ABI office and of course Shelby police department were working on the accident."

She swallowed. Blinked. And though his mind told him to stop, to give her time, he trusted something deeper and kept on talking. "I remembered the truck, remembered having seen it before, at the bar...the day we saw Oscar. Welding put out an APB on his car and person, found him at the closet clinic to Shelby, compelled a DNA sample and had forensics start running the rapid DNA. Welding called another officer to sit on Earnhardt until he could be booked and headed back here to pull up every description of every crime scene, checked them against Oscar's known whereabouts during each incident, and by the time Oscar was stitched up and his broken leg had been set with a cast, Welding had the warrant for his arrest and the prosecutor standing by to press charges."

He'd skipped some interim stuff. But she had the gist of it.

"But...*why*?" Mouth open, she was staring at him. And for a second there, he had a glimpse of the woman he'd slowly begun to understand had changed him forever.

"First place, he was drunk—partially why he escaped the crash with no internal or head injuries. But after a few minutes with Peter Welding, he confessed to the rest." Mitchell paused before addressing her question. And then, when he meant to state the facts, said, "He was a man not in touch with deeper truths, Dove. He didn't understand that the power to change his life came from within himself."

She blinked. Twice. Hard. Trying not to cry. The conclusion was pretty obvious. What he didn't get was why Dove would hold back tears. It wasn't her way. And he said, "He blamed everything bad that his drinking had brought onto him on you and your dad. Your father for firing him because how could he? He drank right alongside him. And then you because his wife was your client and he says you filled her head with crap. If you hadn't done, she'd never have kicked him out or filed for divorce."

Why he was just putting it right out, almost as though placing blame himself, he had no idea. He just had to get it done. Have her hear it all at once because she was going to find out at trial, anyway.

"His wife… I never gave her any advice at all," Dove said, as though that was the key point in the moment. "She came to the studio for exercise, *quiet exercise*, as she called it. I didn't even know she'd filed for divorce until after Dad told me. I knew she was troubled. I told her I was available if there was anything I could do—more because of Dad's friendship with Oscar than anything else. But she said that Oscar needed our friendship more than she did. And that…" she paused, frowned then said, "…she'd gotten far more from me than she'd paid for." With a blank look, she stared at Mitchell, as though he had answers she couldn't access.

"I'm guessing she learned how to find her inner peace through your example," he told her. And then, for no logical reason whatsoever said, "I know I have, Dove. Before you came barreling into my office I was living a two-dimensional life. You showed me that the way I feel matters as much as how well I think. That trusting one's instincts matters as much or more as facts. That loving is far more than doing. It's living through heart as much as mind."

He was beginning to sound like a damned greeting card.

And had one more thing to say. "You mentioned once that you were led to me so that I could help you. Well, you were only partially right, Dove St. James. You were also led to me so that *you* could help *me*."

She started to sob then. Big, painful, ugly sounds that,

strangely enough, sounded a bit like heaven to him. A heaven that acknowledged pain and suffering, that wouldn't stop challenges and couldn't always spare tragedy but that would be there always. With warmth, a steady hand, healing. And more joy than there would ever be sorrow.

And he had Dove to thank for showing him it was there.

She'd come close to losing her way. Would never have believed there could be a time when she'd be unable to access understanding. Unable to feel. To believe.

And yet...even then...her spirits had been there. She hadn't had to believe in them. They'd been there anyway. In the form of Mitchell Colton.

Lying with him in his bed that night, Dove couldn't find the passion for lovemaking, but she found everything she needed. A safe place to grieve. To be. To breathe.

Her head on his chest, her arm around him, his arms holding her close, was as close to heaven as she was going to get in that lifetime.

"Right before the crash, my father told me that I should have just let him die and be with his wife." The memory stabbed her, but not as deeply as it had when she'd first heard the words. "He got his wish," she said softly. Wishing she understood better, but knowing that, in some space, at some time, she would.

She'd had a dark night of the soul. Her mother had taught her about them. She just hadn't recognized what was happening at the time. Maybe due to the crash. To the shock of losing her father on top of everything else. To an emotional blow out that prevented her from accessing her cortex. And maybe a dark night wasn't really dark without that total separation.

Because within the darkness, light shone the brightest.

"I want more than just sex," she said. It was truth. And she wouldn't deny it its say. She was who she was. Probably more so after all she'd been through. Had yet to get through.

Her father's funeral. Cleaning out his house. Selling his business.

"Yeah, well, you have no idea how relieved I am to hear you say that." Mitchell's response was so unexpected and sincere-sounding she raised herself up to look him in the eye.

"I love you, Dove St. James. I want more than just sex. I want a lifetime. Forever. However we can make it work. Marriage, no marriage. I don't care. Just together. A couple. For the rest of our lives."

She didn't try to stop the tears that fell. The effort would be ludicrous. But she did smile through them. A day ago, she might have struggled with his declaration. Needing to meditate over it. Right then, after suffering the dark night, she just trusted. More deeply, more fervently than she ever had before.

"You don't need to worry about the *forever* part, Mitchell," she told him, meaning far more than the single lifetime he spoke about. "I knew almost from the beginning that we were destined to travel through life together."

"You did not," he said, frowning. "You were the one who said *no commitment, no expectations*."

"I didn't say I knew we'd be lovers or a couple. Just that we were soul mates."

Shaking his head and grinning, he said, "Soul mates. I can see I have a whole lot more to learn."

He might have. And might not. Mitchell was Mitchell. The world needed him.

But not as much as she did.

And that was as it was meant to be.

"I just figured something out," she told him.

"What's that?"

"The deepest level of truth and learning isn't inside yourself. It's in joining your deepest heart with another's."

"It's called *home*, Dove."

She kissed him then. Needing more than words. More, even, than understanding.

She needed to rest. To heal.

Because finally, she'd come home.

Epilogue

Mitchell woke up to a text message. Long after dawn had arrived. Careful not to disturb the exhausted woman sleeping with her head on the right side of his chest, he reached for his phone with his left hand.

Read the message. And knew he had to wake her up.

There were times when family was a pain in the ass. The thought was quickly quashed with another. There was never a time when family was a bad thing. Not ever.

Then he glanced at the hour and woke her up quickly.

"Dove, it's almost noon." He was texting Wes even as he said the words.

Only to hear back, immediately, that the morning had gone like clockwork. And asking how soon he could get there.

Right. About that.

He hit the bathroom. And found Dove gone from their bed when he came out. As had been their way all week.

Nervous, needing to get a whole lot done in no time at all, he cursed his overemotional, wayward tongue of the day before. And realized he was also going to have to start to accept it. The task would be arduous. Likely slow. But worth the effort.

He was a Colton, an adventurer. He knew more than

most that the more effort one put into something, the more benefit that came out of it.

By the time he'd made his coffee, Dove still hadn't come out from her bathroom. Knocking on the door, he received no answer and moved at lightning speed to her room. No Dove there, either.

But he thought he heard a footstep above him.

Climbing the stairs he found her in his room, walking around naked, chomping on…a bunch of what looked to him to be grass.

Seeing him, she said, "I thought it'd be cool to shower together," she told him.

Taking her hand, he led her to the bed, handed her the clothes that she'd obviously brought up with her and laid there, and said, "As much as I want to take you up on that offer, we don't have time." He was already at his dresser, pulling out underwear.

"I have something I have to tell you."

And hurrying into clothes without a shower wasn't the way he'd wanted to go about it.

"I want to buy St. James Boats," he told her, rushing into his explanation even faster than he was getting into a pair of jeans. "You love the place, even if you don't have the interest in or the skills necessary to run it. Living alone as I have all these years and investing well, I can easily afford to give you market value plus a bonus for selling it to me without trying to get other offers. And…"

Still naked, she stood, came over to him and lifted one finger to his lips. "Mitchell, you had me with the first sentence. You can buy it for a penny. Or I'll gift it to you. The fact that you want it is of the greatest value to me."

She had tears in her eyes again. Happy tears. And in

spite of the crowd he knew was waiting for them, he took his time kissing her. Sharing his deepest heart.

Just in case she changed her mind.

And then he went right back to dressing. Hoping she'd get the hint and do the same.

He had no speech. No plan.

He would have had. If he'd woken up at dawn, as he'd done every morning since he was a teenager.

She'd pulled on panties. Was in the process of putting on a frilly purple crop top and stopped. Frowning at him. "What's the big rush?" she asked, as if only then realizing that his talk about buying her father's business had nothing to do with their need to forgo a shower for rushed throwing on of clothes.

"Wes texted," he blurted. Truth. Absolute truth. "He needs us at the marina. Something about a party that is asking for the owner's attention..." The truth. And...so much more than that.

"A customer?" The fact that she translated his perfectly normal sentence into legalese had to be a sign that he was supposed to go with it, right?

He might be aware of an inner knowledge, but he wasn't so great at listening to it yet. Or understanding if he did.

"Right," he told her. And did his best just to get himself downstairs and into his car without giving her a chance for any further conversation about the docks. He asked her how she was feeling.

Listened while she told him what she could do to ease her stiffness, her soreness. She just needed to get her oils. Some bath salts. And a diffuser.

He knew what the words meant. Had no concept of what she was going to do with them all. Asked if she'd taken the muscle relaxants or pain pills the doctor had prescribed.

And was a bit frustrated, but not all that surprised, to hear she hadn't filled the prescription before she'd left the medical center as she'd been told to do.

By then, he was pulling into the marina. Not breathing deeply. And beginning to think that he'd made the biggest mistake of his life.

He'd loved the idea when he'd heard it the day before. From Hetty Amos in the waiting room at the trauma center.

Had forgotten all about it. Until Wes's text.

But after the night he'd just spent, the conversations, the understanding he and Dove had reached…

He never should have told Eli that he wanted to buy St. James Boats before he'd told Dove. Not that Eli would break his confidence, it just hadn't felt right after the previous night's conversations. His brother knowing before she had.

He crested the hill and—holy hell!—the crowd was five times bigger than he'd heard about the day before, and…it was too late to figure out a plan.

And definitely far, far too late to avoid the consequence. For which he had no solution.

"What's going on?" Dove asked, leaning forward to stare at the hundred or more people blocking the docks from view.

For a second he thought about playing dumb. Except that he was not going to lie to her. Ever.

And his family was at the front of the crowd, waiting to show Dove St. James just how much she was cared about. Respected. And even loved.

They'd spent the morning cleaning up the marina, mowing the grass, cleaning all the boats, draping a partially repaired *Wicked Winnings* with a colorful cloth bearing angels' wings.

And loading *Ladybird* with the food they'd prepared for a family day on the water.

The rest of the crowd, he'd known nothing about.

He came up with no words to answer Dove's question. Just got out of the car, hoping she'd join him. And, taking it as a sign when she did, took her hand, linking his fingers through hers and walking with purpose toward his mom and dad. His brothers and sister. His aunt and uncle. His cousins.

All of whom walked out to meet them, wrapping their arms, their mass around them, each hugging Dove in turn.

Showing her what there were no words to say.

What apparently so much of the town had felt, based on the numbers that weren't going to fit on the boat that day but were there just the same.

Dove let go of Mitchell's hand. She cried some. Okay, a lot. She returned hugs. And she seemed to glow with a sense of something Mitchell couldn't put a name to.

Something he might not ever understand.

But when she looked at him, as she did often over the next hour before they finally made it to *Ladybird*'s deck, he fully understood the message she was sending him.

The townspeople meant the world to her.

His family's welcome even more.

But he was her soul mate.

And together, they'd always find their safe place.

Their peace.

And a love that didn't die.

* * * * *